Across Open Ground

Across Open Ground
Heather Parkinson

a novel

BLOOMSBURY

Published by Bloomsbury, New York and London
Distributed to the trade by Holtzbrinck Publishers

The Library of Congress has cataloged the hardcover edition as follows:

Parkinson, Heather, 1974-
Across open ground : a novel / Heather Parkinson. – 1st U.S. ed.
p. cm.
ISBN 1-58234-243-1
1. World War, 1914–1918--Idaho--Fiction. 2. Idaho--Fiction. I. Title.

PS3616.A755 A63 2002
813'.6--dc21
2001056527

Paperback ISBN 1-58234-289-X

First published in hardcover in the United States
by Bloomsbury in 2002
This paperback edition published in 2003

1 3 5 7 9 10 8 6 4 2

Typeset by Hewer Text Ltd, Edinburgh
Printed in the United States of America by RR Donnelley & Sons, Harrisonburg

for my mother

ACKNOWLEDGMENTS

For his unending faith and invaluable insight, I would
like to thank Robert Olmstead. Thanks as well to
Tom Hoffrage, Scott Lung, Leigh Feldman, and
Karen Rinaldi.

Chapter 1

L E G D E E P I N mud, the sheep stuck in their own tracks and the blue heeler dog moved like an elk in heavy snow, bounding and lunging as if he might somehow find a surface that would hold him. But the corrals were wet with spring runoff and the ground gave way and the dog sank deeper the more his effort.

While the snow had melted along the valley floor leaving a mud field for the herders, the surrounding hillsides were inlaid like a kind of marble, whorled and patched white. Far up north where the sheepherders could not see, the Pioneers and Sawtooths still rose bold and white and jagged like broken teeth. Some years winter was timeless – the white clung on forever and the water never stopped coming.

John Wright told Walter earlier that morning he thought it would be one of those years, what with the water table so high, the streams near flood level and their banks still laced with ice. These streams aren't done flooding, John had said. It won't be until late June, July maybe, when the tributaries feed out. This here is just snow. Spring rain and snowmelt.

Be all right? Walter had said.

With some luck, John said, swirling the heel of a mud-splattered boot in a puddle at his feet before mounting his horse. We'll make out better than some.

Everything about that year of 1917 began in a struggle, what with the weather so bad and the war moving the price of mutton and wool up and down. But men and animals stood living proof of the conviction people still held, that a field torn into dark clods could still be born up green and something eternal could still spring from an earth steaming as if breathing with a bloody fire.

1

There were but a hundred sheep to go and the blue heeler was forcing the stragglers forward. Walter was standing at the gate channeling them in and John was still on his mare holding them deep into the corral so they wouldn't get boxed on top of one another.

When the last of the sheep were penned Walter pulled the gate shut, hauling his mud-clogged boots out of the sucking earth where the sheep had tread. He had to lift his toes and brace his feet to keep the boots on, and more than once he reached down and pulled at his boots to free them before taking another step forward. After he clasped the gate shut, he bent down and retrieved a horseshoe.

Your horse threw a shoe, Walter said, holding it up for John to see.

John shook his head and cursed under his breath and told Walter to hang it on the fence and he'd nail it on later. He dismounted the bay gelding, used his hands to fling the packed dirt from its hooves, and when he could be sure there were no nails still stuck, he set the foot down and led him out of the pen.

He tied him to the sheepwagon and John and Walter began piping water to the sheep through fifty-gallon drums they had hauled down earlier in the week. The sheep would be watered and grained, but there'd be no hay.

Hay was selling in Picabo at thirty-five dollars a load, and ungettable at that the sheep were suffering. Operations farther south had sheep so weak that on cold nights many of them died to be found in the morning frozen to the ground. Those not quite dead still could not be saved, for the melting snow made the ground so slick the starving sheep tripped over their own legs and fell down and froze before the herders could get around and drag them upright.

With the sheep watered John pointed at a fence rail indicating they should sit and take a rest. They climbed the fence and sat and both men stripped off their gloves, cupped their hands to their mouths, and blew and then rubbed their hands together quickly.

Walter pulled his gloves back on and slapped his hands on his legs a couple of times to keep them awake and feeling. Surveying the ashen sheep he began to imagine just what kind of fight they'd put up when he went to hold them. The thought made the muscles across his arms and chest go tight.

Not that cold is it, John said.

There's a nip to the air.

You weren't shivering just then?

No.

Good. We'll be getting back to work soon enough.

This was Walter Pascoe's first season with John Wright. He was seventeen and just coming on to the belief he could hold his own in the world and do as good a day's work as any man, which made him eager to prove himself.

My father says you've always had the best, Walter said, pointing to the sheep spread in the pens before them. They were thin but not starved, as John had extended his credit at the mercantile to get them grain.

Not always, but the Panama's been good for me, and like I said earlier, with some luck things will work out fine for us this year.

Walter didn't know about luck or whether he much believed in it. His thoughts were on picking out a quiet sheep, one he might grab as soon as John was ready to commence with the marking. He drew his arms tight across his chest and antsy to be moving, he let his legs to rattle on the fence rail. He blew out as if he were smoking and watched his breath float in the air in front of him.

John pulled out a cigarette, offered one to Walter.

No thanks.

The sheep did look weak, but Walter knew they had spirit. There were two hundred of them confined in the pen before them, two thousand total. They were all wheat colored and matted with mud and twigs buried deep within the fleece. They had grown a bit restless and agitated in all the waiting and John motioned the blue heeler out of the herd to quiet them. John kept smoking and looking over his sheep as if calculating their size and weight in his head.

Walter picked at the loose slivers of wood coming off the fence and split them with his fingernails, seeing if he could make them thread thin, waiting for John to tell him it was time for them to get back to work.

Now and then the sheep raised their heads to stare at John and Walter suspiciously, before dropping their noses to trail the wet ground for grass they would not find. John and Walter stayed on the top rail of the fence

3

for some time, letting the blue heeler do her work, and soon the sheep were quiet and milled about patiently.

Lambing and shearing and the rest of the sheep operation had a way of running together. It was all one big project: marking, lambing, shearing, and herding them up the valley to the high country, the Sawtooths, for summer grazing. They'd herded John's ewes into corrals south of Bellevue, a place called Slaughterhouse that was below Timmerman Hill, just that morning. The sheep would be separated and John would teach Walter to clip the fleece around the ewe's bags to help the new lambs find their mothers' teats. Not all men followed these practices so carefully, but it was another means by which John claimed to propagate his lamb crop.

Others were on the move that cold and unfavorable spring, moving their sheep up from winter range between Rupert and Bliss. Some were en route to lambing sheds at Sid Owinza, Picabo, Carey, Macon, and the Neusiis corrals; others would lamb on the surface of the desert and take their chances with the weather. John was one of these men. Land and wide open space were critical to surviving in the industry, and with cattleman and herders in contest for open range, herders could see their own forced exit from the business if they were not careful. For that reason, John tried to stay his sheep on the range as much as possible and penned them in only long enough to get them marked and ready for lambing.

They were still seated on the fence rail when John pointed below them to a sheep pushed up against the fence. Got to clip them close, he said. You don't shear the hind legs, flies and maggots, they get bad, real bad.

Okay, Walter said. I'll make sure to get the hind legs.

Handle them firm. Stay clear to the side of them, but keep yourself pressed close. You get behind them and they don't know where you are, you'll get kicked.

Yes, sir.

Good and short, John said, holding his hands not so far apart. John was wide across the shoulder and he looked grounded as he sat there with his shoulders rolled forward explaining to Walter the ways of the business. There was a sense about him that he had what he deserved. Then you make sure you cut the hair around the bag. You don't and we got trouble. You ever see a lamb nurse?

4

Yes, sir.

You ever see a lamb nursing that couldn't find the tit? No, you haven't. You never can. See, they'll go right ahead, start sucking on a tuft of wool between the legs if they can't find a tit. That doesn't do them a hell of a lot of good and none for us either.

No, sir.

I like that.

What?

Sir, John said, smiling.

Walter didn't know what to say. John's idea of fun would take a bit of getting use to. His own father had taught him respect and how to listen and follow by example and to be careful with his words. John seemed to be just as careful with his words, but his words seemed to require response, and Walter didn't yet feel sure what kind was in order.

Worse than sucking a tuft of wool, John continued, they suck in all that dirty stuff. John spat and lifted his hat to run his fingers quick through his hair and to scratch his hat line where the hair was matted. They get the maggots and other stuff and they can get real sick. They get the scours sometimes, the shits. That can take 'em down. They do that for very long and they're clear dried up. Kill 'em dehydrated.

That's bad.

It'll take the heart right out of you, son, John said, replacing his hat.

John took the shears he had resting on a nearby post and slid down from their perch on the board fence, and Walter followed. John waved a hand in the air and his blue heeler separated a ewe. John took hold of her and drew her back against him, flipped her into sitting position, and dragged her to an empty spot on the far side of the corral. Her front legs flailed for a moment and then she went quiet, her whole body still in submission.

Once he had her positioned he quickly began clipping around her bag and then he turned her on each of her sides to get a better angle on the fleece around her haunches. Not once did the shears leave the wool.

They would clip around the ewes' udders to prepare them for lambing, but then John would hire out an outfit to do the spring shearing, for the crew men averaged ninety to one hundred head a day. While the shearing unions were pushing for rates as high as fifteen cents a head with the war

5

on, John still couldn't see another way around hiring them. Woolen mills paid premium prices for uniform grades of wool and John could not afford to have Walter, so new to shearing, cut the fleece into ragged patches of uneven length.

Walter was bent next to John, watching him intently as he handled the shears, clipping another ewe. Letting the second sheep go, John pulled from the back pocket of his overalls a second set of shears. He handed them to Walter and pointed him toward the adjacent corral, where another two hundred of John's two thousand sheep were gathered. Walter felt the steel of the shears cold in his hands. John offered nothing else in way of instruction then.

Called it the season of bad feet that first year, John said, hollering over to Walter who was climbing the fence to the other pen. John was bent over his fourth ewe and spoke without looking up. Went from one rotten hoof to the next pulling twigs out of cloven hooves. Bacteria soaked so deep in there, turpentine ridded them of it only for but a day or two. Maybe not even that long. By the time I made it back again to check their feet, it was back. That smell, just like piss and Pomade hair grease.

I smelled it in the sheep in our field at home, Walter said. It's bad. It stays in your hands.

That's right, he said, wiping the sweat across his forehead with his coat sleeve. Get yourself a ewe, Walter.

Walter hadn't been standing there long, and it wasn't that he didn't know what to do, but he knew John probably thought it looked that way. He raised his hand and circled it in the air as he had seen John do. The blue heeler, not more than twenty feet out, intent on his lines, paid him no mind and lay crouched to the ground trembling as he studied the herd.

Is there something special I should do to get him to go? Walter said.

Point your finger. Flat hand raised in the air makes him stay put.

Walter circled his hand with his index finger pointed to the sky and the blue merle-colored dog leapt off and then broke to a trot as he fell into the band. He crept up silently behind a ewe on the outskirts of the herd, nipped its heel, and then clapped to the ground to avoid being kicked. And then the blue heeler was up again, driving it in Walter's direction with another nip. It kept on like this, diving and nipping and then ducking again, until the ewe was finally at Walter's feet. Then it slunk off stealthily to circle the herd.

John had bought the blue merle-colored dog as a pup from a breeder in Caldwell three years ago, who made promises he'd kept the bull terrier out of his dogs. The dog was more thickset in the shoulder and a bit slower than the traditional dingoes he was use to working with, but he had a bigger heart than any herding dog he'd ever owned.

After an hour of shearing Walter felt like he was picking up speed. It wouldn't be bad to have two dogs between us, he yelled back over to John. He kept his head down so John couldn't tell if he was serious or not.

You ought to know better than to get me started this late in the morning, John said, shaking his head.

John's other dog, his lambing dog, was an Australian shepherd and not so willing. While the blue heeler worked the sheep, attentive to John's every gesture, the lambing dog slept in the open door of the sheep wagon. She preferred her small and boxy outpost, with its two beds on opposite sides of the walls, and guarded it like a nesting den. She was a year younger than the blue heeler, but lazy. John cursed her daily and called her good for nothing and said over and over he ought to get himself a real dog, but he kept her. She had a white blaze running in between her eyes and a short stubbed tail and a black nose that saved her. She could smell the lambs coming days before any of them, so when the ewes started wandering out of the herd to drop, she was the first to find the lambs.

That morning the lambing dog hadn't even bothered to get off the front step of the sheep wagon to do her morning business. John had to rouse her out by the scruff of her neck.

You'd think she was nursing pups in that wagon, John said.

You never know.

Know what? John said, letting loose another sheep.

Maybe she's pregnant.

Then she's been pregnant since the day I bought her, John said, with his hands on his hips, bending backward to stretch out his back. Hope to hell she's not pregnant. Sure don't need any more like her hanging about.

The blue sky and the still biting cold air made Walter feel like he was growing inside himself and his bones were stretching. He felt lucky to've hooked on with John Wright, being as he was just out of high school. His

7

father knew all the sheep men. He'd been one himself, liquidating in 1907 to buy a mercantile that same year in Hailey and moving the family into town. Walter's mother couldn't be on the land anymore. That was ten years ago when Walter was seven.

Walter's mother never asked to live in town or move anywhere they hadn't already been heading. She wasn't that way, but there came a point when even prayer and belief no longer kept her standing on both legs. Two years after Walter was born a paralysis began its degenerating move up the right side of her body. Some days the right side of her face looked limp and staggered, half drunk, as if the left side had been mismatched with the right. Other days it was her feet that gave her away, and with one wrong step it was everything she could do to catch herself and remain standing. She believed her mind and spirit would ultimately triumph over her failing body, but it hadn't gone that way yet.

In Hailey they built a house sided with shiplap on Croy Street. It was the first time home was just one place. No longer would they follow the sheep from ridge to valley and back again. But something got into Walter those first ten years on the land so they weren't surprised when he said he wanted to leave school early so he could be out moving with a herd.

You can always come back and work the mercantile, his father'd said when he left for John Wright's. You go, son. It's all right with me.

When it was time for Walter to go his father handed him a double-bladed pocket knife with mother-of-pearl grips. Then he put both hands squarely on his son's shoulders. He looked to have a thought and then to say something, but he removed his hands and stood there.

Walter nodded. They'd see each other again in May when Walter came home for graduation.

Walter let go a ewe and again thrust a hand into the air and circled a finger above his head and John's blue heeler swept under the bottom rail and parted another. He grabbed the ewe with one hand under her chest and the other around her hind end and turned her over into a sitting position. With the shears in his right hand, he used his left to gauge the thickness of the wool. He dug his hands into the fleece, feeling how thick and dense the hair was, and he rubbed his fingers together and felt the oil, like a salve on his dry hands.

His life was marked by a rhythm now and even when the days were long and his back ached low down from so much bending over, he kept going. Part of it was that the work never ended. Sheep were not something you could take a break from and he took a certain comfort in the prospect this work might go on forever without end.

But it was more than the routine of their work that had made him rise early for the past eight mornings. It was something about the land, the way the valley floor gave way to mountains that rose to the sky, white and blind, reflecting white, even late into spring. The white made things seem larger than they were and sometimes standing between those distant mountain walls Walter couldn't help but feel small. It was strange to him because he also felt to be resized and made over big. Here, even the sky climbed high. Everything collided – the sky, the mountains, and the valley – and it was hard to tell where one started and the other left off. He could never be sure where that left him, and some days it meant all there was to mean just to know where he stood at a particular moment in time.

Bent over, working the shears, he listened to the sheep as they wandered aimlessly and out of the corner of his eye he watched John's bay gelding turn his head and rock back on his haunches, ready to shy. But hobbled, he simply dropped his back end with his hocks flexed and crow-hopped on all fours. He snorted and flared his nostrils and pawed at the earth twice, almost to spite it, and then he stood. It was the nervous kind of still of something untold, of something invisible to most.

The wind seems to be kicking his heels up, Walter said.

He's all right. He's just that way, John said. The gelding remained poised in his nervous readiness as harmless as John indicated.

Walter went back to work and a ewe separated on her own. She moved toward him on legs so thin he marveled they could hold up the weight of a body. Then she stood there and bleated out of her bowed head. She was an easy catch, and Walter gathered her up in his arms. But she had more nerves than he thought, and he could feel her body coiled and quivering all over like a taut rope. He angled his body over her, trying to get a solid grip on her before flipping her on her back. He kept one hand around her chest, but she began to squirm, and before he knew it she had pulled away from him. Scrambling forward to be upright, she threw out a kick that caught him in the crotch and knocked him down.

When Walter stood up, his hands cupped over his crotch, John was at the fence line, his elbows on the top rail and his hands loose. He wasn't laughing, but the sides of his mouth were turned up and his green eyes were bright with the thought of laughter.

You got to quiet them, he said softly.

She didn't give me time.

Just let them know you aren't leaving and hold them tight. They'll settle for you.

By noon Walter was stocking them and keeping up one for every three of John's. John said he was doing just fine and at the rate they were going they might even be done by June.

Chapter 2

J OHN POURED OUT the last of the coffee into their tin cups. It steamed in the cold morning air, bathing their faces as they hovered together over their plates. Nearby the cookstove clanked as it cooled, giving up its heat to the cold air.

He told Walter he'd be needing a horse now that they were going to start moving. It was the last week of March and the ewes were clipped and near ready to lamb.

Walter nodded as he forked scrambled eggs and hot sausage into his mouth. The month had been good for him. His hands had blistered and toughened and he was sleeping tired and waking up rested. When the weather broke in the middle of the month he and John rigged up a lean-to with a tarp stretched over the top so they could sleep outdoors. The first night was cold, but Walter slept more soundly than he could ever remember sleeping in town.

The morning was also different insofar as John didn't eat his usual breakfast but picked over it, watching it go cold, as if he were by nature a finicky eater, which he wasn't.

I get a pretty good horse at a fair price from a fellow named Cliff Bolles in Ketchum. Do you know him?

No, Walter said, but my father probably does. He trades with about everyone for a hundred miles around.

Well then, after today you can say you know him too. Though it wouldn't be a proud thing to say.

Why is that?

Did I not say he was a horse trader?

Not in so many words, but yes, you did.

John's bay mare was hobbled on the far side of the sheepwagon and she whinnied out into the thin morning where there were no horses to hear her. John twisted his body around to scan the horizon, thinking maybe another operation was coming up on them and they'd have to start pushing the sheep north sooner than he'd planned.

What are you looking for John?

Not like we don't share this range. Other herders, ranchers try to pass us at any time.

The sausage was spicy and Walter swallowed some coffee to cool his mouth.

Something wrong? John asked.

No, sir.

Well, you're acting funny, picking at your food, John said, setting down his own fork.

I didn't mean to, Walter said, not sure what John was getting at, as his plate was empty and John's was still full.

That's all right.

I guess I didn't know I was.

No matter. We've got to travel to get you a horse and there's no two ways about it. You can get worried about traveling. You get pretty settled down here. Don't like to leave. It's understandable.

Must be, Walter said, still not understanding the conversation he was having with John but somehow knowing he was managing to say the right thing since John kept talking.

You going to eat that? Walter asked.

No. Go ahead if you want.

Thanks, Walter said as John passed over his plate. Walter set down his own plate behind the log he was seated on. The lambing dog was watching him from the sheepwagon step and she trotted up close to them. Before John could tell her to get away, Walter was pointing at his plate that was clean, except for a bit of grease she might lick up.

She's already lazy and now you want to go and make her a lazy beggar to boot, John said.

She'll be all right.

I understand getting nerved up, but you are not to worry.

I didn't say I was nerved up, Walter said.

But you're acting it.

Walter kept eating.

Then John told him that his wife, Annette, was driving down from Hailey to take them to Ketchum. Walter would ride back on his own with the horse.

We won't be gone but the day.

Walter raised his head and both men exchanged looks. Walter tried to read John for what he was and what had been said, but there was little he could say.

Sounds all right, Walter said. He was surprised to hear John get around to telling him he had a wife in such a way, but then he figured there was really no good reason he should've known about Annette before.

Only it means we have to do a day's work this morning before she gets here.

That'll be all right, Walter said, his mouth full of eggs and sausage.

Good God, Walter, you can eat enough for six men.

I guess I'm hungry.

No need to eat that fast, John said, pressing his knuckles with his thumb.

I thought we were in a hurry.

We've got work to get done, but I don't want you choking down your food like a dog. He began sliding his ring finger up and down over his thick knuckle, without watching what he was doing.

When Walter was through eating and John had boiled water for their dishes, they cleaned up camp and got to work moving the sheep into stock pens. They weren't more than a mile north of Gannett on a vacated homestead. There was a large wood corral opening up into a pasture. They'd walked the wire fence line the day before to make sure it was enclosed and decided it'd be a safe place to leave the sheep for the day.

Late that morning when they were holding the sheep into the pasture, Walter looked up at the sun crawled almost halfway up the sky and then to the dirt gravel bar northwest of them and in the distance he could see a black vehicle. He watched the truck come on, telling John that someone was coming, but John paid it no mind. He waved his hat in the air driving a few sheep and kept at his business. When the sheep were caught up at the gate, confused and moving in despondent circles while the blue heeler dove at them, John made his way in their direction.

Come on. Get these sheep now, Walter.

Yes, sir, Walter said, stumbling to keep up but keeping an eye on the approaching truck.

When Annette pulled in they were putting the last of the sheep in the corrals. For the second time that morning the lambing dog rose from the sheepwagon step where she was curled up sleeping. She took off barking only to sit at Annette's feet with her head bowed for petting as Annette stepped down from the running board.

John was leaning against the fence rolling a cigarette while Walter dragged the gate shut. With a hand still clasping the gate bar, Walter turned to see.

Annette was standing holding up the hem of her blue gingham dress. The dress was drawn tight about her waist with a matching blue lace sash the color of the sky. She wore a Dolly Varden hat, the kind his mother wore to civic club meetings. Annette's hat was trimmed with fresh-cut daisies and blond strands of hair fell from underneath it. She took a step toward them. She had only a few steps to go, but that was as far as she went. Her face softened and she smiled, and it looked like she might just stand there forever.

That's Annette, John said as he stepped past Walter.

She bent down and patted the dog's head, gently at first, and then she roughed its neck and scratched its ears and it sprang to life, twisting round and round in circles at her feet. Then the lambing dog was jumping high into the air and yelping and raising its lips smiling at her.

Glad to see at least someone is happy to see me, Annette said. My old girl still remembers who her mama is.

As best Walter could tell she was younger than John by at least ten years. John moved toward her and she let go her hem and both her hands came to rest at her side. Her skin was fair except for her cheeks, which were flushed in the cold morning air. She was thin and looked even smaller beside John. Walter thought if the dog were to jump on her she might be knocked down and he waited for John to call the lambing dog from her, but he didn't.

Walter couldn't see John's face because his back was to him in his walking, but he watched Annette tip her head down, shy-like, as John neared her.

I just wanted to look nice, she spoke out to him, as if finally declaring a thought she'd been holding for a month or more.

You do, John said. He reached to take her hands in his own. You look real pretty.

I brought a change of clothes, she said, becoming shy with his touch. I'll just go in the wagon and be out quick-like. The supplies are in the Ford. You two might start unloading them if you like.

John said that was fine and that he and Walter would take care of it and for her to go right ahead and change. He motioned to Walter with his arm to come join him. Packed in the Ford were two coal-oil cans, a hardwood barrel for smoking meat, a twenty-pound bag of rolled oats, and two grub boxes stocked with sourdough starter, black beans, garbanzos, rice, sugar, saltpeter, cooking oil, pepper, and a supply of spices. Walter and John each took an end of the box and set it beside the sheepwagon. The bagged goods they would set inside as soon as Annette was out. The rest they piled under the lean-to.

Then John went to a grub box and found an egg. He opened the hardwood barrel and dropped the egg into it and watched it bob in the brine.

Floats, John said.

So?

You're mama never taught you how to tell if a brine was strong enough?

I guess not.

This barrel's ready to soak some meat for smoking, Walter.

How so?

A brine strong enough to float an egg or a potato, that's how you tell. John dipped his hand into the syrup-colored brine to retrieve the egg and then rinsed it in water left over from the morning dishes and replaced it in the grub box. Make a bit of coffee before she's ready? John said.

Sounds all right.

Then they waited, John seated on a bucket and Walter stretched out on the ground. The earth was hard and it felt good to be close to it. The sun warmed Walter's cheek and though the sweat from the morning's work had left his shirt damp, he was not chilled. From the northwest was coming the last cold wind of the season, sifting flurries of lacy clouds across the sky. Walter watched the clouds take shape and then split and part ways. He breathed in deeply and could smell the sweat from his body, ammonia left from sheep manure, the lanolin on his hands, and the musty scent of earth and dirt drying out after a long winter. He took another drink off his coffee.

She'll be our camp tender, John said.

She'll stay on for the summer?

That's what a camp tender does, John said. You know as much.

Yes, sir.

John told Walter how Annette would get along just fine, that she had a tough side to her and he should not underestimate her.

You mean she doesn't wear dresses all the time, Walter said, putting his hand over the sun so he could see John's face.

I didn't say what she wears to get her work done in, only that she does it.

Annette would go on ahead of them and pick out suitable places to bed down for the night. She'd have a fire ready and the Dutch oven buried in the ground by the time they arrived at the sheepwagon. Often she'd wander off to tend the sheep during the noon meal so John and Walter could eat in peace without having to look over their shoulders at the sheep. Then when supplies ran low she'd take a day and go into town to restock. And when lambing time came they'd need all the extra hands they could get and she'd work the days beside them.

Reckon she'll want to go into town a bit more than some camp tenders, but she'll keep the mail and any news we need coming to us, John said. He got up then and went to the lean-to and brought back rawhide rope and tossed a few lengths of it on Walter's chest.

Don't go thinking we take naps around here on any kind of regular basis.

I wasn't, Walter said, propping himself up on his elbows. She ever been your camp tender before? Walter said. He sat up when he saw John meant for them to do some work. He pulled out his knife and began whetting it up one side and down the other on a stone until it was sharp to his finger.

Not exactly.

John watched Walter and then handed over his own knife for Walter to sharpen. John did so without asking, as if Walter had always been in charge of the knives and it was something they both knew he did better.

Annette came along here and there, but I didn't need one before I lost Baptie, John said, taking up the rawhide and beginning to twist it into a braid with his thick fingers. He intertwined the three cords, plaiting the rawhide so tightly, not even a hair could be thread through the braid's links.

John had never operated before with any other man except Harry Baptie, a one-armed Scotch. Baptie was slight in build, wiry, and tough and came from the state of Texas where he'd been a one-armed bronc-riding star. He'd never had to worry about being penalized for holding on to the saddle horn with one hand because that hand wasn't around.

And before he was a bronc star, he'd been a cook for more than thirty buckaroos, and before that he claimed to have rode the sea. Baptie was inclined to the riotous life, which included whiskey and plenty of what the men in town and the men of the hills and all of the men who had ever known too many nights alone called pleasures of the flesh. He never wanted the women he was with and always the women he'd never have and so he drank to reconcile the difference.

John told how he kept Baptie on as long as he could before the whiskey and the women did him in and finally burnt his stomach so bad Baptie said even the tallow couldn't save him and he pleaded to be quit of the land and the sheep. Each year John managed to bring Baptie out of his dazed and drunken winter stupor. But last year things had changed. John picked Baptie up in town and it was the same as every other spring when he'd brought him south, back down to the herd. It took a few days to dry him out. He butchered a mutton that had to be culled anyway and took the leaf fat and boiled it to get tallow. He made Baptie swallow down the tallow, and after two or three days Baptie said his ulcers were cured, or at least so coated he could walk upright without the hunch of a man with cramps. He was sixty-two years old.

Did you manage to keep him dry?

Wouldn't quite go that far. You don't dry a man like Baptie out that easy, or for good. There were still days I'd catch him by the creek bed puking up blood.

What was he bleeding for?

His insides coming out. When he coughed real hard it was the same, blood coming up.

Never heard of that.

Well, you never seen a man like Baptie. Lot I put up with to keep that guy.

Was it worth it?

I'll say.

It'd made Walter a bit uneasy and none the more confident to be taking Baptie's place because he knew if he failed, his failure would be all the more great as when backed up against a man not so reputable. But listening, he could tell John still had admiration and affection for the old man and behind his complaints and hardness there was sadness over the loss of him.

Do you figure Baptie might want to rejoin you sometime? Walter asked.

He won't be back. Baptie gave up trying to prove anything to anybody. He cut out early on me and was done.

You don't leave midseason, Walter said, handing John back his knife.

Sure as hell don't, John said, putting a finger to the blade and then trusting it on his rawhide. He cut three more cords off it before passing it to Walter. Said the tallow washed off his ulcers. Offered to make up some more for him, but he said that wouldn't be what he was needing. We let it go there, but he and I both knew where we stood.

Did you see him in town?

Said he was done, didn't I? There was a gruffness to John now, like he couldn't afford to talk anymore about Baptie, like he might be bringing up some weakness or failure of his own if he did so.

Yes, sir.

Don't much matter at this point, does it?

No, sir, Walter said. Walter cut off three cords of rawhide for himself, knotted them at the ends, and began braiding. There was the creak of the leather being won into place, and the occasional bleat of a sheep, but the wind was quiet and carried no sound through the hollows of empty sagebrush.

Then Walter heard the sheepwagon door open on its rusty hinges. He set the rope aside. They had not been properly introduced, which was not strange or awkward in itself, since each knew who the other was. Still, introductions of another kind were being made. There would be things about Walter that John had yet to make his mind up on, and he knew Annette would likely play a role in shaping these opinions. He stood up and brushed his hands on the back of his jeans and with the palm of his hand he tried to smooth the sides of his hair back.

John stood up as well.

She stepped out of the wagon wearing a sweater and a pair of pressed blue jeans cinched at the waist with a wide black leather belt. The cuffs of her jeans she wore rolled to midcalf and on her feet she wore low-cut shiny white leather boots. Her blond hair was tied back and she looked even younger. John stood, and this time she went right to him and wrapped her arms around his shoulders and he kissed her.

You ready to go? John said.

If Walter is, she said, looking him over.

Yes ma'am, Walter said.

Walter Pasoe, you're kind of cute.

John laughed and started to turn her in the direction of the car. Come on then.

Fine then, she said and put her arm through John's.

Walter held back as they made their way to the truck, waiting for John to slide in next to Annette, but John told him to get in.

Go ahead, Annette said. I'll drive and John can ride next to the window.

So Annette drove and Walter sat in the middle and John rode with his head to the passenger window. They were leaving out of Slaughterhouse and would drive up through Bellevue to Ketchum. But they hadn't even pulled out of the yard onto the road when Annette slowed and reached across Walter to take John's hand.

Her sweater slid up her arm, and two bracelets chimed on her thin wrist as she reached across Walter. Walter was struck by how small her bones must be for how thin her wrist. Her wrist looked like that of a child's and her skin was so fair and white he couldn't imagine she'd spent a day in the sun. Her hands were made even more white when held in contrast to John's, which were dark and brown and spotted in places from

19

sun and weather. She was so unlike any woman Walter would have ever imagined John with. Their was something so fragile about her and yet Walter hadn't doubted John saying there was a tough side to her.

Don't mind me, she said to Walter. You okay? Annette said to John.

Yep, John said, but when Walter looked over John was using his coat sleeve to wipe sweat beaded at his brow.

She then concentrated on her driving, but still she kept hold of John's hand across Walter's lap, looking over at John from time to time. John's not much of an automobilist, she said as they picked up speed.

He doesn't drive? Walter asked, thinking it odd to be talking about John in his presence that way, but it seeming like a thing okay to do.

He gets carsick and he can't sit still too long in a truck. He likes me to hold his hand if you don't mind.

No ma'am.

It was like John wasn't even there, caught up as he was trying not to be sick. Walter was surprised to see John would allow Annette to take care of him the way she seemed intent on doing. Their was a sweetness between them he had also not expected.

I may ask you to do the stick shift if he gets worse, she said. He doesn't like me to let go of his hand.

I'll be all right, John said to the window, this time a bit more gruff. John did seem okay, riding all quiet and to himself.

He bought me this truck three years ago and he has never put his foot to the pedal once. It doesn't seem right to him.

Not right?

He figures it's mine.

Sort of like the way a man never rides another man's horse, Walter said.

Or lends a fellow a gun, Annette said.

Sometimes you have to, John said, as if trying to pay no heed to his condition, his voice dry and reed thin.

Yes, like that, Annette said. I told him once I didn't mind so much if he wanted to get rid of it, seeing it makes him so sick. He wouldn't hear of it. Said his opinion didn't matter in the slightest. It wasn't his to drive to begin with and it would never be his to sell. He says it suits me well, the truck.

That late morning they drove up through Bellevue, Hailey, and on into Ketchum not talking much. The sun was high and the air was thin and cold rushing through the car. Walter kept his arms folded across his chest staying the heat around him. For outside the car, the land did not look cold so much as ashen and washed out and it seemed something you ought to keep your distance from. The sage was almost vibrant in its pallid hue, set against the dark dirt of the valley floor, and ahead of them was always more and more of this expiring color. But for a few scattered Douglas firs bent upright on the rising bluffs the valley might have been mistaken for some perished place coming to its end. The fescue and bluebunch wheatgrass were still brown this time of year, gray like wind and sun-worn bark.

Chapter 3

W H E N T H E Y M A D E it to Bolles's place in Ketchum, there was
a narrow footpath leading to a one-room log cabin. A wood plank
porch stretched the front of it. There was a rocking chair on the porch and
a milk jug set beside the front door and a pair of leather boots gone soft at
the calf and bent over.

John slid out of the truck first and stepped down to the hard dirt road, cut
a foot deep in places by wagon wheels and expanding snow and ice. He
walked slowly a few steps as if he were finding his legs and Walter walked
behind him ready to reach under John's arms and catch him if he should
stumble. Annette came around from the other side of the black Ford and
put her arm through his and they all walked toward the house. They could
hear a dog barking from inside and John turned to Walter and in a hushed
voice told him to keep his eye on the dog, that he was one crazy-ass dog.

Bolles stepped out onto his porch to see who it was and without waving
he walked out to meet them. A tan dingo dog trotted behind Bolles with
its ears pinned back and its tail tucked under. He looked shy more than he
did mean.

Bolles shook John's hand and said, Fine day to be out.

A beautiful one, Annette said.

Found me a hired hand, John said, nodding toward Walter. Here to
find him a horse.

Fair enough, Bolles said, folding his arms to his chest. I'd say it was
about time. Bolles was tall, thin, and straight legged, and his brown hair
was balding on the top of his head and he had a mustache. Last I heard
Baptie was camped up in Mackay, he said. Breaking two-year-olds. I
guess he can sit a horse.

John cleared his throat and spat and didn't answer Bolles.

I see you're getting used to the black Ford, Bolles said.

Don't you start in with him Mr. Cliff Bolles, Annette said.

Bolles reached out a hand to Walter and introduced himself. Pleasure to meet you. Your father's a good man.

Thank you, sir.

I've known him for a good number of years. A practical man. Give you the coat off his own back, I figure.

And then Bolles inquired about the health of Walter's mother, saying he knew how tough that disease was on her. Walter'd never thought to call his mother's condition a disease, and his eyebrows narrowed, and all the while Bolles watched him steadily.

She's doing all right, Walter said.

I remember first time she bought a horse from me, so she could ride aside your father. I imagine it's hard for her, having you away. But, my god, she's a tough one, fighting her health the way she does. She gets by just fine, doesn't she?

I believe she does, Walter said, confused as to how Bolles should have any idea how his mother got along. Bolles seemed a decent enough man to Walter, but still there was something about him, the way he kept his arms across his chest and that he should presume to know things about Walter's life and family.

Shaping up pretty bad down there? Bolles said, tightening his arms to his chest as he pivoted to face John.

Seen it worse.

Do you think high prices will pull you through?

Don't like making money off the misfortune of others.

Sometimes I think you're just too honest, Bolles said.

I warned you, Annette said.

Bolles smiled and tipped his hat forward to her. I won't be starting nothing you don't approve of, Annette. We won't have it.

You have some horses to show me? John said.

Bolles shoved his hands in his pant pockets and turned around to lead them out back to a large pasture where twelve horses grazed. The dingo trotted behind Bolles, stayed off about ten feet and watching that distance if it were something to measure. When John and Walter quickened their step to keep up with Bolles they got too close to the dog and it yelped before loping off to the other side of Bolles.

When they got to the pasture, Bolles stopped at the gate. There they are, he said. There's my beauties.

Walter started to raise his hand to point at a little red dun mare in the corner of the field.

You mind if we just go have ourselves a walk around in there? John said.

Wouldn't expect you to do anything less, Bolles said. He held out a halter and lead hanging over the gatepost and told them to take it with them. Annette stayed back with Bolles.

When they were off the fence line and their backs to Bolles, John spoke in a hushed voice. I know which one you're looking at, but don't act so sure. We'll work our way out there to her. But we're going to act like we've taken a fancy to that gray, John said, pointing to a gray gelding that stood at least sixteen hands high and too high behind.

They walked toward the horse and John patted it on the neck and it lowered its head to be scratched and Walter walked a full circle around it. Then John haltered it and trotted it off while Walter watched. It was slightly off in the right front.

You sure? John asked.

She's lame, Walter said. Might just be a splint, but you can't tell.

Just puts a few more cards on my side of the table.

They let the gray gelding go and slowly made their way out to look at the red dun.

She looked at Walter and John as they approached her and did not begin eating again. For a moment Walter thought the horse would bolt so as not to be caught. But she stayed, paralyzed at what they might do there.

Might be skittish, John said.

Walter stepped in close to her and leaned against her as he ran his hand along her withers and down her back along her spine. She did not flinch. He patted her belly and behind her shoulder a little harder.

She's doesn't seem girthy, Walter said. Trot her out for me, would you?

Didn't know you knew so much about horses. Hell, you didn't have to bring me along on this trip, John said, trotting the mare off.

When John came back, Walter looked her over once more. He walked

25

behind her and studied her hindquarters. They were full and round and she was legged up. He ran his hands over her hocks and down her cannon bones. They were smooth and there were no lumps in the tendons or splints to be found.

We're not buying you a goddamn race horse you know? John said, coiling the lead in his hand.

She quivered a bit while standing and her flank never quit trembling, but that didn't bother Walter. For he could tell she was thinking, trying to figure them out, and he liked that in an animal. Lastly, he ran his hand over her eyes and looked into them. She had large soft eyes – he looked for that in a horse too.

She looks good to me, Walter said.

That's it.

I'd be proud to ride her.

Fair enough, John said, releasing the clasp on the halter.

You going to bring her in or not?

John told Walter that while he might know something about confirmation he didn't know a damn thing about horse dealers. He's got to think we don't need this horse. He indicated that Walter should go back to the black Ford with Annette. You stop and pretend like you're studying the confirmation of a few more as we walk out of this field. You understanding me?

Yes, sir.

When he got back to the Ford, Annette patted the running board and told him to set himself down next to her.

She offered him a cigarette but he declined. This is going to be fun, she said, touching a match to her cigarette.

What are they doing?

This is the famous event where Mr. John Wright buys a horse from Mr. Cliff Bolles. Maybe you've read about it in the newspapers. It only happens once every three or four years and it got started long before I knew John.

Something bad happen?

Annette shook her head. I don't even pretend to understand this one. It's the damnedest way I ever heard of buying a horse.

You think Bolles is all that bad?

I don't know, Walter, she said. You'd think John would just go elsewhere to do his business, but he keeps coming back. Like he's got to prove something.

I don't see what John's got to prove.

We all got something to prove, Walter, she said, turning her head to face him and smiling. We just don't choose the same people to prove it to, and I just say thank God he doesn't have to buy a horse that often.

Walter leaned over and picked up a stick at his feet and began to dig in the dirt, making small tracks and indents in the earth. It was good to be away from the sheep for the day and to sit and not feel the weight of work that would have already settled in his ankles if he were back with the herd. His body felt light, and even the wind coming out of the west felt warm for the first time all year.

You hearing much news about the war from town? Walter asked.

They're still drumming up support. I figure it's any day now and we'll be going over.

Annette picked up a stick and began digging her own scratch marks in the earth. So, Mister Walter Pascoe, I say we all got something to prove. Just what is it you've got to prove?

He set the stick across his lap and leaned back against the truck and his hollow shadow stretched out longer in front of him. Crows that seemed to be exploding from their voices in the bare scrub oaks in front of the house cawed and flapped their wings, moving from branch to ground and back again.

He sighed. Knew just as soon as you said it I ought to be ready to tell you just what it was I aim to prove in life.

You're learning quick Walter.

I suppose I am, but it's not helping me much now, is it?

I'll let you off the hook this time, she said. And when you know what you're here to prove, you be sure and come up to me, any old day, and let me know just what it is. I sure know I haven't figured it out for myself.

Walter didn't say anything back to her. Her request was said lightly and in good fun, but it did not weigh in as such. Ambition wasn't something you explained to anybody; it was how it was, like a good secret that you didn't give away because as soon as you did it no longer felt like your own.

27

Walter'd tried to explain the way he was to himself countless times as if that would somehow stay the questions and make him content inside himself. That he was born with ambition and will he knew, but that it had any more of an explanation than the fact some people were born with blue eyes and others with brown eyes, he wouldn't say.

There didn't seem anything to say.

Annette and Walter sat facing the trees, looking out beyond the house the open hills that fell away to a stream and the sun began its descent down the brown pasture. A hush rose around them, as if a kind of dim ghost of what they saw, to which they would each offer and owe their days, hovered. It could not be pointed to or even spoken of, for it vanished quickly and had no place before them. It resided far off on the land's edge and had crept in faintly gleaming under a lowering sky, only to slip out before either of them could trail it to its end.

The birds drew closer in the trees and a lone crow sounded.

Annette tapped him lightly on the shoulder and then poked him in the arm with her elbow. Neither of them had said anything for a while as both had been content to feel the warm sun soaking their faces and warming their skin under their layers of clothes. He lifted his head and he stared at her and then smiled. They began to talk of other things and he did not say what it was he feared.

You thought much about the war? she said.

Yes. I've thought about it.

Do you want to go?

I'm not eighteen yet.

Then wait until then to start thinking about it. I don't much like bringing it up so I don't know why I did.

Do you think it's going to be hard on the business?

Already is. There's talk of fixing the price of wool.

John's sheep are better than most it seems.

Yeah, but it's early and we got lambing to come. Always lose some there, she said, giving her stick a fling.

It grew silent between them again and they continued to watch John and Bolles talking, with neither hearing a word of what was being said. So close to the ground, Walter could smell mulch mixed with the dry smell of trees not yet with blossom. A half dozen sandhill cranes lofted down from the cottonwood trees and landed in the pasture to feed. Their bodies tipped downward and they looked like they would topple, but their long stilt legs held them fast, and they pecked at the stray kernels of horse grain left from the morning.

Look at 'em, she said, motioning over to Bolles who was shaking his head and John who had his hands up and flying in the air. Neither one's going to give up until he's sure he got the best of this deal.

Figure they're dickering over price, ma'am? Walter said, finally looking up.

I'd imagine they're dickering over just about anything and everything right now.

Does John owe Mr. Bolles something?

Just his pride and mistrust.

John ever left here without a horse?

Nope.

Then out from under the truck they heard a low growl. Annette turned her head and looked at Walter, who started to stand. The dingo crouched with his shoulders close to the ground as he scooted out from behind the wheel well of the truck and went for Walter's ankles, growling and lunging at his leg.

Get. Go on, Annette yelled.

Walter kicked at the dog and caught it in the rib and it went off yelping to the porch stair. John and Cliff turned to see the dog running toward them.

Get over here, Bolles said, pointing his finger to his side and the dog slunk his way. Then John and Bolles went back to talking.

There was the clop of hooves on hard dirt, still too damp to turn over dust. It was two of Bolles's hired hands. They seemed to be snickering to themselves, Walter thought, and he assumed they had seen what happened.

But they didn't let on. They dismounted, said good day to Walter and Annette, and one pointed toward the porch.

I take it we'd be interrupting something? the one with dark hair said, shoving his hands deep in his pockets and looking right at Walter.

Annette cut in. I think you might be best off going straight about your business today.

The dingo trotted back over to them, stayed off by about ten feet. He lifted his head high in the air and his nose pulsed as he tried to get a scent of the two men and who they were. Then he seemed to, for he trotted off toward the porch.

The other one nodded and said, Let's go.

They walked their horses toward the hitching post, and in between the rear legs of the horses, white foam was lathered. They tied their horses to the hitching post and threw the saddles off them and the steam clouded over the horse's backs like it does off a river in early morning.

Did he get you? Annette asked, once the men were out of earshot.

Walter sat back down on the running board without lifting his pant leg.

No, I'm all right.

I didn't ask you if you were all right, Annette said, bending down and lifting up his jean leg herself. There was a little blood trickling down from a puncture wound at the top of his shin above his boots.

Damn, that dog gets everybody new that comes around here, she said. She sat down beside him then.

You saying the dog got you once? Walter asked, still watching the men and their ways but keeping an eye on the dingo.

No, never. Suppose it's just men it don't like. Once, he got Baptie so bad in the hand John had to take him down to Dr. Fox to have it sewed up. It was a bit of a scare, it being his one good hand and all.

Did you like Baptie? Walter said, spitting into his hand, rubbing it over the bite once and pulling his jean back down over his boots.

It wasn't so much about like or dislike. He saved John's life. She pointed at his leg and told him to get it cleaned up as soon as they got near water. I'll clean it myself if you don't. We don't need anybody turning green on us.

Yes ma'am, Walter said.

The dark-haired man haltered the gray gelding Walter and John had stopped to look at. The other, a short, bowlegged man, took a medium-sized bay horse that Walter had hardly noticed. They led them out of the field and tied them to the fence, as their own horses were at the hitching post. Walter watched them begin to saddle the green-broke horses. They ran the warm blankets from their own horses down these young horses' necks, legs, and hind ends before easing them into place on their backs. Then they went for the saddles. One of the men threw his on too quickly and the gray horse pulled back, stretched his neck out long, caught himself on the rope, ran forward, and rammed his chest against the fence. Then he swung his hind end over against the fence, dumping the saddle to the ground. The man booted the horse in the belly. To Walter's surprise it did not pull back again but merely cocked its neck to stare back at the rider, lifted its front leg up as if the man were going to pick its feet, and then placed it down and stood.

I got it in me to give Mr. Cliff Bolles some hassle as to the men he hires, Annette said. The way he goes on about Baptie with John you'd think he hired the cream of the crop.

How'd Baptie save John's life?

It was a long time ago, Annette explained. It's not something John likes to talk about.

All right.

John thought he'd give up herding one season and try mining. That's when he met me. My parents were miners. John was going in with dynamite, up in one of the mines in Copper Basin, when a shaft collapsed. He was one of the lucky ones. He got out. Baptie dug him out. But John didn't want to get out. A beam was cutting off his leg and John had in his head they'd have to amputate. He told Baptie to get a pistol and shoot him.

Doesn't sound like John.

He didn't want to be a damn cripple. But it didn't do him much good, being that he was talking to one. Then he told Baptie to hand over his pistol and he'd do it himself. Baptie wouldn't loan any man his gun. He set to work getting John out and worked for six hours straight. That was the last day John stepped foot in a mine. He still don't feel much in his right leg. You can pinch it or stick a cigarette to it and he wouldn't feel it. It's like it killed off some feeling in there, but you don't see him limping none, do you?

No.

Well, when he was as recovered as he was going to be, he went and hired Baptie out of the mine and they were partners from there on out.

John never said anything.

I would guess that, but I sort of figure you have a right to that bit of history so you know where things began and left off. He saved his life.

Somehow in telling him the story of how John almost died, Annette was also telling Walter how much she loved John. Her face went quiet as if she looked into her heart and she smiled. Then she lifted her head, elbowed Walter, and gave a short laugh, knowing he'd caught her daydreaming.

They stared at the two men and neither had to say anything more. Walter thought back on what John had told him about Baptie and how he had told him where things left off, as he watched the unmounted rider fumbling, trying to get the bit in the horse's mouth. But the gray kept spitting it out and tossing his head.

John had his back to Annette and Walter, but he turned suddenly with his hands up in the air, gesturing there was nothing more he could do to make the deal work. He began walking toward Annette and Walter. Annette started to stand to meet him, but Bolles yelled at John to not go walking away so quick, and she sat back down and let out a sigh.

Don't go falling asleep yet, she said to Walter.

Giving up on me mighty quick today, aren't you, John? Bolles said as John neared still closer to the Ford. We haven't even got started.

I don't aim to get started, John said. He took a few more steps toward Annette, winked at her, and turned around to face Bolles. You're going to have to do better, or I will just start driving myself and this boy up to Mackay to find ourselves a horse. But you know as well as I do I'd rather not have to do so.

He's playing him, she said. I'm just not sure it's working.

Walter heard John ask what it would take to get a fair price on the horse, and then he was out of earshot again, climbing the stairs, and the two men were back up on Bolles's porch. Bolles put a hand in his pocket and twirled one end of his mustache and leaned into the porch rail.

Mr. Cliff Bolles just might be getting the better of John today, Annette said.

Why's that?

With you here. He knows John won't embarrass himself in front of you. He also knows John didn't drive all the way up here for nothing. You think John would walk away from here without a horse for you?

I reckon not.

Annette leaned her head back against the truck door and let the sun hit her face and set her hands on the top of her legs, palms skyward as if the heat might pool in her hands and stay.

Something about the sun, she said. I should have lived in California where the sun never quits.

You ever been there?

I was sent there once. Supposed to live there, but it never suited me. There were always too many people coming and going down there, drifter-like. I was never sure I'd find my own two feet. The sun, that was the only thing that suited me about that place.

I'd like to go.

Never know, you just might. You're young. Plenty of days before you. You got a girl, Walter?

Not really.

I imagine you got your eye on one.

Yeah, but I don't think you'd know her.

Try me.

I've only seen her though.

That's good enough for me.

Trina Ivy's her name.

The oldest one of Frank Ivy's?

Probably so, but I'm not sure.

I see her now and then in town with her father and I've always thought she was real pretty-like in a rough and tough sort of way. She's not from any fancy family, but she carries herself real nice and I don't figure she's short on brains. Her father may be a bit crazy, but my dad always told me that man knew what was coming and going.

Walter couldn't help recalling the first time he'd seen her, about a year ago, when she was in town with her father. They'd come with a string of pack mules and she'd been riding doubles with one of her brothers. They stopped at the mercantile to order traps and Frank had bought a pair of coveralls for himself. His father had quickly pointed to Frank Ivy as a trapper not worth messing with. The Ivy family was big, eight kids in all. He was told how they lived in the hills and surrounding mountains of the Wood River valley, trapping and coming down only when Frank needed a good game of poker and what Walter's father called a good pickling up. Despite what he'd been told about the family, Walter couldn't help being mesmerized by Trina the first time he saw her. He was so taken with this vision he had of her moving lithely through the store, skimming the tips of her pale fingers over everything that seemed to pique her interest. She'd looked back at him behind the counter now and then and smiled, almost impishly, as if she were giving him permission to catch her stealing. When he looked at her, she looked away, and he had the sense she was wise to the world in ways he could not yet put names to. She kept moving through the store, touching things but not picking a single thing up to hold.

I guess it's been a long time since I seen her, he said.

Well, you keep your head up and you won't miss her, Annette said.

Annette, you think John would mind if I stopped at my parents' place on my way through town?

Oh, of course not. You go right ahead. I should have thought of it myself. I'll tell John, and you just come back on your own.

They watched as John handed over a set of bills, which Bolles took with his left hand so he could shake John's right hand. The two men nodded and parted and the deal was done.

Go get her. She's yours, John said, motioning to the pasture. John looked at the two men on the young horses, somewhat nervously, as if he might have overlooked the two horses and made a wrong choice.

They'll leg up real nice, Bolles said, as if he'd already caught on to what John was thinking.

John didn't say anything. He just watched the men and then he saw, as Walter had, that the gray was off, just a hair lame, and he smiled.

Walter led the red dun mare around to the front of the place and heard Annette tell John he was right to keep his temper and not go about getting himself into trouble with Cliff again. Walter didn't ask any questions, but he'd come to learn from Annette later that Bolles would be paying John back as long as they were both alive.

She'd tell him one night by the fire, with John out on night watch, how John bought a horse from Bolles that died the day he got it to his place. That was ten years back. Bolles said the horse was fine when it left his place and he refused to give John another horse, but he promised he'd make John a special deal on every horse he bought from then on. The special break he was suppose to receive with each sale would remain the point of contention for as long as John would know Bolles.

Walter mounted the mare and thanked John. Annette reached up and took Walter's hand. She held it and told him to have a safe ride to his parents' place on Croy Street.

Walter dismounted when he arrived, and his father came out the front door wiping his hands with a dish towel. He studied the mare from a distance, the way he had taught Walter to do and the very way Walter had done that day. Then he came up, ran his hands down the length of her neck, felt along her back, and gave her a firm pat on the shoulder. He told Walter she was straight in front, said her neck had a nice curve to it, but that her withers were a little high, which might make her short strided.

She's nice, his father said. What will you call her?

Rosina.

Inside, his mother was not at the kitchen window but sitting by the wood stove. She smiled and held out a hand for him to come to her. Bandages were piled in her lap and she did not try to move them but left them resting where they were, to be rolled by day's end, when they would be picked up by a Red Cross volunteer.

The wood table was spread with the morning's paper, and in the center set a lemon pie heaped with meringue. Walter looked at the headline of the Wood River *Daily Times*: TO BE CALLED OUT, HOW THE PROPOSED NEW ARMY WILL PROBABLY BE RECRUITED. Walter's father was studying him and he did not break in as he usually did to summarize the news for them. They were accustomed to having George give them the daily news, for he had always woke long before Walter and his mother, and so by the time they joined him at the table for breakfast he had the paper read.

What's it say? his father asked.

Walter read to his father how there were plans to recruit an army of three million men and that there would be a call to the colors either by volunteering or drafting. First priority was to be given to unattached, unmarried men under thirty years old. Secondly, unattached, unmarried men under forty-five. Thirdly, married men under thirty. Lastly, married men under forty-five.

His father got up and came and stood next to Walter and looked to where Walter read.

George, I saw you with the paper this morning. Why is it we have to talk about this now? Ann said, bringing plates from the kitchen.

Ann, it has been a while since he's seen a paper. Let him look.

Walter trailed the lines with his index finger where it said not a single dependent would suffer, no indispensable breadwinner would be taken under the current recruitment plan.

George nodded to where Walter pointed, but he might as well have been shaking his head. Doesn't quite figure, does it?

Sit, both of you, Ann said. We have Walter home for such a short time and all you two want to talk about is the war. I want to hear about something else.

They sat and ate the pie and he felt himself come home from a long journey and it seemed like years had gone by and miles of distance grown between them. His mother stayed quiet and didn't converse and ask questions as he had expected. It was almost as if he were a guest she was trying to make welcome by being calm and soft-spoken. His father abided his mother by sitting in a mighty silence, lifting his head from his plate of pie now and then to look at Walter but offering little. He seemed older and more tired and resigned than Walter remembered.

Twice Walter tried to ask his father about business at the mercantile, which usually got his father telling a story about someone from town. But today the conversation continued to turn away from people Walter might have known to how sales were down as a result of war conservation measures and how customers were expecting larger and larger store credits from him. Then his mother would cut in and ask him how herding was, whether he was too exhausted, and whether he was getting enough to eat or not, just to change the subject.

Walter realized that in the short time he had been gone the war had spread about his house, not unlike the way sickness does throughout a body. A presence had come over the place. It fell about them all like a breath taken in suddenly, and there was nothing to say, as there is so little to say about conditions of life that fall on people without their asking.

When they seemed to have nothing more to say to one another he rose from his chair, went to his mother, hugged her so she didn't have to get up, and went for his coat. His father was at the door by the time Walter got there, and he patted Walter on the back and said, We'll see you soon, son. Walter said good-bye, already eager to be out on his own again, fearful if he did not leave soon they might offer up some reason as to why he might stay longer. He trotted the horse down Croy Street away from the house and waved his hat in the air.

When Walter made it to camp it was late in the day and John was waiting for him. Walter dismounted, pulled the reins over the mare's head, and unfastened the headpiece so he could turn her loose for the night with the band to graze. When he released the clasp on the bridle, her neck flipped back in the air. She spun around and galloped, dead north.

John raised his hands up in the air as if he might catch her and then fell them down again. By God, John said, where's your head at? You should have cobbled her. Then he shook his head.

Walter wanted to say he was sorry, but he was too angry with himself and the horse.

John waved his arm in the air and bent his head. I might have done the same. Not like we're going anywhere you can't find. You set out early tomorrow morning and we'll catch up. You go ahead and find her.

Annette was standing in the sheepwagon door and she just shrugged her shoulders and held her hands up for a minute.

It happens, she said, and then turned back inside to leave them alone. John kept watching Walter.

I'm sorry, Walter said.

Like she said, happens. We had a big day.

Annette's pretty.

She is, John said.

You get sick coming home?

Yeah.

You better?

Yes, I suppose I am.

That's good, Walter said.

They stood there on the edge of the arriving night. The wind had cleared the day and the stars stood bright overhead. There was an awkwardness to the silence settled about them. Walter understood that

Annette's coming to be with them was as much a change for John as it was for him.

Did your father have any word from about the countryside? Any news besides the war and the blasting cold winter and what it did to the price of crops?

It's like Mr. Bolles said, the prices are going to be high.

Fine, he said. What I expected. Well, looks like I'll be sleeping indoors tonight. John slapped his hat against his overalls and made his way to his sheepwagon.

Walter didn't want to climb under the gray tarp John had bought for them to sleep in for the summer. The sun had just set and the mountains were cast purple, a purple that receded into a diminishing skyline faded lavender. Sagebrush dappled the surrounding hills and dead tree stumps rose up like apparitions. Up the draw just north of him he thought he saw a figure moving. Maybe the red dun.

He stared for a while, drawn into the distance to a dark silhouette, thin at its base, gnarled and unshapely at its top, but he gave up on it after a while when it didn't move. All seemed still except for the crunch of the tarp on its frame as he moved under it, putting down his bedroll. He thought of just sleeping under the cottonwoods, beneath the stars, but he knew that by morning the frost would be heavy.

Settled in his bedroll, he wondered at the clear and quiet of the night where everything seemed to have a place and where his body again, unlike at home, felt grounded with a weight all of his own making. He thought about his parents and the day and realized it was perhaps not their physical beings but he who had changed and become different in his seeing. The world seemed weighted differently and resized and he felt farther away than ever from them now.

He reached into his satchel for a leather-bound book he had not taken out since he'd left home. His mother had given it to him when he left and told him to remember prayer and faith and something larger than himself.

Oh, here. Open it, she'd said.

A Bible?

Go on, she said.

The pages were white and blank and there were hundreds of them and he knew she expected him to find his own God somewhere in the empty space.

Tonight he rifled through the pages and then noticed his thumb smudging a dark print in the corners where he touched. He blew at the white pages and used his shirt to dust them and did not take out a pen.

You write, son, she said.

I will.

You promise.

Of course I promise.

He rubbed his feet, tingling with cold, together at the bottom of his bedroll and he stared out at the star-speckled sky and then through the sky to detect the slightest bit of motion. Again, he thought he saw the red dun's shadow, this time wandering across the moon and then he imagined her standing still somewhere near the bottom half of the moon so that he could find her.

Chapter 4

H E W O K E B E F O R E dawn and saddled John's bay gelding to search for the Rosina horse. He headed north early, as they had planned, so he might return before dusk to help move the sheep the three miles to Saunder's Reservoir for water. The gelding was surefooted and kept a good stride, filling the reins and moving into his hands. He stopped at the mouth of the Little Wood and dismounted to cool the gelding and rest him, and while the gelding drank and blew, Walter ate the now cold biscuits and the wedge of cheese Annette had set out the night before, wrapped in a white cloth.

The water rushed over a set of boulders just above him and spilled out into a smooth pool. Walter drank from the river with his hands and then he filled his copper flask. A small hatch was on and a large brown trout surfaced, dappling the water, before slipping back under, and the river leveled again. He remounted and galloped John's gelding through the open stretches of short spiky grass and walked her over the hills cropped out with high sagebrush and the horse was reliable on the ground that was pocketed with gopher holes.

Midday he arrived in Hailey riding down Main Street past brick-faced buildings and storefronts. The town was drawn up and quiet with so many of the town's men locked away in the mountains mining for ore, silver, zinc, and copper. The saddlery shop had its doors open, and he could see people inside, in the shadows, standing over a saddle, examining the workmanship with their hands. He passed on, and in front of the lumberyard there were two stout, broad-shouldered men with beards, who looked to be brothers, loading long planks of undressed timber into a wagon. A straying hog wandered under a plank they were carrying and one of the men tangled his feet up with the animal and almost lost his hold of the wood. He cursed an old man trailing behind the hog with a long cane. The bearded man yelled at the old man and told him he ought to know there were laws to prevent stray hogs from wandering the streets of Hailey. The old man didn't seem to hear, or if he did he paid no mind, for he kept shuffling along.

Walter inquired of a man seated out in front of the post office and learned from him that the Rosina horse had been brought into town by one of Bolles's hired hands that very morning. He was told he would find her tied out behind the Alturas Hotel in the travelers' stable. Walter cut up Croy Street and a block off Main Street was the hotel. He went around back.

She had her neck stretched between two fence rails trying to pick at the few blades of grass surfacing on the other side of the fence. She lifted her head when she saw him and stood there quivering like she didn't know what to make of him. She waited as if in judgment of their fate together. A leather halter was slung over the gatepost and he reached for it slowly and took it inside the corral with him. The pen was small and he did not dare tie her for fear she might pull back and take the fence post with her. He left the halter rope slung over her neck to accustom her, and she stayed still.

He placed his hand on the white star centered between her eyes and then ran his hand gently over the skin above her nostrils. He studied her legs and then with both hands he felt down her front right leg, along the cannon bone and around the fetlock and down the pastern for any swelling. She lifted her foot for him easily and he checked to make sure there were no stones wedged in the frogs of her hooves. He did the same on each of her legs and hooves, finding only a horse bite on her hindquarters. He figured she must have been penned with another horse who ran her around a bit overnight.

He took the white cloth Annette had wrapped his biscuits in, dunked it in the bucket of water hanging in the corral and flushed out the wound. It was not deep and he knew it would heal on its own. Her coat was rough and gathered in places where sweat had dried without being curried out, but the mare looked to be in good shape and ready for the ride home. He decided to give her an extra flake of hay to fill her belly before going south. He had not had anything but biscuits himself all day and he thought he'd go inside the hotel where he could get a meal for himself.

He was alone now and he couldn't remember a time when he'd ever had reason or an occasion to go to a restaurant all on his own and order a meal. He'd eaten out with his father and mother or someone from school, and then there had been town hall meetings where everyone went out for supper afterward. But today he would go in alone, find a table, order what he wanted, and pay up his own bill with the money John gave him just days before, at the coming of the month's end.

After lunch, he told himself, he'd ride up to check on his mother. He thought to do it right then, but going inside and ordering a meal was something that pulled at him. If he were to go home his mother would surely feed him herself. And if he were to tell her he was only stopping to say hello her face would fall and she'd try not to show her disappointment, but it would be there. He went home last time he passed through town, and this time he simply didn't have it in him to return home so soon.

He left the mare with hay and water and John's gelding tied to the fence and made his way to the front of the restaurant. Two old Basques were seated on a bench across the street and he nodded to them and they nodded back. The sun was high overhead and the wind did not bite as it usually did in early spring but sent a breath of life rushing through him, and his step quickened. The thought of a steak and potatoes was already making his stomach rumble.

Going through the hotel and bar he scanned the room. A player piano was backed up in the corner next to the mahogany bar back and counter. Two men sat at the bar with their backs to him. One straightbacked man was scuffing his boots along the brass bar footrest as he clicked his glass on the table for another drink. The walls were wood with Victorian carvings inlaid in the beams and floorboards. A deer, an antelope, a big-horned sheep, and a giant moose head extended out of the wall nearest him. The opposite wall was blanketed with a bear skin, a wolverine, and a mountain lion. On the floor, set near the bar counter, was a cannon.

Sitting at a table with her back to him was a woman, the only one in the place. She did not wear a hat as most ladies did when they went out in the day. Her black hair was loose and curly and hung down her back and the light from the window made it glisten amber across the top of her head.

43

She began to shift in her chair and her skirt swung at her ankles showing the toes of her boots. Then she stretched her hand and ran her long white fingers over the corner of the table and as she did so she turned her face to him and he saw it was her.

For the first time in a year he was looking at her. She kept her chin high and seemed bored with the men slouched over in their chairs and well on their way to being drunk. She leaned forward and, as she did so, a few strands of hair fell over her cheekbones and blew across her mouth. He saw her face, so pale and soft as she dropped her head to piece the hair back behind her ears, and she did it so tentatively, as though she were in deliberation over an important matter. Then abruptly she turned and lifted her face and looked Walter straight in the eye and smiled, as if she'd suddenly remembered who he was and where they first came to recognize one another. He nodded his head slightly in return, and then suddenly she was turned again and somehow restrained by her company as she kept tucking the folds of her skirt more securely under her.

There were two men with her and he recognized the one as Frank Ivy and the other he could not say, for he was turned away from Walter. Near them was an empty table, and that's where Walter sat.

The two men at Trina's table were drinking whiskey. Walter thought about ordering a glass, figuring if they were letting a girl in the bar they'd probably let him drink. On the other hand they might serve him and then he'd have to drink it with them watching for how he drank it. He dropped another cube of sugar in his coffee.

What's wrong, boy? one of the men said, and though Walter heard the words clearly enough he did not at first know they were directed at him. Without realizing it, he had been tapping the heel of his boot against the wood floor. You got the jitters already this morning? Boy's clicking his heels for service or else he's on edge for a good game of cards.

A Chinese man came to his table and asked him what he'd like. The special's chicken and dumplings, he said.

Steak, please. If you have it.

Yes, he said. You like it how?

Medium rare, Walter said, looking up and noticing that one of the man's eyes was cloudy and did not follow the other.

T-bone okay?

Sure.

The Chinese man nodded and said, Very good, and left the table.

The man who had first spoken to Walter swung his head around. It was Joe Moran, a cowboy who'd spent five years in the penitentiary in Boise for shooting a Chinese laundryman in the foot, whose wife he was supposedly sleeping with. There was also a rumor he'd been involved in a killing in San Francisco.

You the Pascoe boy? Joe Moran said. He had a way of talking where spittle came to his lips and hung there and when he was finished he'd lick it with his tongue.

Yes, sir, he said, not liking the man and knowing the man did not like him.

Well, that just about explains it. Joe Moran stood. He wore horsehide shotgun chaps and sawtooth roweled steel spurs. For some reason he seemed to change his mind and sat back down. You been holed up with them sheep? he said.

The straightbacked man at the bar counter turned around when Joe talked and rolled his eyes when he figured out whom the questions were coming from and then spun his chair back round.

Been out a few weeks. Down at Slaughterhouse.

Walter's food came out shortly and he was given a large T-bone steak with a second plate of fried potatoes with green peppers and a stack of toast heaped on top. Walter began to eat.

Boy his age is starting to figure out what it feels to be lonely. It gets damn cold some nights up there. I imagine he gets to wishing he weren't so alone.

The room was growing quiet as more and more of the diners were picking up on the conversation and taking an interest in it. Not for what was being said, but for the way of it.

And I imagine you know what you're talking about Joe, Frank said, and they all laughed.

There was a crash from the kitchen and the sound of dishes breaking and for a moment no one spoke. The Chinese man was pouring a drink for a man seated at the bar counter. The Chinese man looked to the man he had just served and then back to the kitchen and then merely shook his head and disappeared through the swinging wood doors to the kitchen.

45

There was the shuffle of the Chinese man's shoes on the wood floor in the kitchen and the sound of glasses lifted and then set back down on wood tables and the sound of cards shuffling and Walter ate. He ate not knowing the taste of what he brought to his mouth, only the sight of her.

But then came a high-pitched squeal and a snort and the patter of animal feet.

Shoo, shoo, the Chinese man said, coming out of the kitchen frantically waving his apron, driving a hog who'd slipped through the back of the kitchen. The hog was sidewinding and veering every which way, and one of the old men seated at the table near Walter got up to help the Chinese man corner the hog out of the bar.

When the Chinese man came back in, Trina stood up. At first she looked to be only stretching, as she leaned over and pulled up on one of her boots, but then she wandered outside without telling the men at her table where she was going. They paid no mind to her leaving. She glanced at Walter and leaned her head as if to tell him where she was going as she went toward the door.

He stayed at his table hoping she'd come back and watching her table for any word that might pass between the men of her coming or going.

Joe Moran set his two cards facedown and scratched the table. Hit me, he said to Frank.

Anytime, Frank said, laying down a card. It'd be my pleasure.

You working for saintly John Wright this spring? Joe Moran said, with his back still to Walter.

That's right, Walter said, forking in a large bite of potatoes.

You going to play cards or run your mouth? Frank asked.

Your father still selling goods to coolies? Joe Moran wanted to know.

Walter said nothing. There'd been trouble before, at school, kids making fun of the Chinese people because their parents said they were getting so rich they might take over the town. One Chinese man they hung from a tree at Saunder's Reservoir. He came in with the railroad laying ties and then people decided he'd stayed too long. Word was the Chinese could go ahead and serve their food, tend their gardens, but they weren't suppose to make any real money. Two boys a year ahead of Walter had brought up the fact that his father dealt with the Chinese. Walter fought them after school and took his licks but left a blackened eye and a broken nose.

I guess the boy didn't hear my question, Joe Moran kept on. I tell you we got goddamn coolies selling us liquor these days. He pointed to the Chinese man who was now dusting the back counters of the bar. If I were your father I'd tell them to keep them coolie shoes clear of my shop front. You still down below Timmerman?

I didn't take it you were asking questions.

A boy like you don't bring luck, does he? He looked down at his cards and his shoulders rolled as a laugh went through him.

The straightbacked man at the counter who'd been scuffing his boots on the brass foot rod stood up. Standing up, he was bigger than Walter had thought. He had a thick black beard. His eyes were black and deep set and he had a wide barreled chest and a presence that took the air right out of the room when he walked. He put on his hat and as he passed Walter he said out loud so everyone could hear, No need for you to answer this man's questions son. Better to keep an ignorant man dumb and quiet than give him something to talk dumb about.

Walter had never seen the man before. He walked out the door past Joe Moran's table and neither man looked at the other, and Walter couldn't say why this was so, since he was sure Joe Moran had heard the man.

When the man was gone Joe Moran turned again to look at Walter, his tongue lolling at the corner of his mouth. What you doing in town then?

Walter didn't like anything about him and he wished he hadn't lingered at the hotel. His food was growing cold. With his fork he picked at the potatoes, but he was no longer hungry. He let it sit.

Picking up my mare, he said.

The bitch got away from you. I'll see your ten and raise you ten more. Frank put his twenty chips on the table and doubled up.

Walter pushed his plate away and leaned back in his chair and breathed deeply, as if he'd just finished a good meal, even though his plate wasn't half eaten.

Three men came to the bar door, stepped inside, pointed to a back table. One shook his head and all three wandered out again. Walter wondered if it just felt like people were leaving because of Joe Moran or if that really was the case.

It's a woman thing also, ain't it? Joe Moran said, swinging around in his chair looking Walter up and down. Well, I'll be damn. The Pascoe's got a man coming of age. I'll be goddamn and ain't that sharp shootin'. But how's a growin' boy going to get laid eating the ways you do? He smacked his free hand down on the table and spit flew from his mouth.

God damn, Frank said, pulling a dirty bandanna from his pocket. For someone so notorious you are the biggest damn slobbering ass I ever seen. He laughed, one up on Joe with his hand.

Then it was quiet as the game seemed to occupy Joe Moran, but Walter knew it wasn't over and he knew he couldn't risk leaving just yet and have it look like he was running out of there. Trina wandered back in and took her place at the table.

Joe Moran leaned over and whispered something in her ear and she turned red but didn't smile. She started to stand, and he grabbed her wrist and yanked her back down. You been to the ladies' room enough already. Besides you don't need freshening up any more than you is. Joe leaned over, cupped Trina's chin in his hand, and said, Ain't she a darling? Walter, you looking this way? You ought to be. Then he dropped his hand and fingered a card out of his deck and lay it facedown.

Walter was watching her. The way her face had gone hot and then suddenly she'd looked frigid, like one breaking a fever, all the heat and color draining down the body, suddenly gone cold. He wanted to go to her and ask her if she wouldn't care to leave with him, but there was something so removed to her being right then, as if she'd never belonged to their world but was merely set there and would be lifted from it on a day beyond any of their recognition.

For Christ's sake, not like she's for sale. The skins she brings in is worth more than her own skin. I don't even bring in as many pelts as she can do. What are you taking her for, a whore, you ass? Frank said without looking at her. He dealt Joe Moran another card.

This town's gonna have to find itself some more ladies to keep this boy company is all I'm saying, Joe Moran said, bouncing in his chair. Keep him honest and hardworking. This boy wants to get laid. Who knows a woman that'll do this boy? Joe Moran said, turning around, sweeping his arms wide, gesturing to anyone in the room who would pay him any attention.

Trina turned and looked at Walter for the first time since she'd come back in and her eyes were blazing with things she couldn't say and questions hung themselves like snow-white bones in the whites of her eyes. Walter had the sense he wanted to run his hands over those eyes to quiet them and make them forgetful. She looked back at him as though to challenge him to do so. All the while she watched him as if she worried he was deceiving himself in her and finally she shrugged her shoulders just slightly, telling him he did not know all there was to know and her eyes dropped. And yet they rose again and she kept testing him this way, for how he watched her. Her look, bound not by mistrust but by a fear of being misunderstood, was so sincere. He felt he would be consoled by her forever.

I've heard just about enough of your tapping. You might just shut the hell up as I'm trying to do you a favor here, Joe Moran said.

What would that be? Walter asked.

Frank put down his hand of cards, faceup. I call you.

Fuck you, Joe Moran said, staring at the cards. And he stood from the table so quickly he lifted it off the ground, spilling his whiskey over the top of the glass and scattering their cards. He put his hand down, looking to steady the glass, but then he picked it up and hurled it back toward the bar where it shattered against the wood. The Chinese man ducked.

Then Joe Moran turned all the way around to look at Walter. What's that you asked me, boy? I got sidetracked. You ask me a question?

I asked you what sort of favor you were aiming to do me.

Joe Moran stood there deciding what to make of Walter. You've got some fight in you, it seems. But I changed my mind, if I ever made it up.

Walter suddenly stood. He stayed behind the table with his fists clenched.

Let it go, Joe, Frank said, or you'll have a piece of me to tangle with.

And I'm good for a tangle so long as it's with that wife of yours, Joe Moran said, wiping spit from his mouth.

Frank stood up from his chair and swung out at Joe Moran, who leaned back, dodging the blow with a smile.

Frank seemed to need to reason through what to do next. Finally, he nodded and patted his hand on the table as if he'd let it pass. He sat down and it was as if nothing had been said at all. He tossed down another glass of whiskey and shuffled the cards.

The Chinese man came back over, bringing them each a new glass of whiskey, and Frank took a long drink off of it before picking up the deck to shuffle it. Joe Moran stood over his chair watching and waiting on Frank. When sat, he cut the deck for a fresh hand.

Walter knew things weren't set straight, but he decided he had no business hanging about waiting until they were. He stood up and there was the sound of him getting up and pushing his chair in that Joe Moran heard. He turned and watched the boy. Walter walked back to the counter, while everyone stared at him, set a dollar seventy-five on the bar counter, and as he started for the door he caught Trina's eye a last time.

She stared back at him, resting her hands on her chin. He thought he saw her face soften as she stared back at him. She did not smile, but her eyes seemed to glimmer and her face flushed. He looked hard into her eyes thinking they might finally give her away. He learned nothing.

Outside he mounted the Rosina horse and tied John's gelding behind and headed south.

Hey, a voice called, you forgot your change.

Walter turned his horse around and trotted back to her. He was nervous and still a boy in so many ways. I didn't know I had any, he said.

You shouldn't let them bother you, you know, she said, reaching up to place the change in his hand. Her fingers lingered in the palm of his hand and she seemed to smile at him coaxingly and he thought there was something reckless and almost extravagant about her looking at him the way she did.

I couldn't help it. But what about you?

She shrugged, and then from inside there was the sound of Joe Moran's voice. Where's she taken off to now? he bellowed.

She turned back toward the bar, but before she did so she told him to have a good ride and then waved and there was nothing for him to do but turn the Rosina horse around and ride out of town. And it wasn't until after he was well down the road that he turned around looking where she'd gone. There was nothing to see, but he stayed looking anyway, like she might appear if he wished long and hard enough.

Chapter 5

THAT EVENING AFTER they moved the sheep to water, Walter ate while John smoked and kept him company. Walter had been late in finding them, and it having been a long day for everyone, Annette was already asleep in the wagon. John and Annette ate before Walter arrived, but they'd kept a plate of beans, eggs, and links of chorizo warm for him. Annette had brought the chorizo from town and she'd made biscuits and they were still hot inside the Dutch oven.

Halfway through his meal Walter heard a rustling and the sound of limbs snapping somewhere off the far side of the wagon. Then came stillness again as if there'd been no sound at all. He looked up from his tin plate and already John had his eyes cast in the same direction as the sound.

So everything went all right in town? John said, staring intently into the blackness.

Saw the Ivys.

You didn't say that earlier.

Wasn't anything.

Maybe not.

You heard that? That noise off in the brush.

I don't hear anything now, Walter said.

Doesn't mean there isn't anything out there, John said, cupping his lit cigarette in the palm of his open hand.

Well, what do you think it is?

I don't know.

The heeler was discontent and whining, but they could see nothing in the darkness. It would be only a night or two until the next full moon, but the clouds were thick and the sky swirled, half lit by the hiding moon and farther out a splay of dead stars like cast sand. The trees were moaning and creaking from a wind they could not feel. The coyotes were distant and quiet. Walter went back to eating and John lit another cigarette off the one he'd just smoked. He explained again how the herd was bedded a quarter mile back into the thin, steep draw. Walter was to follow a line of firs running along the ridge just west of them and so long as he didn't go back into the trees, but stayed low and followed them, he'd end up at his tarp.

I know where we put up for the night. I was there.

Kind of dark though, John said. Easy to get lost on a night like this.

I set it up. And I'll find it.

Something got into you today?

No.

Walter decided to leave the Rosina horse tied to the sheep wagon for the night and walked just over a quarter mile to his tarp and bedroll that were near the herd. The blue heeler followed behind him despite the stones he tossed at him telling him to stay back at the sheepwagon. But the dog wouldn't listen and he decided he'd let the dog sleep at his feet. There was nothing to be scared of, but the night felt restless and inside him was the beginning of a longing that he had not known. Up on the ridge, sidled up against a wall of firs, not a leaf stirred, but something watched and he could not sort it out.

He stripped off his overalls and coat and slid into his bedroll with his long johns still on. The ground was cold beneath him and he rolled from side to side trying to get warm. Finally he got up and cut a few boughs from a fir tree to sleep on. He knew he might have told John about Trina, how pretty she looked. But John would have asked Walter if they talked and he'd have had to say, not really. He wanted to be back in the bar and wished he'd gone straight up to her at the table and said, let's get out of here.

He straightened a green bough against his knee, trying to take the bend out of it.

He figured by now she was far into the mountains with her father. They'd be packing the metal claw traps for muskrats, beavers, and minks. He imagined her in her own bedroll, bedded down for the night waiting for sleep under the sky. Her skin would be moon white in such darkness and her eyes black as an agate and her face warm to touch.

He slid back into his bedroll and worked his back into the boughs trying to get comfortable. He thought on what John said about things being out there even when you can't hear them. He shut his eyes and let Trina come to him. He knew it wasn't women John had been talking about, but he ached for her all the same.

She stayed with him, came to be with him, had never left him, he imagined it as so. He did not try to hear her voice, and she did not speak and he still knew her to be there. And in his dream he began to trust she knew something of the life carried on in the unspoken and she began to teach him how to hear and in hearing he saw a field of silence rung out before them, not quiet, but trying to sound like a bell in water. Until finally the words seemed fallen away and not important and he couldn't remember if there had ever been such a thing between them. All he could think to do was touch her face and her hair and run his hands along the inside of her legs and she wanted him to hold her while they slept.

He slept so wakeful that in the morning he would be tired and believe he had not slept at all. He would think he had stayed up the night long and been beside her through the hours of darkness.

The top of his tarp was beaded with dew and thin rivulets were dripping off its edges and falling to the ground. The sky was steel gray and a cold seemed to be settling back in stalling their hopes for spring. Even in March, when he and John sheared and moved the sheep out of Slaughterhouse, the skies hadn't been so heavy and wintry, nor the mornings so cold.

Walter stood and stretched and pulled on his overalls and coat. He walked back into the woods and pissed in the moss and felt his stomach gnaw with hunger. He waded through the herd, the sheep beginning to stray even though the signs of day were few, and it was like someone wading through a thick fog. He raised his hands to his eyes to rub them and make sure it was the day and not his eyes blurry with sleep. A slack wind blew and the blue heeler had his nose to the air and his hair bristled on his back. It was clear that he'd not slept well either but spent the night wary and vigilant.

What is it, Blue? You smelling something ol' boy?

The dog growled low and lifted his head higher as if he was just trying to get above sheep level to follow the scent. He whined and darted about Walter's feet for a few steps but went quiet again as Walter said, No, Blue. Quiet now, boy.

The dog knew better than to get excited and start the sheep running. Coming out of the band, Walter spotted a trail of blood but no carcass or new lamb close by. A ewe could have easily lambed overnight, for many were now so near to their time. But then he saw in a stand of willows near the creek bed, the limbs parted like they remained permanently passed through, and there a carcass lay stretched. Before he even got near, it was clear to see that it was the whole of a sheep.

The hind end looked to have been ripped off and the animal was smeared in its own blood. He crouched down and rolled the animal over to find the other side removed in the same way with cold blood matted into the remaining fleece. The work was fairly neat and he figured the animal couldn't have been too hungry to be this selective. The sheep in the herd had turned and were looking at him. They'd followed him a few steps behind and were intent on him as he crouched under the mass of willow limbs. Blue sat at his side and remained alert to the herd. A few of them started running into the center and this caused others to follow and soon they were milling in a great swirl.

Walter stood and motioned the dog to settle the sheep. Blue trotted off and he watched as the blue heeler sifted through their depths staying on the outside for the most part, diving only a few times to nip a ewe's heels and send her into the herd. And then where a large number of sheep were now massed shoulder to shoulder, the blue heeler sprung on top of them, ran across their backs to get to the front of the herd, and then jumped to the ground and began driving them in Walter's direction to break up their moving formation.

Soon they were settled and Walter started back down the draw. He sidestepped down a ravine of river rock where a tributary once fed out, and where it leveled he followed a gravel sandbar, winding his way south on the flat. As he neared the wagon, he was greeted by the smell of woodsmoke and cooking.

Annette handed Walter a plate of hash and he told what he'd found. A coyote got it, John said, and grunted, more annoyed than angry.

It's just that it was so quiet last night. I didn't sleep much, so I figure I should have heard it.

They're always a problem.

I just don't get it.

They're always going to be a problem, John said.

I don't know why I didn't hear it.

Maybe it happened before you got up there.

But Walter could tell John's mind was somewhere else, the way he sat on the log, his upper body leaned over, and the way he kept smoothing his hands on the knees of his trousers.

Annette poured coffee for Walter and a cup for herself. Then she sat on the ground between John's legs, her head back.

You can shoot the damn things if you see them. Likely, you won't, John said, kicking at a stone with the toe of his boot. The stone sailed into the fire along with a pile of dirt. The fire was down to just a few coals and began to smoke.

I brought the traps, Annette said. They're still in the back of the Ford.

We ought to set them today, Walter said.

Setting them where? John said.

Up on the ridge and a few down by the stream, Walter said. Tonight I'll keep a fire going extra late.

Won't work, John said. They're too damn smart and it's because they've only one thing to be smart about.

You think it could have been something other than coyotes, Walter said.

What are you thinking John? Annette said, looking up at him.

Nothing. Just the plain bad luck that runs with coyotes. They figure out the traps or chew their own damn legs off to save themselves, or you see one in perfect shot but you don't have a gun. That's how it works. He gently pushed himself up off the log, letting Annette settle against it. Almost got to respect them, but you hate every minute you do. I see your mare made it over the night? John said.

Yes, sir. I plan to leave her another day, tied, grazing off the back of the wagon.

That's fine, but you're going to have to hobble her one of these days, Walter. Get her used to it.

I'll see how she does. Walter wouldn't hobble Rosina, he knew that, but he wasn't going to say so to John. She was stuck where she was in her training and he knew she'd stay right there if she could not come to appreciate her lessons.

That night another lamb was taken. Blue woke him early, and he followed the dog to a thicket of brush just west of the herd to find it. The dog danced at his feat and leapt in the air yelping, excited to share his find. In the morning he brought the lamb to John who only shook his head, grunted, and said, Damn it.

It rained all that day as they moved north, deeper into the high country, keeping an eye out for a suitable meadow should the ewes begin dropping. They were heavy about their middles, and John said it could be any day. Daily, he checked the udders and vulvas of the ewes for swelling. Just that morning he had said that a few were bagged out and would drop any day.

They had spotted a clear basin that wasn't overridden with sage a couple of miles back at Deer Creek and they talked about settling down for lambing. But they knew the higher they could get before lambing started the better chance they'd have of staking out the best grazing area later on.

John said they'd best keep pushing up higher and try to make it to Greenhorn Gulch. There they would have a nice empty draw and they could get water out of the Big Wood.

It was wet and the men sat stooped on their horses, riding through the weather and feeling themselves chilled and cold. Even the dogs fell back, dulled by the wet and endless gray skies. And the Rosina horse walked on with her ears bent back so the water would run right off the sides of them, and she kept her head down, as if that would distance her from the rain. The land they left behind them had been overturned with their passage. It lay in their wake a dark upheaval of brown clods or dirt, written all over by tracks, and it was hard to imagine grass ever growing among such wreckage.

That night when they stopped in a clearing just a mile south of Greenhorn Gulch, Walter decided he would let Rosina loose. She did not run but followed him and showed no interest in wandering and when they ate, she stood off behind the sheep wagon with her neck lowered and tired.

You got yourself a goddamn dog, John said that night at supper. Before you know it that thing will be following you to take a piss.

Don't be nasty, Annette said.

They hurried and ate. John said he smelled rain and as each of them was eager to be bedded down out of the rain for the night, they said little during dinner. Walter went to his bedroll, wrapped himself in his tarp and like almost every night since he'd seen Trina, he thought of her as he shivered and tried to quiet his chattering teeth.

Just before daylight Walter heard the lambing dog barking and he knew a ewe was dropping. It was dark, but John called to Walter from the sheepwagon and told him to pull his coveralls on quick.

It's starting, John said.

He was at Walter's tarp in a few minutes and they hurried into the night, following the lambing dog's cries. There was a full moon overhead and the sky was studded with stars. The clouds had passed and the rain let up. In the flat light of the moon they had little problem seeing. They trailed the dog's cry to a gully and John ran down into it, sliding sand and rock with him. He yelled back to Walter, who was not far behind him, to hurry.

A ewe had dropped along the stream edge and the lamb was down on its side wet and still tangled in its own sac. John ran to it and, using his shirt end, wiped the mucus from its nose. He pulled some sagebrush ends off a nearby bush and began tickling the lamb's nose.

It's not breathing, John said.

Walter was crouched down at the ewe's head and looked at John, trying to read what was next.

Hold that sheep still for me so I can try to put the two of them back together as soon as I get her breathing. Else we got a bum lamb on our hands.

Walter rested his body over the ewe and held her front and back legs down.

For Christ's sake, she's not a wolf that's going to bite you. Ease up.

Walter let go of the ewe's legs just as John lifted the lamb at his side up by both back legs and gently began to swing it in a vertical circle overhead, trying to give it breath through the up-and-down movement.

John circled the lamb in the air again and again and then gently brought her down. The lamb was breathing and John nudged her from behind, the way a ewe would, encouraging her forward to her mother.

As soon as Walter let up on the ewe, she sprung up on all fours.

Christ, John said, spitting into his hands.

What do you want me to do? You want me to hold her down again?

No. Just make sure she doesn't go anywhere.

Walter watched her nervously, expecting he might have to dive if she bolted out of the streambed and up the gully. But she didn't run. She began pawing at the dirt beneath her, panting as she walked in circles, mindless of the trees and limbs about her, as if she were blind.

All right, set her down again.

Walter looked to John to make sure he meant it this time. It seemed to Walter the last thing they'd want to do if they wanted the lamb to start nursing. But John was shaking his head and wasn't going to say anything more. Walter then wrapped an arm around the ewe's chest and another one around her back end. She squirmed and tried to break free, but Walter held her.

She's not giving up, John.

The lambing dog sat behind them and whined.

Goddamn it. Ewe's got another one coming. All right, let her go, John said. She didn't run but took a few steps forward and then heaved over on her side.

The ewe was down grinding her teeth and her eyes were dull and her breathing labored. Her breath smelled of alcohol and the ammonia of urine-soaked pens.

Is something wrong with her? Walter said, running his hands down his coveralls.

John watched the ewe and ran his hands over the tips of the floppy ears.

She's not making it, Walter said.

Give her time, John said, backing up to nudge the lamb as close to its mother as he could get it. He'd had his hands all over the lamb and he knew that didn't help if he wanted the ewe to accept her lamb.

The ewe going to take her?

Probably not. John suddenly stood, folded his arms across his chest defensively and kicked the heel of his boot into the dirt.

They waited and after a while the head of the lamb wedged its way out of the ewe's birth canal.

She's breeched.

Damn. I knew it, John said. He ran his hands quickly over his trousers again as he stared intently at the ewe. He looked almost like he was grinding his own teeth, his jaw clenched so tight.

Walter didn't know quite what to do and he stood up beside John for a minute and then came back down squatting beside the ewe.

Her sack remained unbroken and John quickly bent down and cut a slit in it with his fingernail and fluid seeped out. We got to be quick now or this one won't make it. Lamb will drown in its own fluids in there.

You want me to do something?

No, I got this one. First of the season. You best just watch.

He stuck his arm inside the lamb, trying to get hold of the legs that were crossed over one another and then he began to pull.

The ewe strained and panted, but the lamb didn't come any farther.

Roll her over Walter, John said. Might just ease her up enough to let this lamb out. And hold her front legs.

Walter did as John said and the lamb came out a bit farther.

I think I got it now. You hold her front legs tight. John pulled again and the lamb finally came out, covered in a reddish fluid and draped in its own afterbirth.

Walter motioned the lambing dog to move in closer to them, and she did so. He had heard that a ewe's instinct to protect her lamb from a dog was sometimes enough to reestablish the bond of ewe and lamb. The lambing dog circled the two lambs and then lowered her head to sniff them, but the ewe did not rise.

Should have culled her last year. I know better.

She old? Walter asked.

She's dropped her share, John said, lowering down on his knees and leaning over the ewe's head. He lifted the skin about her mouth and pressed a finger into her gum. Her gums were a pale pink, almost gray, and when he pressed down the skin went white and when he let up the color did not return for a number of seconds.

We're losing her, John said. You go see who you can match those two

59

lambs up with and I'll take care of her. Who knows, maybe there's another ewe already lambed while we've been stuck here.

Walter picked up a lamb in each arm and with his back to John he walked to the herd. He knew John stayed not to be with the ewe but to kill and skin her. He would strip her of her skin and bury her. If Walter didn't have the lambs nursing by the time John came up from the stream, they'd drape the skin of the dead ewe over the twin lambs and hope another ewe would smell the skin and accept the orphaned lambs as her own.

By the time the sun crept up over the mountains, Walter had matched one of the lambs with a ewe and he'd managed to get the second lamb a bit of milk off another nursing ewe. But the second lamb's ears were droopy and it was hunched up behind. The lamb was going into shock and Walter knew it had to be dehydrated, so he was glad when he saw John walking across the field with the ewe's skin in his arms.

John looked like a man bearing a gift born out of an exhausted earth. The thing in his arms was flaccid and altogether changed from what it was, a long strip of bloody hide and brown tick-burrowed fleece. He did not turn his head about to look around or to plot the least intrusive course through the herd. He moved straight toward Walter as if by instinct and without eyes to guide him, and the sheep parted for him without running or growing nervous as they would have done confronted by any other stray wanderer unknown to them. As he neared, Walter could see that his face was still and tensed so as to remain without expression. Walter had assumed that death had stopped getting to John long ago, but he knew that morning that it had not escaped him. It hung about him, and there was nothing to say, as there is very little one can say about the timeless season of birth and death.

Chapter 6

B Y T H A T   S E C O N D week of April the band was spread out and the ewes were dropping their lambs too fast for Walter and John to keep up. They were both staying awake nights taking turns watching the sheep and each was dying for a little extra sleep. Annette helped out too, rising early to cook for them and giving each a rest into the late morning. One of them had to be awake at all times because it was too easy for the ewes to wander off and drop their lambs and never find their way back. One night John told them he saw a wolf and they started keeping the rifle nearby and each night after coyotes could be seen skirting the herd and waiting patiently for the lone sheep to fall out, to give birth, and to fall prey.

Walter became such that he was walking blind and pulling lambs and matching bum lambs with any ewe who'd take them. They didn't speak much other than to curse an aimless sheep or yell a command at the lambing dog. They were no more than moving figures sharing nights over wandering sheep, while both men and sheep longed for a pasture stay and a bit of rest to soothe their weariness.

Finally came the day when, at its end, they were matching a bum lamb with a ewe, and Walter looked up and it seemed for the first time in weeks a sheep wasn't lambing. He mentioned it to John and for a moment neither of them knew what to do. The afternoon was going orange in its lateness, broken with streaks of lavender-colored clouds and the sky was warm like summer. But the turn of the season was still a good month off.

John pulled his hat off and ran his fingers through his hair. The smell of the campfire curled up from the nearby knoll in the shape of a ribbon and Walter breathed in the burned cinder and could almost taste the coming meal in his mouth.

But it was John who pointed to the boulder-strewn creek bed, signaling cleanup time. She might just be about finished, John said, referring to the whole season of lambing.

And Walter thought how the season was said to be a woman, just like ships and storms. Do you really think so? Walter asked, trying to imagine so abrupt an end to something that had consumed them day and night for what felt like months.

A break won't be so bad.

There wasn't much to say about what had just happened, though to Walter it seemed there ought to be, for the herd had doubled in size. At times it seemed to jolt forward in fits and spurts like an engine being cranked. It would get ahead of itself. The ewes were nervous and the young lambs curious and wary and one was always overstepping the other. Walter did not share what he thought with John, for it all seemed too obvious, the fact that a ewe would be changed by a lamb just as a mother was by a newborn baby. He walked with John toward the creek.

Then it wasn't long after when Annette sounded the dinner bell that rang over the sheep who for once seemed to be resting in one quiet drove. John and Walter walked east, one behind the other, slantwise along the sloping land angling down to the creek bed. Walter followed John, who moved almost in a stagger, bent over at the waist and beat from tiredness. On his way down John caught his toe on a river rock, fell to all fours, and came up laughing. They both laughed then because it could just as well have been either of them.

Just about tuckered me out, John said.

Walter laughed again and told him he better remember how to pick up them damn lazy feet or they'd both end up toppled on top of one another, fallen down, before they could even put some food in their stomachs.

Where the gully leveled at the stream's base they found the boulder where Annette had left clean folded shirts, dungarees, and soap. Both men kneeled to wash their faces and clean their hands and arms. Their arms were slick with lanolin and the afterbirth of lambs, which made their skin shiny in the late afternoon glow. With their hands rinsed they began to strip down, for there was no part of the body spared of sweat and the grease of the day. Among the sheep they did not notice the smell of their own bodies, but alone by the creek the smell of sweat and blood and animal rose thick.

They tossed their dirty clothes on the river rocks and both men waded calf deep into the creek. Goose bumps stood on Walter's legs and a chill ran the length of him. He waded deeper. John was next to him and off the dark water their skin had a pale ghostlike sheen. In their whiteness, which might have been the boldest color to be found in that place, they stood out the way the moon does. Chiseled out and their muscles taut and their chests, which had not seen sun, white, they looked like two things who might flourish mightily for a brief while and then expire, foreign as they appeared in this dusk-colored scene. Walter shivered.

A bit of the fading sun cracked through the clouds and lit the river rocks before them and then fell away, and the creek bed was gray and the water flat and green and a midnight blue where the willows bent over it and cast their shadows. John plunged his head underwater and came up for the bar of soap set on a rock near the dead tree stump. Camped out in the meadow for lambing, John had insisted they make themselves at home and have a proper wash station complete with a soap stone. John soaped up his body and then tossed the bar to Walter.

It slid right through Walter's hands and bobbed in the water before Walter caught it. The soap felt a bit like wet newspaper in his hands, but as he worked it into a rich sandpapery lather on his skin, the dirt and film of body fluids and the blood and the grit of the day washed clean. He ducked his head under and wet his hair and put a bit of soap in it too and then went under again. Underwater he paused and listened to the silent flow of water rushing over and around him. Then he came up for air and turned his body around so he faced west to feel whatever was left of the sun.

These moments of cold, with the initial tingle of the water gone and a slow penetrating cold settling in, didn't bother Walter. For it seemed to shock the two of them into another sort of being and the quiet intentness of their day's conversation that had been centered on which ewe was lambing, which lamb was lost, and which ewe was about to lamb was replaced by an openness and a lightness that came only after they were out of the herd. There was a calm that settled around them and part of it was the exhaustion finally settling into their bones and making even the weight of their skin feel heavy.

Wood ducks paddled upstream from them and dove their heads under and up, caught up in their own washing. A mallard drake began clipping another duck from behind, grabbing at her neck and ducking her under in their customary mating ritual. They went on like that, the one forcing the other under and the other flailing to be free, as if it were some tormented dance. The two struggled, and the quacking persisted even after the female had freed herself.

You'd think they were trying to kill each other getting like that, John said.

Walter laughed and splashed another handful of water onto his face and let it sluice off his chin and down his neck.

Walter had never made love, though he had kissed a girl at the church dance last summer and held her close with his hands in between her shoulder blades. He hadn't moved his hands because they'd fit somewhere in that indent of her spine. At the time he thought he wouldn't have minded leaving his hand there forever. Then when the music stopped he took her hand and led her out back behind the dance hall to kiss until there'd been the sound of a door slamming, another couple coming out to do the same thing, and she'd said they better go back. They'd wandered inside past trees where boys' bodies were pushed up against girls whose heads were tilted back, their necks gaped wide and exposed, and boys taking them as if they were the very air their life depended on. Long after, he remembered the feel of his lips on hers for the first time and the taste and smell of her in his mouth and it was like something of fire and ice lingering making him go numb as if he were caught in sleep.

John?

Yeah.

You think I'll run into Trina again?

Have in the past. Don't see why you should stop now. Then John told Walter that Joe Moran was coming.

How do you know? Walter asked, scanning the seed-lit horizon.

I saw him. He's about a mile off north. He don't make no bones about letting you know he's coming. If you just look up he's riding straight toward us. See him?

I see him.

It'll be fifteen minutes or better.

A thin lift of steam had begun to rise off their bodies as the day was fading quickly and they hurried to be finished scrubbing and in fresh clothes and ready for Joe Moran. Coming out of the water Walter glanced again at the whiteness of John's back and stared down at his own body to see if it too looked so out of place and foreign, but he didn't have to look to know it did.

They unfolded the shirts Annette had left on the boulder behind them and John stayed facing east as he dressed, with his back to the now red sun and his front side facing the approaching horse and rider. In a short time they finished dressing and bundled their dirty clothes in the crooks of their arms to take back to the sheep wagon.

As they walked south they kept an eye on the distant moving figure until finally Walter could distinguish horse from rider. Even then Walter still wasn't sure he could tell it was Joe Moran. Looking sideward and not watching where he was going, John slipped and went down again on the rough ground and banged his knee and caught his hand on some sagebrush and this time neither of them laughed.

At the sheep wagon Annette took their slick blood-battered clothes and set them aside to be boiled clean after dinner. John paced the camp quietly loading supplies into the sheepwagon they'd left out all spring – a branding iron, the mess kit, and their raincoats. Annette did not question him and in a while she was helping him load things she sensed he'd forgot. He picked up the rifle and made to go to the sheepwagon and then seemed to think better of it and propped it against his campstool. He examined it and its location, then turned and went to fill a tin cup with coffee. Finally he sat and calmly built a cigarette. Walter filled his own evening tin with a first cup of coffee and stood watching Joe Moran come on, bowling dust behind him as he worked his horse their way at a gentle trot.

When Walter went to sit, John wagged his finger indicating Walter should sit on the blanket directly across from him, facing west, with the campfire between them. Walter trusted John had some reason for directing him so and fully understood when he sat down and found a revolver tucked in a fold in the blanket.

Okay, it would be best we get heating some extra beans and bacon tonight, John said. The words were spoken to Annette, but it was Walter he was staring at. Walter nodded and John returned the gesture with a tight smile.

Walter hadn't told John that he ran into Joe Moran in Hailey the month before and now regretted it.

Your father tell you how Joe Moran took out two of Randy Laidlaw's men last year?

No, Walter said. He didn't say anything about it.

Right on Laidlaw's property he took them out.

I never heard that one.

We don't have time for that one now, Annette said.

I can tell it fast, John said. See, Laidlaw was moving cattle off his ranch. He hired Joe Moran to help him, but then some stock turned up missing. Joe Moran felt like he was getting the blame from the rest of the crew. They had it out and Joe Moran galloped off the property, lots of bad feelings all the way around. The crew started firing at him. Joe grabbed his rifle and then he fell his horse over to its backward side, pretending to be shot. Two men came riding out to him, for to be sure he was dead. Joe Moran let them have it. He shot one right in the face when he leaned down to see just how dead Joe Moran was. The other, he shot him in the breastbone.

Hush now, Annette said, as Joe Moran was nearing on them.

They stood waiting, watching him as he closed the distance. He dismounted and left his horse standing a few paces off with the reins still over its head and waited for John to speak.

Grab a plate, Joe, John said, pointing to the camp box unloaded behind the sheep wagon.

I appreciate that. Thank you. Thank you very much. Mrs. Wright, he nodded to Annette.

Good evening to you Mr. Moran, Annette said. You better hurry if you want some, and she pointed at the stove. My men are hungry tonight.

Joe Moran lined himself up first, dipping the ladle into the steaming pork stew. Then he asked what they were all up to.

Walter could feel the weight of the revolver against his leg. It did not give off heat or cold but was merely something hard.

They were doing what they did every spring day and it was known among them that it was Joe Moran's presence and arrival that were curious. But Joe's business was his own or he made it his own and not even John asked him why he had shown up in their camp.

Just finishing lambing, Walter said.

What's it been? Three weeks? Joe Moran asked.

Sounds right.

John lifted his head and looked at Joe Moran and then back at Walter. Three weeks since what?

Something like three weeks, Joe Moran said, when you was up to Hailey picking up a mare. I gave you a bit of a time how you'd be back in town for something more than a horse. Herders, I hear they're worse than a dog in heat when they come to town.

You hear that, Joe, or is that what you say? John asked.

Joe Moran walked to the stool that had been empty when he arrived and set his plate down on the stool and leaned over and spat before fingering a chaw of tobacco out of his mouth and into the fire.

Figure I might be of some assistance growing this boy up.

Walter does just fine on his own, Mr. Moran, Annette said. He doesn't need any help from you.

You're right, Mrs. Wright. He'll get his own. He'll do just fine. With his soup tin rested in his lap, he rubbed his hands together and spat in them and wiped them on his jeans before he began eating. Fine stew, Mrs. Wright. My compliments. He blew at his spoon and took another heaping bite and began to chew, but suddenly he spat it out. Damn, that meat's hot.

They all looked at him, but no one said anything.

How are the numbers looking? Joe Moran asked, looking right at Walter.

Walter turned his head toward John. He wasn't going to answer the question. John was still the boss of the operation and it would be best to let him deal with this one.

Had a couple of my ewes torn up a while back, John said.

Animals, Joe Moran cursed. I ever tell you how much I hate mice. Fucking mice drive me right up the wall.

John nodded as if it were part of the course of his eating habits and not in response to Joe Moran. We are doing all right. I figure the coyotes are pretty bad this year. Haven't seen but a few dancing around in the evenings, but then come morning and I'll find the hind end of one of my ewes gone. They aren't taking the whole thing, so they can't be that hungry.

The Bascos been doing their share of eating around here. You hear what I'm saying?

People like to talk. Doesn't mean anything.

Joe Moran belched and sopped up some gravy with his bread and put the whole slice in his mouth. His cheeks were full and he didn't talk, just chewed and smacked his lips.

Frugal little bastards, Joe Moran said when he could talk again.

They got credit at all the stores in town, John said.

All they have to buy is supplies. It ain't healthy what those men do. I mean without being with women. They're a merchant's dream, though.

Different ways of living, Joe.

Living? I call that something bastardly. Joe Moran took out his tobacco tin and placed another chaw under his lower lip. Mighty generous you've been tonight, Mrs. Wright. This is real fine, he said, nodding at the fire.

Thank you, Mr. Moran.

Then with not a moment passed, he said, Excuse my French, but those boys are cocksuckers.

Who? Annette said, taken aback so that the question came out before she could think not to ask it.

The Basques same as any other, John said.

You going to tell me they're something else besides bastardly and plain fucked in the head. Pardon me, ma'am, Joe Moran said, laughing but without so much as turning his head. That's funny John Wright. That's a hoot.

Annette said nothing but stood and went to the dogs' bowls to scrape the scraps of pork fat she had left on her plate. Joe Moran didn't seem to notice she'd gone, for he stood a short time later and said, I might just have a second helping, Mrs. Wright. And it was only after he'd said it that he looked around puzzled and turned once in a full circle as if he'd somehow overlooked her.

Help yourself, John said.

Convinced she really was gone, he ladled out another serving for himself. He held the bowl to his face to smell it and then asked John if he ever cooked rattlesnake.

No.

Joe Moran nodded and then looked like he decided to save the thought, for he sat back down. Walter waited for Joe Moran to pull the tobacco from his lip before he began eating, but he did not this time.

I got some cattle to run north, come the end of the month, Joe Moran said.

That right? John said. He set his fork in his tin and stopped eating.

I'm going to push ahead of every one of them Basco-run operations.

Who you running them for?

Billy Obenchain.

That's a lot of cattle.

It's a couple weeks of good work. I want to ask if I can run my cattle in front of you.

You asking me or telling me?

Good God, John Wright. Talking with you is like talking with the Old Testament.

You asking the Basques as well?

I don't ask a Basco nothing. Ever. John, are you a believer?

Don't have a personalized God, if that's what you mean. Mind telling me why I'm getting a special courtesy?

Joe Moran burst out laughing and took another bite. John, you never ever eaten rattlesnake.

No, Joe, I can't say I've needed to.

I was down near the south fork of the Boise couple years ago, Joe Moran said, before setting his plate at his feet and grabbing his right ankle with both hands. He bowed his head like he was trying to touch his head to his foot. Sucker got me right here on the anklebone when I was coming out of the river barefoot. Sucked all that poison out myself. Joe Moran drew his cheeks in and held his breath and kept holding it until his face reddened and then when he finally let his breath out he started laughing and couldn't stop. Walter looked at John, but John wasn't taking his eyes off Joe Moran.

I sucked the snake snot right out of there, he said, still holding his ankle. Finally he let his foot down and picked up his plate again and blew on his fork before taking another bite.

The ground ought to be dry by the time you're back down in the valley. You'll be breaking a few horses? John said. He leaned forward and set his palm on the ground and patted it and felt to see what water was left in it.

I got a special service I do on my most favorite Basco folk, Joe Moran said.

Might guess.

I break their three- or four-year-olds to ride. I let them watch me work them for a bit, help them mount up their first time when I think the horse is fit for it. Once they're in the saddle I run my hand down their horse's haunches like I'm steadying it before I walk behind it. Joe Moran stopped and put his hand over his gut and burped. Some rich stew you feed up here. Then he spat.

He pointed his index finger straight up as if he were testing the direction of the wind and left it there. While they're getting the reins in their hands, he said, I get my special sauce out of my pocket and quick slide my finger under the tail and up the horse's ass. He was shaking his finger in the air so no one could help looking at it. I lodge some cayenne and Toabasco up there, he said jutting his finger forward. If I'm lucky I gets some down one of the horse's ears. Then he pointed his finger straight at Walter, who had a coffee cup in his hand that he hadn't taken a sip off since Joe Moran began his story.

You, boy. You know what happens next? Joe Moran asked. That sorry ass don't know what's hit it and that saddled son of a bitch can't hit the ground fast enough and be done of that horse.

Joe Moran might have kept on, but Annette came out of the sheep wagon and he stopped to watch her walking toward them. Your wife's got a good stride, John Wright.

Walter looked to John and Joe Moran and then back to John, who nodded as if to tell Walter he was right to let him handle this one.

So, what happened to the horse Joe?

What?

I said, what happened to the horse. You ever get the horse trained?

Joe Moran screwed up his face and his eyebrows pushed closer together. What do you mean what happened to the horse? I wasn't telling a story about a goddamn horse.

I wanted to hear about the horse.

70

Joe Moran bent over his plate. Anybody ever tell you you're strange, John?

Annette moved to the kettle of boiling water and took it away from the fire to signal cleanup time. Walter thought to get up and help Annette as he did every other night after supper when they began evening chores. But he was situated on one side of Joe Moran and John on the other, and it was clear he held a position John wanted him to hold.

You stay right there. You've worked hard today, she said, almost reading his mind.

You got any other business you got to say? John said to Joe Moran, flinging the rest of his coffee in the fire. It hissed and sputtered and blue smoke rose.

Walter stayed bent over, listening but trying his best to stay out of the conversation. Before him the sky was bent orange and layered with pinks and corals as the sun was slivered over the horizon. Such nights made the sage turn soft like gossamer, and in the fading light all was gentle and slow moving and nothing could be expected to bolt or dart. Birds did not ride the air. The sheep did not bleat. The coyotes did not howl. Nothing intruded. Everything simply mingled, sidled up closer than would otherwise have been comfortable, basking in the warm evening glow.

Suddenly Joe Moran laughed. You can be mighty sanctimonious, John Wright. Meanwhile them Bascos are eating lamb and beans for dinner and good-size servings at that. Now, it's been a rough winter, I get that much, but it wouldn't make much sense for them to cut their own herd any shorter than it already is. So you tell me what's wrong with your numbers, Joe Moran said, then he laughed.

John didn't say anything and picked at his food, even while the rest of them had long finished. Finally he passed his plate to Walter, who handed both of their dishes on to Joe Moran to clean up. It was sort of a contracted law of the range that people were always welcome to eat in a sheep camp as long as they washed dishes before leaving.

Joe, you got a reason for everyone else's business but your own, John said, putting a last piece of wood on the fire. And we know the Bascos are on your mind, Joe, and I guess we could talk about them, but what do you hear of the war?

The war? Joe Moran said, looking puzzled. He stood up and his knees creaked and he squatted slightly, getting the blood back to them. Then he reached deep into his pocket and pulled out something that fit in his palm. He lifted it to his lips, smelled it and then blew on it. He walked over to Walter and held his hand out for Walter to take it.

A little present for you.

Walter could feel John watching them, trying to make them out and whatever was going on. Walter leaned over a bit, reaching to take what Joe Moran held out to him.

Careful there, Walter, or that heavy you got packed away is likely to go firing off right through that foot of yours, Joe Moran said..

John suddenly rose and came to stand next to Joe Moran.

Walter looked down at the gun. His hand was already on it, and in his other hand, still held out before him, was the tail of a rattlesnake that felt like the broken end of a beaded necklace. Joe Moran turned around and stood face to face with John.

Are you brooding tonight, John? Joe Moran asked, as he walked passed John slow and controlled. His back was to Walter, who still held the gun. He sat back down and took a deep breath and spat into the fire and began to pick his teeth with his fingernail. That's not a bad thing, you brooding. After all, the Lord is watching over every supper.

You never answered my question from earlier, John said.

What's that?

Why'd you tell me you were moving them cattle?

Maybe so we could blow more smoke up each other's ass, he said, slapping his hand to his leg and letting out a small laugh.

Annette did not so much as wave or say good night. She had already slipped off to the sheepwagon, escaping all of their notice.

John lit a cigarette while standing and smoked it, and Walter couldn't keep his eye off the red-tipped embers on it. He offered one to Walter who shook his head.

Didn't think so, but you keep looking at it like you want one.

Walter shook his head. Walter didn't smoke but John had been offering him cigarettes since day one.

Joe Moran seemed content to have gotten out of John what he had, and he stood again and this time he stayed up. You know how I said earlier your wife's got a good stride. That's 'cause she's got a nice ass to move herself with.

Finally John dropped the cigarette butt and rubbed it dead with the heal of his boot. I'll kill you, you know.

But John, you're a believer?

You dim-witted bastard, John said, slinging his arm around Joe Moran's neck. Before Joe Moran had time to resist, John spun him around and kneed him in the back of his legs so he hung off balance in John's clutches. Then John had Joe Moran pressed into his body, gripping him so he couldn't move. Joe Moran reached to pull John's arms off of him, but his arms were all muscle and hard like rawhide.

A rattling chain of phlegm sounded out of Joe Moran's throat and then ceased to a gurgle. Walter stood with the gun pointed at the ground. John loosened his grip.

You got me, John, Joe Moran managed to say. In the name of God, you got me.

I don't want to see you in my camp ever again.

Let up, Joe Moran said.

John let go and Joe Moran went straight to the dishes, rinsed them and nodded at each of them, then mounted his horse and set out.

They watched him ride out of camp alone and his shadow dug into the hillside before him and he seemed to be staking some claim on the land simply through his passage. He moved slowly, and though the light was flat in the coming dark, the night waited for him and his figure remained black and bold against the sloping land he moved not across but through.

When he was over the next ridge and out of sight Walter began stirring the dying coals with a stick. You think the Basques been taking our ewes in the night John?

Not only Basques out there. Not every enemy that you can see.

Right, Walter said.

Annette creaked the door on the sheepwagon open enough to stick her head out and told John she was ready for bed. They knew she'd been watching from inside.

He waved his hand and said he'd be in soon.

Soon, John. Right? I need some lovin'. John turned around and smiled at her and nodded and spoke again only after Annette was inside.

She can be a bit forward and open about things, John said. It don't bother you none?

No, sir.

I'm sorry about what happened, John said.

Walter couldn't help noticing that John's thick hands were shaking and his face was still clenched.

There's a little more to men like Joe Moran, John said.

I get that.

You can't figure out what rules he's playing by because he don't have any. All the while he's moving his cattle in front of us and getting the best of the grass. You might've learned a bit if you were paying attention tonight.

I was watching.

John nodded and they exchanged silent looks and saw themselves as they were. Then in time, John pointed back to the sheepwagon and left Walter, asking if he'd mind putting the fire out that night. Walter waited and watched the coals burn blue and exhaust themselves gray before taking a bucket and heading to the creek for water. When he came back he could hear a moan come from the sheepwagon and he hurried to get the fire out and be gone and to leave them to their own doing. He poured the water over the coals, listened to it sputter and hiss and watched the smoke rise and disappear into nothingness and he coughed when the wind turned suddenly and blew it his way.

Then he wandered off to a cottonwood tree at the far end of the field where he'd start his night watch. The sky was black and in this dense time of evening objects overflowed from their contours, while the night itself was gutted out by its own quiet. He wondered what all was out there in the night that he could not see. He wondered if it was the imagination and the unknown that posed the greatest danger to a man's sense of safety and well-being.

The trunk was cold against his back and slick to touch and Walter was no longer tired. He pulled his pocket knife from his satchel and began carving on the tree, a pattern of arrow shaped mountains and a coyote's head. He admired his tree quaking, though there didn't seem to be any wind.

The limbs were tangled above him in a webbed pattern, their connection untraceable. He squinted his eyes and imagined them as the reflection of trails, escape routes traced across the desert. He fingered the rattlesnake tail he had been given and replaced it in his trousers where it would stay for some months.

For a while he listened for the coyotes over the howl of the wind, but he heard no distinguishable call, and then he fell back into the Alturas. He thought about Trina and her father, but mostly he thought of Trina with her distant look that resonated and captured everything around her. She appeared without sadness, but it seemed there was a loneliness that clung to her.

He fell asleep slumped against the cool back of the aspen and woke to a morning that left no trace of Joe Moran having ever crossed it. Walter made his way to the wagon early for coffee, looked once behind him to make sure Rosina followed, and then he heard the snap of brush just along the tree line. It was Blue. He kept walking.

Chapter 7

WALTER SHOT THE Rosina horse the second week in May. The sky was the markings of a deep sea, hued with ashen tones and lavenders and striated with royal purples and thickened by a consuming dark blue the color of a bruise laid over an eye. They were moving north, across a tanned ridge, banked by a fallen ravine on the western side that was sheer and steep and one to guard the sheep against. The sky felt to be closing in on them as it grew heavy and deeper in color yet, and off some miles, bolts of lightning forked down and the sky churned as if from boiling. All day, leaned over their horses and bracing against the wind, they'd watched the sky unfurl and waited for the coming rain, never once believing it would spare them.

Keep them straight and tight, John yelled, his words trailing in the muffle of wind.

John was pushing them from behind and Walter was working the west side with the dog Blue, trying to keep the sheep from running the edge. The edge fell nearly straight off and Walter spat out over it just to watch the distance his spittle fell before landing.

Then he looked east over the cracked and yellowing earth, the grass gone straw color in the glow of the storm and he couldn't hear John's voice for the wind, but knew he was yelling his way. He halted Rosina, letting her trod in place and giving Blue time to catch up, and all the while waiting to make out John's words if he should yell again. Her shoulder quivered and then she began to shake, nervous and anxious to be moving.

Walter patted her and spoke softly and said, Easy girl. Whoa. Easy. You're all right.

She relaxed her stand and her breathing quieted. He could feel her giving up the tension that'd held her. Then Blue came running up behind them and again he felt her seize up, sudden and abrupt. Her haunches dropped and her back rose as if she would bolt, but he sat in a little deeper and steadied her with his seat and gentling hand. He whistled up Blue and swept his hand to the front of the herd and then he waited for more of the sheep to pass the point they held.

The wind was high now and the thunderstorm, threatening them since midday, had yet to settle on them. The Rosina horse was trodding, nervous in what cowboys called bucking weather. She wanted to move from that exposed place, but they had to stay put or they'd leave a gaping hole for the sheep to push into. Too close to the edge, sheep might tumble off the ravine, down the cliff, and others could follow. So he held Rosina in his hands, holding the line on the ridge's edge high over the plain, and he looked behind them from where they'd come and onward over the next rise of mountains where the storm was cloistered.

Standing there Walter felt the whole range posed for some great wheeling change. He looked about him as if to locate this feeling, but it could not be found for it was a heaviness riding with him across the foundering purple sky. The air had a charge to it and hundreds of still-winged sparrows were perched in the surrounding cottonwoods as if they'd already been electrified into stillness. But at any moment they might take flight and begin diving like bats. The dogs sensed the hush before the storm as well. They ran the lines but moved a little too quick, stirring the sheep who no longer walked but trotted, their heads turning from side to side in the thick and heavy blue white air mounting all around them. Blue and the lambing dog dove in between the sheep, trying to break their confused and desperate weaving lines, but there was no way to quiet them.

Then Walter could hear the storm pushing silence before it and huddling them all in that void of nothingness where everything hovers on the possibility of its own undoing. The reins were sticky in Walter's palms and all over his skin, damp and muggy with the hovering air laced to their bodies. The clouds began to pick up speed and swirl overhead, everything moving while soundlessly still. And suddenly there was no wind at all, just the whirl of masses of animals in motion and the straw smell of the coming storm in his nose and mouth.

In his head he saw sheep stacked nose to tail, climbing one another, urgent like people fleeing a burning church only to be fired upon. He saw lambs trampled and sheep tangled up and packed so tightly they suffocated, and their legs, twisted together, snapped. Walter waved Blue forward to hold the line in front of him and licked his lips for how dry his whole mouth was.

The band moved in the shape of an urn, narrowed and then wider in the middle and then funneling narrower still to make a lip out of which they all funneled, over rock and sage and hard dry dirt. John was east of him now, working the other side and he held his head high with his nose tilted slightly up like he were trying to smell which way the storm would end up taking them from. The sheep kept moving and the dogs kept working and then all seemed to be moving steadily forward again, and already a hundred, by Walter's calculation, had streamed off the bluff to band together in the flat draw below. But that didn't mean they were clear, only that for now the sheep were spread evenly and still channeling through. Once they hurried them to the bottom of the draw they'd have to move them out from under the trees, for the sting of lighting could strike and kill all those gathered at its base. For the time being it was everything they could do to keep them moving forward.

Walter was still holding his line when the last five hundred head were making the bottom and the thunder sounded out of the still. There was no wind or rain, just thick purple air broken on the far western horizon in a yellow sliver, a crack of light where mountains and sky collided. He hollered the sheep forward and backed Rosina to let a straying sheep past him. She shied at the sheep and bent her ears back and veered, and her hooves grated on the granite rock beneath her.

Then the thunder sounded and then sounded again and became a rolling of thunder and whirling wind. For a moment Walter looked down, half expecting to see the earth and rock shuddering and collapsing, for it didn't seem that such a furious sound could be born out of the air. Almost instantaneously there was hard driving rain coming down in giant slantwise beads and more thunder sounding. Walter felt it on his backside and the Rosina horse felt it too, for she shied forward a few steps before he could get her back in his hand.

A second later there was lightning that lit and lit again in great connected flashes that blinded and then cracked in the sky as if the sky were splitting from the earth. And the thin strip of yellow on the horizon glowed gold and the mountains turned silver black in the bright light.

With his whole body pounded through by the sound of the storm, a pain shot into Walter's back and at first he wondered on being struck but realized it was his neck pulling into his spine. The pain made him cry out and he looked for John, finding him slipped farther behind than he thought. Walter waved his hat in the air and yelled to get John's attention, but the thunder was so loud he could not hear his own words.

I'll circle, Walter yelled, drawing his hat out in a great loop so John might understand him, even if he could not hear him. The air crackled and echoed under the weight of the water falling on leaves and limbs and rock, pinging like chords sounded on a tight strung guitar, zinging fast and hollow, causing the land to sound off as a series of fast, shallow riffles, deepened only by the churning wind.

If they could only get them off the ridge and down into the basin draw without losing one to the edge, Walter thought it might be some miracle. He would circle the herd once and then try to get the lead sheep stopped and cornered in the draw for the duration of the storm. John motioned him on and to go ahead and he would stay behind for any stragglers.

Walter lifted his hat and flung the water from it and then began to angle down the western facing bank. The rain was coming down in a torrent now, shining the ground over which the sheep covered. He couldn't help bracing his feet in the stirrups as he pulled his hat over his brow, steeping more water down his chin and chest. He felt Rosina's back drop and he shortened his reins to keep feel of her mouth.

Walter said, Easy, and patted her, and she flinched again under the compressing weight of his hand and tried to shake the bit from him and snorted. Then she proceeded to chomp nervously on the bit, the metal clanking against her teeth.

Lightning struck again not more than a half mile behind them, this time in a large fork. With the sky gleaming white, Walter looked down the steep ravine below him at the wet shale, shining clay red under the light. Part of the ravine base had already washed out and rocks were littered there in large mounds. He made out a fallen lamb stretched out on the ground and taken by a pair of ravens who would continue to peck at its eyes long after it was rid of sight. The ravens had indulged in their share of feasting during lambing, scavenging on the blood and life a birth affords and then surreptitiously they were gone.

Walter tried to hiss at the birds, though it would do him no good, and so he watched as their crude bald heads bobbed. It was then, with the sky lit up as if it had been turned on its head, that Walter understood they could not be through of the ravens, for with their long black wings tipped to the sky and flapping like black sails caught in a changing wind, he knew the ravens would follow them as long as wind was bound to air.

He leaned over farther to his left, his weight settling into his left stirrup as he tried to see where the rock slide began and ended. But as he leaned over Rosina shied right while he leaned left. His body turned in the air as if without weight and he was staring into the pines and then through their trunks and then beyond, and it was all black sky and darkness for the infinity of miles he could see. He felt as if he were not airborne but lay at the bottom of a creek bed, for all the rush of water falling around him and then he knew the rush to be air and he was weighty again and passing down through stratas of sky and he landed.

A rock seemed to rise up to meet him. It found his rib cage and sent a sharp pain into the middle of his back and then coiling down the length of his leg. His head was still tilted forward resisting the fall and it came down next and he felt the next blow behind his right ear. He could hear Rosina's hooves grating against the shale, fighting for traction as she scrambled to push her hind legs back up onto the ridge, but she remained angled off the ravine, clamoring for the evading ground she continued to kick out from underneath her.

Mounted in a frame of time that seem to run on so much longer than time itself, Walter saw the moment for what it was and felt it would all be over soon, and he convinced himself that the silver of her hooves, now sliding close to his face, would disappear. But the bumping and grating of skin and rock in traction didn't stop. His arms came to cling to his chest as he tried to hold the blows from his body, all the while his spine bouncing across the hard, shiny, wet earth.

He was getting pulled and then one leg was caught under him and he felt his legs stretch into the splits. He looked up to see his right foot was still caught in the stirrup and he felt himself dragging all of the earth he had passed that spring along with him. Her hoof rose to wave him off and the silver slant of her hoof veered dangerously close to his eye and then was gone and then back again, landed in the middle of his face.

He could feel a wetness running down his neck and under his shirt collar and he knew it to be his own blood. He reached for his foot, dangling in the stirrup, as if he could pull it to him, as if it were that easy, as if life were that easy to grasp and hold on to. His heel was locked against Rosina's barrel, pressing her forward, kicking her onward, and her legs were thrashing the air to be free of his boot in her side. They were now on the ridge and he looked through thousands of sheep legs running and then it was as if the Rosina horse had made to have him dodge the legs, for his body flipped from his front side to his back to his front side as Rosina dragged him with her on her start down the bank.

He fought to see and level the earth, but the whole landscape blurred together. It wasn't long after he saw the sheeps' legs disappear and thought to wonder why it was he couldn't see them that his foot finally slithered out of the boot. His body fell limp, but all around him was a steady hum and he could not know if it was his own body making that sound, or the earth. He swallowed down the metallic taste building up on his tongue and he thought of the horses being hot shoed and the smell was the same as the taste in his mouth. He was on his chest and he raised himself up on his elbows and coughed. His jaw felt to rattle under the strain of such a movement and then he tried not to cough anymore, but the blood rose to his mouth and he couldn't help it.

Before he knew it John was over him on his horse yelling down at him. He wasn't yelling down at Walter but out over the ravine and for the pounding in his head Walter could not make out why John looked where he did. He was yelling at Rosina.

Walter turned his head in time to watch Rosina sliding down the ravine on her haunches until her front leg wedged in a rock, and she began buckling over herself. She rolled once, caught herself, and then continued her slide to the bottom, balanced back on her hind end. There was the sound of John coming off his horse, his boots clapping to the rocky ground and then the steady buzz again of his ears ringing and the water sluicing its way into every open crevice.

Without saying a word John lifted Walter up and draped him over the back of his bay mare.

You hold on. Can you move?

Walter strained and started to lift his upper body.

For God's sake stay still and let me get you down off this bank first.

On his stomach draped right behind John's saddle, Walter couldn't see John's face. They walked down off the ridge and Walter shut his eyes and the water ran over his face. He opened them once and they burned as the salt and blood and sweat ran into his eyes.

John reached back to hold his hand to the cut laid deep in front of Walter's ear. As soon as John set his hand down on it, Walter's arm lashed out, barely missing John's as he struck the air. Then Walter's arm fell limp against the horse's flank.

When they were down off the ridge Walter felt the horse halt, but he stayed where he was, slung over the horse's back.

It's up to you from here, John yelled, louder than he needed to.

He slid down, reaching to feel his feet land on something solid. He grabbed John's saddle blanket to stabilize his balance, but when his feet touched down, his knees gave and he almost fell over backward.

John leaned down to him with his Winchester rifle spread between his two arms like a gift. Take it.

Walter spun around too fast and it was like he'd been punched in the jaw again for how his whole face pulsed. Rosina stood hobbling around in a small circle on three legs not more than one hundred feet away. Her neck was bent low to relieve the weight on her right front leg, which she was keeping off the ground. She took a few steps into the herd, lame with her front leg barely touching the ground.

Goddamn it Walter. Go over there.

She'll be all right.

Shoot her, John yelled, over the wind and rain cutting through both of their clothes that were now soaked even beneath their ponchos.

It might be a sprain.

Don't tell me what that might and might not be.

She could just be lame for a few days.

John and Walter stared at the Rosina horse.

The next step she took her shoulder sank in, collapsing under the pain, and she stopped moving in the tiny circle she had been tracing. The sheep crowded around her and she seemed unreachable.

A man doesn't shoot another man's horse.

I'm not shooting her, Walter said.

To hell you're not, John said, swinging off his horse. He shoved the gun into Walter's arms, and the stock smacked against his shoulder as if it was being fired. You put her out of her misery now, John said. Now, I tell you. I won't say it again.

Quickly, methodically, Walter drew the stock tight against his shoulder. The sight of the rifle found its way to the horse's head. Walter quickly pumped a bullet into the chamber. With his left eye closed, the bullet in its chamber, Walter felt oblivious to the world around him, concentrating only on the pressure of the rifle stock on his shoulder, the cold steel of the trigger, and the horse's head.

Suddenly the sight was no longer at the horse's ear but at the sky. He turned to his left and saw John, his right hand grasping the barrel of the gun.

Christ, not right here. What do you think you're doing? he said, finally letting go of the barrel.

Walter stared at John with his look of raging indignation and upon the instant he saw how old and hollowed out a man can look when he's unarmed and passing off that which is his own, that gape of quieting despair sometimes called wisdom, sometimes good practice, being handed over to another over the long sound of rain. In Walter's own arms the weight of the flanked gun, a hot rod of something not so akin to fire as steely metal and wood bound like bone and flesh and so suddenly a part of him there would be no limit to what he was capable of for he was young and his capacity for physical grief untried.

John's chin depressed down like a breath spent right out of it.

Walter slung the rifle over his shoulder and walked on foot through to the middle of the herd to reach Rosina. She lifted her head as if she might shy and veer off, but even raising her neck placed an added weight on her front leg so she stood still. Her rein had been torn off and Walter grabbed the shank on the bit to lead her. She walked lame and three-legged behind him and he didn't turn around to see how she walked, though he could feel the bob of her head trying to balance out the work her legs could no longer do. All the while John watched and could not believe what he saw, for how businesslike Walter had become.

Walter led her into a stand of cottonwoods and only then did he finally turn to face her and let go of the bit. He uncinched the girth, pulled the saddle from her steaming back and walked ten paces away from her. When his left foot hit the forest floor, he dropped the saddle, pivoted, and turned around. He went back to her, grabbed the shank once more to steady her. She was already in her place. He raised the gun just below her ear and fired. Rosina's body fell out from under her as if suddenly her legs were retracted, as if she had no legs at all and there was no going down, only a complete descent as if she'd always been steeped and blanketed to the now noiseless earth.

Chapter 8

WALTER SLEPT RESTLESS and woke himself snoring through his battered jaw. He dragged himself up so he was propped on his elbows and slipped his hand under his leg to pull out a branch from beneath him, and the pain shot up his leg and he could feel the rocklike swelling of a bruise. He held the bruise in his hand sizing it and recalling the pain of being unhorsed the night before. Behind his ear he scratched at a hard mound where blood crusted until it turned cool and he knew he was down to raw skin. He bit down on his lip and the dried blood gathered there tasted of metal. He spat and rolled to his other side and held himself for a minute before thinking of getting up.

At first he heard it as the sound of hooves and he braced his hands against the hard earth and started to ease himself up and then he could hear the kick step of John approaching, his boots skidding over rocks as he walked. His shirt was untucked and misbuttoned and his collar bunched around his neck. He walked quickly, but his hands swung unevenly at his sides like a man with one leg longer than the other. John's face crinkled into a smile and when Walter did not rise to meet him, but merely watched with wary detachment, John stopped and held his place.

Morning. You up? he said with some hesitation in his voice.

Not yet, but I'm getting there.

Your head all right?

What's left of it.

You didn't break it, did you?

No.

It looks a little broke up to me.

I didn't break it, Walter said, just cracked it some.

That's good. Annette was worried you might've broke your head, John said, talking low as he shuffled a few steps closer.

No, nothing so bad as that.

Just some bumps?

Just some bumps.

And a small leak?

Leaked some last night, but I think it might've stopped.

Walter told John again that his head really was fine and that he'd go down to the stream and wash up and be at the sheepwagon shortly.

I'm not hurrying you, John said quickly, and almost added the word, boy, but caught himself. You take your time.

Give me a minute. I'll be right down, Walter said.

It's just that Annette thought you might have broke your head.

Walter let John's words come to him and again he nodded but did not try to speak. That it had been Walter and Rosina dangling off the ledge and not a hundred head of sheep was the difference between a season of profit and one of loss. There were no two ways about it. If one man died and a hundred sheep were saved, his death would have been for the greater good. Even if he had broken his head up worse, he knew they'd still be just as lucky.

More footsteps and she seemed to come out of the currant trees like she'd been asleep in them. She pulled at her hair and acted to gather it up but had nothing to hold it and so she let it fall. She looked thin and bare in her nightshirt and Walter wondered if she'd been hiding all along and how he could have missed her, but she hadn't sounded before then. She seemed to glide toward them, ghostlike, and all of their eyes gravitated toward her so she couldn't have helped looking at herself too for what they saw.

She was thin but her cheeks were pink and full and flush and he thought all the heat of her body to be congregated there. And when he realized she might have caught him staring he looked down to her feet and they were bare and small and deformed in their gray whiteness. John wrapped his arm around her and his hand rested under her breast.

She reached out for John's hand and wrapped both of hers around his. He leaned forward and whispered in her ear and then she looked at Walter again and her face was suddenly thin and choked as if she'd remembered something she'd lost.

I'm sorry, she said. John told me about yesterday. That's not an easy thing to take.

Walter, still propped up on his elbows, nodded. Ma'am, I'll be fine.

Don't ma'am me this morning, she said, tucking her hair behind her ear. I thought you and I were beyond that. Don't go regressing in whatever fragile condition you might be in to calling me formal-like. I worried about you sleeping out here under these trees without your bedroll or anything.

Yes, ma'am, Walter said, still staring and not giving in to her.

She took her hand from John's and began to bunch her nightgown in her hands.

You aren't Catholic, are you? she said.

John was still holding her and she seemed to bend into him so the whole of her was touching him and the only thing free of him were her hands, which still fidgeted with the material at her sides.

No, I'm not Catholic, he said, scratching behind his ear where it stung.

John smiled. I said to Annette this morning that if I found you dead I might have to fetch me a priest.

That's crude-like, John, Annette said. You didn't have to say that aloud.

You just asked him what he was, John said, seizing her playfully around the waist, stretching her gown over the fullness of her swaying breasts.

You wouldn't a had to call anyone out because I'm not anything, Walter said.

Best we could do was at least call for a laying of the hands, John said, speaking right over the top of Annette's ear so that when he spoke her hair whistled up under his breath.

I'm not sure that'd be in your jurisdiction, John Wright, Annette said.

And you're saying you know whose it would be in? John said.

I'd say I might, but that's one thing Walter ain't.

Don't get ahead of yourself, Annette. We don't know what the boy is.

Walter pawed the air with his hand and said, Pffff, I said I wasn't anything.

You don't have to explain anything to us, Walter. She clapped her hands together and rested one bare foot on top of another and suddenly she was long like a tree trunk.

Don't believe there's a man out there that doesn't have a God, John said. You might say your prayers different than the rest of us, but that's about it.

Annette laughed and patted John on his chest and slipped her hand into the opening of his shirt where Walter could see only the rise of her fingers scratching his chest. Walter, don't go listening to him. He doesn't know who he prays to at night, but I can tell you I don't think he's saying, Oh, God, for the same reason he's suggesting you ought to be.

Walter laughed and then he eased himself up so he was sitting and tried to move his lower jaw from side to side, but it clicked when he got it only so far on one side. He licked his lips and wiped his sleeve across them to take the blood from them.

You got something against drink to explain why you wouldn't drink the whiskey I tried to pour down you last night? John said. You sure you're not Mormon?

No, that's not why.

Just checking.

I got unhorsed.

Might a made you sleep better.

I slept all right.

To hell you did. That's why I came up here and you were shaking in the night like you was having some kind a seizure. Then I thought maybe you'd come down with the fever.

Walter sat, the thin wind barely lifting the leaves, as he ran his hand over his rounded knees churning like something hot'd been poured straight over them.

Annette slid her hand out from his shirt and without saying anything she started to turn from them as if she were somehow intruding on their privacy, but John held her and she stayed half facing Walter, with one shoulder wedged into John.

John, he doesn't have the fever, she said finally. He near broke his head.

Well, you never know, it's going around. They shut up Sunshine Mine and they've got guards won't let anyone come or go from the camp. You told me so yourself.

And how, John Wright, does that relate to Walter? she asked, her head bent up to him. I'm inclined to think one wouldn't know whether they broke their heads or not, so you two speculating whether it's broken is about as helpful as you thinking he might've got the fever.

When John shook his head she turned and Walter expected her to meet him with a smile. But she looked him over hard, and there was a coolness about her, a certain reservation and watchfulness to her looking as if she half expected to find something or see something in him she'd never seen there before.

Glad to hear it, John said. Would have been sad if you died of fever or a broken head before you had a run at little Miss Trina.

How come I never heard you got something with Trina? Wasn't I the one telling you to keep your eye out for her? You trying to make a fool of me? she said, shouldering her body back into John's.

No, ma'am.

Well, I can tell when I've missed something, but don't mind me, she said, waving the air. You two go about your business.

John turned her around so they were facing one another and held her for a moment laughing at her playfulness.

Staring at them, Walter suddenly felt a bit woozy and his jaw was starting to pulse. He lowered back down onto his shoulder once more and then rolled onto his back and turned his head from them and all the sudden it was like he had the spins.

Walter? Annette said.

Leave him alone, John said. He's had enough of us already.

He did not answer her, but he heard John whisper something else in her ear, and John pulled her with him as he began to turn around and leave Walter where he was. There was the sound of their steps fading into nothing and then the leftover ringing of noise and silence settling together without his asking.

When he turned over to finally get up, John and Annette were down the draw walking shoulder to shoulder near to where the tree line broke, giving way to a large meadow where the grasses still leaned on their sides, gray, brown, dark, and not yet out of hibernation. He saw them as being alone and yet bound by the land and something larger than the sheer proximity of their daily routines. They looked content and settled, sturdy together. He would remember this too, seeing them walk away and John's arm go up and reach across Annette's back to her ribs. She let her near shoulder drop under John's arm and her head tilt toward him. John turned and kissed her hair and they walked.

He imagined last night's conversation between them.

Do you think he'll make it? Annette would have said.

He will or he won't, John would have replied.

In his imagining he did not hold it against them.

He caught the flicker of a fire burning down below, and he knew that Blue must be waiting near to it like a sentinel on guard, waiting for them and the morning scraps they would toss. They wouldn't wait on him for breakfast. Annette would set a tin aside on the coals, a biscuit, a few strips of bacon, maybe a slab of salted pork.

Standing, after their figures had dipped into the trees, he brushed his pants of leaves and dirt and twigs. He smelled the wet morning grass. He smelled the fog and the clean that comes after a rain. He stepped back in the trees and took himself in hand and pissed. Another pain flared, one that took him in the ribs when he breathed in deeply.

The thin white trunks of aspen ran forever before him, down the draw of the mountain where he had slept, and he felt almost like he was home. So many of the valleys and mountain draws they had camped in were spotted with aspens, cottonwoods, and pines; nowhere yet had they camped in a forest of pure aspens.

A tiny creek meandered down the mountain fed by the previous day's rain and the remaining patches of snow were less than a thousand feet up. Walter dipped his hands and felt the cold travel the inside of his arms and down his sides before sinking somewhere in his ribs. He patted his face, rubbed his hands together hard as if he were ridding himself of something, but the memories pressed harder into his hands. He stopped as suddenly as his mother would have done kneading her bread, not wanting it to go stiff, and rested his hands on his legs, which were folded under him. The morning light cracked down through the canopy of branches overhead and the top of his head grew warm and the rocks and the pebbles in the stream glistened skyward like the eyes of the living.

He didn't like being watched for what he'd do. But he knew they had the right. He wanted to go down there and say, I'm up and I'm fine and I know things die and others move on, but he knew it could not be said in so many words.

Not twenty yards away a deer stepped out from behind the trees and dropped her head for a drink before she spotted Walter and bounded back up the hill from where she had come. The dead tree limbs crackled under her feet, breaking the stillness, but she stopped somewhere not far up, grew quiet and Walter was alone again. He could still feel a pair of eyes watching him and he stayed alert to the slightest rustle, believing she would reemerge from the trees for a drink higher up. She was traveling alone and this seemed odd to him. Deer tended to move in herds in the winter and early spring when grass was scarce and spread out only later in the season when the grass became more plentiful.

He wondered if she had always traveled that way, for he marveled at the willful capacity of certain animals to move through life without a herd. Some he realized did not choose to move on the outskirts but simply found themselves displaced due to some weakness or deformity the human eye could not discern. Walter had seen it countless times with the sheep, for that was how he ended up with the bum lambs as a boy. A ewe would refuse to nurse a healthy-looking lamb, or she would bear twins and mother only one, and such animals were left to their own recourse, to grow weak with their infirmities or to flourish in their abandonment. The same held true for all animals and the deer was no exception.

And yet that she had emerged before him this morning seemed to foretell of the possibility of lasting aloneness and he thought to startle her and send her running. But he waited. She moved out from behind a tree higher up with her head turned, her ears perked to gauge Walter's movement and with neither of them willing to make the first move, they remained at rest and alert for some time. She was smaller than Walter had first thought, round barreled but narrow across the chest. She held her head high with her eyes steady on him and kept her chest pointed into the thicket and her flank quivered in readiness. She kept a widespread stance so she could at any moment scoop her hind legs under her and bound off and be seen no more.

She was an easy target, but the longer she stayed hovered in her alertness the more Walter wondered why she had come and appeared in his world, for she seemed to stay too long.

He remembered the summer he hiked up Proctor Ridge. He sat down at the mountain's summit before noticing a coyote seated twenty feet from him. He didn't know whether to stay still or run so he just sat there staring into the coyote's eyes until much later when it trotted off, more irritated than scared by his presence. The eyes haunted him for months thereafter, gold colored to their core and relentless in their refusal to submit. He felt he was looking at some part of himself. And the minutes they sat on that ridge had seemed like hours looking at one another, looking at themselves, until the wind picked up and ran through his parka and he shivered and realized his mother would be waiting on supper for him. He descended the mountain.

He had been told from a very young age not to stare a wild animal in the eye or it might be provoked into a fight to prove its dominance. He had gone ahead and done it anyway that day on the ridge. And it was the same again today with the deer. She stayed.

The gun wasn't too far downstream and he knew if he were quiet he could retrieve it and still have a chance for a killing shot at her. The rifle John had given him yesterday and the two shells were at his bedroll. He began to crawl on hands and knees toward it and when the palms of his hands, cut up by the shale, winced back in pain, he struck them harder into the wet dirt and dead leaves. On all fours, his head was up and alert to any movement, but he could feel the fall, where the muscles had been strained and twisted in his neck. He kept pushing forward until the gun was beneath him.

He moved slow so as not to startle her and she stayed poised in watchfulness. Slowly he rose up to his feet and still she did not move. And then as he raised the gun her rib cage bent as she meant to turn, but he took her first.

He dragged her down into camp, the blood slipping between her breastbone and down along the front of her legs. John did not get up from his place next the sheepwagon. He surveyed the boy and told him he'd heard the shot.

Why didn't you come help me, then? Walter said, letting the deer's hind legs drop from his hands and fall to the ground.

I didn't much know what I'd find, John said, taking his coffee tin to his lips.

What if something'd happened up there? Walter said, pulling his shirt cuffs back down over his bare wrists.

Like what?

What if I'd got shot?

Got shot by who, Walter? John said.

I don't know.

Figure I know better than to think you'd stay seated on your ass waiting for me, Walter.

94

Chapter 9

MANY DAYS THE spring clouds were sobered somewhere halfway down the mountains or hunkered in some draw, making herdsman forget and become baffled as to how high the mountains did in fact rise. They kept pushing upward, testing the mountains' limits and height, against their own ambition as men, as if one day they'd break from the mountains and be walking the air itself.

For days John and Walter rode, pushing onward and upward, steadily to the northwest, trying to outpace the grass left short and stiff behind their shadows. They spoke of nothing and looked at all that was spread between them, all that lay before them, and they felt held by that space in which they were confined to travel. There seemed no other direction in the world to travel but up and north because the walls rose more than ten thousand feet on both sides of them, east and west.

They could either go back to where they had come from, someplace dry and barren, or forward and onward in this seasonal cycle to the higher lands where the sheep would find the green grass they would need to feed themselves. It wasn't a choice to be made.

The lambs were all dropped and the crew had already moved through completing shearing in under a week's time. And their seamless work of shearing was not unlike that of tagging or lambing or herding, for finally it had come so that the work ran together. The sheep had been made familiar to Walter and now there was a certain idleness to the passing of days that had grown longer and warmer as the season pushed into June.

They moved along the winding dirt road from Galena up toward Stanley with the dust piling under the sheep and then rising in a great cloud of billowing beige smoke that hovered in the air long after they passed. Walter rode an old brood mare of John's that he had brought out of pasture. He took the end of his rawhide reins and flipped them from one side of her neck to the other and she stretched her neck out long and lengthened her stride. Her stride was short and Walter had to keep at her if he wanted her to walk out properly.

Can't you get her to go? John said, angling his horse toward Walter. Then he smiled and flipped his reins from one side of the bay gelding's neck to the other and the horse loped off a few strides without ever trotting. And when he brought him back, the bay gelding dropped his haunches and went right from a lope to a walk. Then John halted the horse and yielded him back four steps and spun him in a circle without touching his spur to the horse's side. When he was through he looked to Walter and bowed his hat as if it were now his turn.

Walter kicked the mare and she lifted her head for an instant but lowered it down just as quick and then plodded on without ever breaking her gait.

You trying to make that horse walk or gallop? John said, halting the bay gelding and waiting for Walter to catch up.

Whatever she'll give me, I'll take, Walter said. But my God, she's damn lazy.

John looked at the boy settled deep in his saddle with his hat slanted low across his face so he could get but a scant glance of the boy's expression. Walter's free hand rested casually on his thigh and the other he held just in front of the saddle horn. The boy no longer needed his help, not with a horse, not with anything, and that's how it was and John did not think one way or another about it but simply realized it to be true.

Get yourself rigged up with some kind a quirt with a bit of sting to it.

Her hide's so tough I don't figure she could even tell a whip from a pat.

She's got a breaking point like the rest of 'em.

Probably right.

Then it was quiet as it had been earlier in the morning and so many mornings past, Walter alone with his thoughts and John unknowingly pressing at his knuckles with his thumb until his knuckles were red, kneading the silence so it might well up into some other sound, not so quiet. With the exchange of a few words like they'd just had, the silence would most often return but not be so silent with the memory of those few words, and John would hold his reins steady and his fingers still.

When they reached the sheepwagon, Annette pointed at a pot she had over the fire. Then immediately she headed off for the shade of an aspen tree, complaining of the heat and how it made her feet and fingers swell.

She had a small fire going and a metal screen on which to dry the deer they'd shot the day before. Walter was looking to where Annette had walked, though he could not see her anymore, her figure fallen into the grass where she was probably reading. He backed off from the fire and crouched out of line from the smoke carried by an eastern wind. He took out a knife and a whetting stone and began to work the blade.

Ought that knife be sharp by now?

I just took it out.

No, I mean you take that thing out nearly every goddamn day.

Walter stroked the knife up and down the stone listening to the slick whooshing sound it made. Something on my mind lately, Walter said.

What's that?

I think I am ready.

Ready for what, Walter? John said, rattling the screen, flipping the peppered meat over.

Jesus, John. You know what I'm talking about. Why do you have to make it so hard? He held the knife against his thigh and stopped sharpening it.

Help me out, Walter.

I have been having these dreams I can't quit.

The blue heeler, noticing Walter crouched down, ran to him, burying his nose in Walter's lap. Walter tugged at the dog's ears and then gently pushed him off, telling him to go on.

That's right, go on with your story, John said.

Don't say anything to Annette.

Cross my heart, Walter. I don't have to tell Annette everything, like you might think.

It's not exactly a story. I just keep dreaming of these girls.

Not a law against that.

Probably not, but I wake up and I feel like I've been with one of them. I'll have dreamt I was touching their hair and holding their wrists.

97

You're on them, you mean?

Well, you put it like that, yeah, that's right.

You kissing them?

Yeah.

You making it with them?

Yeah.

I'd hope you were dreaming stuff like that. I'd think there was something wrong with you if you weren't.

Walter thought about the girl he'd dreamt up the night before. It was Trina he'd been dreaming about, but he wouldn't say so to John. Her skin was that of stone rushed over and over again by water until smooth and like nothing of this dry land. Her wrists were small and tapered like blades of grass. Then there was the pale of her white belly so like a ghost he almost thought he could take his hand and run it right though her.

She occupied his dreams and came to him nightly and in the early morning he ached for her.

I don't know.

What don't you know?

I get up and I feel like she was there.

Walter, you'll know when you've had a girl.

That's not it, Walter said, taking up his knife again and whetting it up and down the stone before asking John if the meat was dry enough.

John poked it with his own knife and said it might be getting near there.

Walter stood and bent over the meat and prodded it himself until he had a strip stuck to his knife's tip. He ripped a bite off with his teeth and the pepper caught in the back of his throat and made him cough and he spat the meat out at his feet before crouching down to sit over his knees.

Well, what is it then? John said.

The girl always disappears.

What do you mean?

I have her and then she falls asleep and I can't wake her. Like she's suffocated or something and then suddenly I can't see her anymore and I'm not sure if she's ever been there at all. I reach out, Walter said, touching the air in front of him with the palm of his hand, and there's nothing there. Walter retracted his hand delicately from the air like it was some sort of instrument, and then he brushed his hand down his pantleg. Then there's just nothing there, Walter said aloud.

Well, you probably are ready then, John said, crouching low to the fire to blow air under it.

What do you mean?

You said you thought you might be ready, and I'm telling you you are.

Oh.

Crouched for so long Walter could feel his pants pinching at this waist so he stood and nervously slapped his hands on the front of them and the dust rose and he told John he'd be back in a minute, he had to take a piss.

When he came back John had the meat put away and the screen was on a rock cooling. Underneath the sheepwagon with his hat over his eyes, John was laid out flat sleeping.

Walter started to walk away quietly on the toes of his boots.

If I get you another horse will you ride it? John said without raising his head.

Walter turned around, but John did not so much as lift his hat from his face.

I got to be getting back to Hailey soon anyway.

What's that mean?

I thought I'd take care of it then. Find a horse.

Is that right?

That's right.

You aim to buy a horse on your own?

I figure I can handle it.

You're probably right. You aiming to come back?

If you mean to suggest I'm quitting on you, I'm not. I'll be back.

You going to enlist?

I don't know.

Figured you might.

I don't know, he said. All he could think of then was getting back to her and finding her.

Then it was time. No one told him when to go. But early one morning the next week, when the rain stopped pattering on the tarp over him and the sun was still under the horizon, it was time to leave for Hailey.

The stars were backing off and looked like pale gray pebbles spattered across the sky and Walter dressed shivering and pulled on his socks which had slipped out of his bedroll during the night and were damp with frost. One star high up over the sheepwagon was still lit with the night's brilliance, and he pretended to let it guide him to the camp, which he could no more lose than he could the sheep he slept by.

What the hell you doing up? John said. He had a cigarette lit and was sitting on a log near the dead fire. And he gestured with the hand holding the cigarette, to the east. It's not even half up yet.

I know.

You hear something?

No. The rain stopped.

John nodded because he too knew the way rain lulled one into a deep kind of mesmerized sleep ridden by pounding images and so unlike the sleep fallen into on the dry quiet nights. One became dependent on the water falling, for it was the rhythm that held one fast asleep, so that when the rain ceased it was as if a spell was broken and a different restfulness had to be found. Sleep after rain was sometimes difficult.

Walter sat on a log opposite John and stretched his legs out long in front of him, crowded his arms to his chest to stay warm, and watched his breath melt into the morning in front of him. The smell of wet coals mixed with John's smoke and Walter felt he could sit there a long time just breathing.

Did you hear something? You're up too, Walter said.

I've been sitting out early the last four mornings.

Can't sleep?

I ain't heard nothing worth being awake for.

But you're up.

I say unless you just want the quiet of this sprawling prairie all to yourself for a little while you're better off in your bedroll.

Probably.

Few stars left this early you can put a wish on. You ever done that? John asked

Wished on a star? Yeah, sure.

It work?

Some of the time.

About like life.

Are you wishing on something, John?

Maybe. Don't know if wishing does a whole hell of a lot of good. It might give you what you don't have, but I never known it to take away what you don't want. You ever had something you just didn't want? John said, dropping his cigarette and stamping it out with the heel of his boot.

Might've.

His face fell gray in the light, shadowless. Something you know you just don't need? I got that feeling right now.

John turned like this some days, quiet and subdued and his face appeared without a care in the world, but the way he talked you knew he was punching the world wide open.

The numbers are turning out all right? Walter asked.

The numbers are fine. Lambing is going fine. Sure, it's a good year that way. Better than expected. We've been lucky.

That's what I thought.

I'm not wishing we had fewer sheep. The operation is fine. It's all right.

Walter knew everything wasn't all right, the way John kept on without getting to his meaning. But if John didn't want to talk about it there was no point contending.

He pulled out another cigarette and a match and offered Walter one before leaning back again. Annette's going to have a baby.

I didn't know.

Now Walter, I wouldn't have expected you to know.

Well, hell, I guess I just didn't know what to say. You said it like you'd just lost your only cousin to the war. I mean, what am I supposed to say?

It's all right, John said, waving the back of his hand in the darkness.

They sat there for a moment and Walter wanted to stand and go, but he knew he ought to hear John out, stick around in case he had something more to say.

So which way were you wishing? Walter asked.

John didn't seem to hear Walter's question, but in John's mind Walter's voice granted him a listener and permission to keep talking and he started in again about Annette.

She's not sure how long it's been. She told me a couple of days ago she was real late. She hadn't said anything for a while. And I didn't know if she was talking days or cycles.

It's hard to understand, Walter said, and while he meant it he wasn't sure how John was taking him.

Said she just knew a baby was coming and that I wouldn't be pleased. Said she waited just to make sure. You know, just to make sure it was for real.

You tell her you were pleased about it?

Told her she should've told me sooner. What the hell difference would that make? But that's what I told her. Don't know what the hell I'm wishing for this morning.

Blue, lying at John's feet, let out a low deep growl and the hair on the back of his neck rose and bristled. John tapped him on the shoulder with the side of his boot and set his hand down on the back of his neck.

Quiet, Blue, John said, without bothering to look around to see what had triggered the blue heeler. His voice was firm and the dog bowed his head to the ground and rested his chin in between his paws.

You didn't expect to be getting a load of this, did you? John said.

It's all right. Like you say, it happens.

Annette's going to drive you back. We talked about it. We're done lambing and she'd like to go into town for a bit. She'll gather some supplies up for us and see what Dr. Fox says.

Sounds all right. You'll be all right on your own?

Not that the doctor's going to tell her anything we don't know. She'll go all the same. You'll make it back on your own after you find yourself a horse.

Yes, sir. How come you never wanted a baby, John?

Christ, we're beyond that, John said, and then he caught himself. It just never suited me, I guess. He lifted his hat to scratch the top of his head. No, that's not really getting at it. You seen how young Annette is. I met her in a roundabout sort of way.

How would that be, John?

Her parents died in the avalanche at the North Star Mine. It buried around forty-five men. Annette's mother was up there visiting, so she was buried as well. It killed both of them. You kill forty-five men you might as well kill forty-five families. Anyway, that was it for her family in this area, but someone got word she still had family in San Francisco so they sent her down there.

You knew her then?

Yeah. I had a thing for her. Thought she was a real sweet girl, but that's all she was. She wasn't but a girl of seventeen. Her father had worked for me off and on a couple of summers and she'd come out a couple of times with us just to ride along. Well, then with her parents dying, that was it. She was sent to California. But I guess you could say I couldn't stop thinking about her.

She told me she'd been to California.

John pulled out another cigarette. Held one out to Walter.

How come you always do that?

Do what?

Offer me a cigarette.

I don't know. Maybe I think one day you'll want to start. Don't want it to be awkward when you decide you do.

She told me she didn't like it much.

Sent there, but she found her way back. She's a tough cookie.

Walter nodded and stayed seated, bent over, just listening. It seemed the most he could do.

John told him how he started down near Picabo that year and when he was on his way to Gannett she just rode up one day and asked if he'd mind if she joined him. There wasn't much I could say, John said, looking to Walter, but knowing he and Walter both knew there were any number of things he might have done to prevent her from tagging along with him.

It surprised Walter that John would admit he couldn't say no to Annette who had been such a young girl at the time. So you let her on? Walter said, easing John on.

John looked at Walter and nodded as if he too were being amazed at what'd happened with him and Annette, even now, so many years later. Then he started pressing his thumb to his knuckles like they were strings of a guitar, the way he did when he got nervous or edged up.

Well, yeah, I let her on, but I told her no at first. Of course, it didn't get me very far.

She had nowhere else to go, John explained, saying he had figured she'd run off into the hills before she'd go back to California. He told

Walter how he decided to let her give it a go, but how he didn't think she'd make it very long, doing real work. Before she had always just come out to ride alongside of John and her father.

I didn't make it easy for her, but she had a certain strength to her. Had her herding all day, and then at night without my asking she'd go right ahead and start cooking. He lit another cigarette and took a drag and didn't seem to notice the long pauses when he didn't say anything and neither did Walter. Last thing I needed was extra work taking care of a girl who couldn't even carry her load.

She did good though?

John blew a deep breath out and smoke rose about his face. He said, Yes she did, and then he stared somewhere far off and his shoulders suddenly rounded in and he leaned farther over himself.

Walter might have thought John was through talking by the way he seemed to be drawing in on himself, but he didn't. He knew him better than that and stayed waiting, sensing that more would come. Most of the time they didn't have to say much to one another, but in the past weeks a trust had born itself up and Walter had noticed John not being quite so careful with his words around him.

One night, John started up again, I was sleeping in the sheepwagon and it was cold out so I had my blankets tight up to my chin. God, it's lucky I didn't have them over my head like I do most nights when it's cold. Wouldn't have seen her. He shook his head. Anyhow, I woke up and she was standing there. I don't even know what she had on, I just knew I was looking at her so finally I asked her what she was doing. She told me she was watching me sleep.

John stopped talking and refolded his legs so his boot was resting across his knee. Then he took up a stick and began to dig at a few stones ground into the sole of his boot. He paused and waited for Walter, half expecting he might just cut him off and say something. He seemed to want to give Walter this chance because they'd never talked quite like this. It was as if he wasn't sure if it might not make them both uncomfortable, him going on. When Walter didn't say anything he decided it was all right and went on telling.

I said, Well it's kind of hard to sleep when someone's watching. She laughed, Walter. She laughed. She thought it was funny. When she laughs she has this way of crowding her arms to her chest, John said, folding his arms to his own chest. You know, she crosses them and then she leans over a bit.

He went forward with his body, imitating her. We were real close with her laughing and just enough light to see her smiling. God, I wanted her, John said. He stopped again and this time Walter did think he had heard all he would hear, for John rubbed his hands together and then began blowing on them to warm them the way he always did before putting his gloves on and heading out to tend the herd.

Walter nodded at John, motioning him on.

I didn't know how to reach for her hand, John said. There wasn't anything else I could do but lift the blankets and let her in.

This time Walter smiled.

John told him how her back was to him and he just knew. He had his hands in her hair and that was it. Against me like that she said, I love you. I put my hand on her shoulder and turned her toward me to try to see her face. And under all the shadows I couldn't see her, only the curve of her silhouette. Thought to say something then, but all I remember is the stillness that came over us. It was like some kind of veil. It wasn't right, but I couldn't help myself and it was something she wanted.

Suddenly John straightened up and looked Walter in the eye. It's not very often I get going on like this.

I know.

I was in love with her long before that night, but I just couldn't admit it to myself or I wasn't smart enough to do anything about it. Let that be a word of advice, he said, nodding.

He said he remembered knowing she was waiting for him. The way she didn't move a muscle and he thought she was testing him.

John looked at Walter who looked like he was listening hard. Walter was listening, but he was also thinking how it might work out with him and Trina. He wondered how he might come to hold her for the first time.

There was nothing to do but touch her. I couldn't say I love you back because even that wouldn't have broken that sort of stillness. So much waiting and wanting. Words can't cut through that.

John finished and sat there as if he had made the final statement on his life and he showed no signs of moving, just kept staring off. Somewhere in the distance the day was breaking from the night and rising venerated in its own bright light.

Then you tell her you love her?

He paused and did not answer Walter immediately.

Yes, Walter, then I made love to her, he said, smiling and leaning back.

Had to cut you off somewhere, Walter laughed. It's nice though.

It is.

You got it good.

I know it. I married her, but I tell you, Walter, this life we got isn't a life you tease others into living.

Walter thought on that and decided John was probably right. Are you saying you think Annette may have got teased into this life, John?

I'm saying I sometimes think she may have been, being she was looking for someone, what with all she'd been through.

But Annette had told John early on no one was teasing her into anything. Said she figured she'd seen the most of it and herding didn't bother her none. Said she didn't expect things, or life, or anything to be all that easy-like. It hadn't been so far and she didn't see why it should change.

John had known she was talking about her own life then, but he also knew she understood. She'd been through enough on her own to make her strong and what he had to offer he guessed seemed good.

John stopped talking and in the gray light of the coming dawn Walter could now see his green eyes had gone wet from his telling.

I figure you'll make a good father, Walter said softly.

John shook his head slowly, not so much in disagreement as in disbelief. I told her this sort of life isn't so good for little ones. I'm not home, Walter, and I can't be. This is no place for a baby, even a young boy.

Not so bad as you might be thinking.

Finally John nodded. Yeah. I got to get that into my head. That's what Annette says, that things turn out not as bad as I think.

Walter could tell then John felt good hearing someone besides Annette say he'd be a good father. And he was right. For it was different than Annette saying things would work out. She seemed to say it to reassure herself as much as him. Because things didn't always work out and over the years their life had been tested and tried together until it nearly ran blue like a wheel run over their faces.

Finally John did start going inside himself. All he could see was the look on her face, the crease on the side of her mouth when she was doing everything in her power to keep him with her. She'd touch him more, grab his hand when he wasn't expecting it and tap it and try to draw him out, and all the while that crease in her face grew deeper as if she were tapping a lifeline, his and her own. And then she'd squeeze it tight, allowing all the hardness to expend itself through their hands locked together. And when all was wasted and her arms were tuckered, her face would go soft, free in the knowing that all was in desperation – once he was gone, he'd be gone. In something he did not mistake for resignation or defeat, but for sheer will, he'd feel her hand ease up and go limp in its understanding.

John sat there wondering to himself if there'd be more days than usual like this ahead with the coming of a baby. It was something they couldn't lie about sharing.

It wasn't her desperation that bothered John so much as her strength, for in the end he knew she could hold out and outtry him. For he would never be able to explain how he kept to himself so much, and in the end she would come to see this as a weakness, for he knew it to be one.

He feared one day she'd look up at him and realize she was really looking down. She'd look him in the eye and tell him how she saw and what she saw in him and she wouldn't lie and there'd be nothing left for them to do but turn themselves around and not look back. His eyes went wet again and he knew Walter would think he was still hung up on the first night he met Annette. He thought it better that way.

John rose first, slid his hands deep into his pockets, and told Walter he'd get some morning coals going for them and they'd have some breakfast before Walter left.

I meant what I said.

What's that?

You'll make a good father.

Thank you, John said, looking him in the eye and smiling. I appreciate that.

Besides, Walter said, it happens.

107

What?

Between men and women.

I think I knew that.

When Annette came out of the sheepwagon she was bright and happy and her step was light.

Walter watched her. There was a confidence about her, like she had something they didn't. She didn't go so far as to flaunt it, but she seemed proud.

She went to the grill and began frying potatoes and onions and chorizo left from the previous night. She leaned her head back once, stretched her arms out wide and took a deep breath in and let it out slowly.

You smell that? she asked.

What is it? John said.

I don't know. The morning. All clean-like out here.

I smell it, Walter said, not taking his eyes off her.

Shut up, Walter, Annette said.

What are you getting after Walter for?

Both of you just gaping at me. You told him, didn't you.

The rain had settled the dust and the grass could breathe again and the trees and plants all seemed to have a new life about them, shimmering in the sun. The fire gave heat and the chorizo began to hiss in the black iron of the frying pan.

Maybe you're just worth gaping at, John said.

Oh, go on with yourself, John Wright.

No, ma'am, John's right, you're worth gaping at.

Oh, and listen to you, Walter Pascoe, like you're a regular candy leg.

Walter smiled at her, but he was starting to feel uncomfortable, like he was closing in too tightly on them. Walter felt a distance growing between them, for John and Annette now had something much stronger pulling them together and it would no longer be about simply moving sheep in Walter and Annette's company. John would now have another life to start thinking about, another future to begin tending to and for. It did not make Walter sad or angry or jealous, he only felt wiser and more aware of the way the coming months would shape them and reposition them on the land. He suspected John might hand over a larger share of the responsibility to him as Annette's date drew nearer.

He finished his breakfast, scraped the last of it from his plate with his biscuit, got up and set his plate in the kettle to soak. He left them to themselves and John to his own to say whatever it was he would say about what he had told Walter and went to his lean-to.

As he walked he noticed that the sagebrush, which always looked muted and gnarled with age, seemed to sprawl across the valley with a rare dignity, just after the rain. The grass on the upcoming ridge was bent on its side by the wind, not forced into submission but coaxed into some gentle waving motion and the whole side of the hill seemed to undulate like a wave that rolls on and on without breaking.

John chatted with Annette and talked to her about moving the herd onto the ridge right after breakfast and leaving them there for the day to graze. He would take them on from there and try to hit Limekin Gulch sometime early in the week. There he would wait for Walter before pushing up into Ketchum.

John fetched Annette's bag from the sheepwagon after breakfast and called for Walter. They all walked the mile to the dirt road where the black Ford had been left two days before when they moved the sheep inland where the truck couldn't go. Annette held John's hand as they walked and occasionally she dropped her head on his shoulder and rested it there in walking and sometimes he turned his head and placed a kiss on the top of her head like he had the morning after the Rosina horse was put down.

Walter followed on their trail a distance behind. He was going home. He hadn't been home in nearly a month.

They waded through sagebrush that rose to their hips and then broke into a field worked over by the sheep where the grass was short and the walking fell into an easy rhythm. Ground squirrels rose and showed their heads before skirting across the field or dodging down into their holes again. The warmth of the morning beckoned flocks of sparrows and blackbirds that flitted across the sky, diving down and rising high in a flight that seemed effortless and wingless and like that of fish schooling in deep pools.

Barometer pressure must be rising, Annette said.

Good thing. I don't need any storms while you two are gone.

Won't be gone long, she said, tucking herself more tightly to him.

Long enough, he said, leaning his head to the side and looking to the ground.

You make out just fine without us.

A small smile bent his lips, but they stayed shut and he nodded.

Walter could tell that their parting was already beginning to happen. Already they were becoming separate within themselves. He waited for Annette to say something more, but she let it go and they made it to the Ford without another word spoken. They loaded their bags and got inside.

John went to the front, bent over, and the black Ford burst into life and Walter and Annette sat there letting it warm up for some minutes. There were tears in her eyes and she quickly wiped them away as they rolled down her cheeks. John waited with them, now leaning against her door with his arms propped on her rolled-down window.

She's steady now. I figure you're ready to be getting out of here, John said when the engine was finally warmed up and rolling even.

You can't get rid of us soon enough.

Not like that and you know it.

John patted both hands on the door, took a step back, and nodded. Then he leaned in and gave Annette a quick kiss before turning and walking back to the herd. She honked twice with her fist, but John didn't look back.

Chapter 10

WHEN THEY HIT the first traffic light on Main Street, Walter told Annette she could let him out and that he'd walk home from there. She told him it was no trouble driving him home, but he declined and said he had a few things to pick up in town.

Don't let me tell a man where he's got to go, she said and smiled.

Thanks, Annette.

And you don't need a ride back to the camp?

No, ma'am. I aim to buy a horse. I will see you soon. Will you be all right?

Yes, Walter. I'm fine now.

Not five miles from where they had left John, Annette had pulled over and been sick beside the road. It was a passing thing and neither of them had spoken about it.

I'll stay in town for a bit, but I can never keep myself away from John for too long.

Walter stood with the truck door still open and waved and went to shut the door, but before he could do so Annette leaned over and extended a hand.

I won't see you before your graduation, so I just want to say congratulations.

Walter told her thank you again and then he thought for a moment. It seems a congratulations is just as much in order for you, ma'am, he said.

Walter, you're turning into a real man and a gentleman at that.

She told him thanks and he shut the door.

He stood on the dirt of Main Street, which was dried out and hard and in another month the dust would rise from its surface. He faced the front of Friedman's general store and three men watched him from the shop entrance. Jesse Stitt, the blacksmith; Arthur Bonning from the livery; and Harry Plummer, a man from the Sunshine Mine. Once they caught his glance, they waved and he waved back.

He took satisfaction knowing things had changed and that now he had business of his own to tend. He felt like a man whose life had finally fallen into place and there was but one thing left to do in the world and that was to find Trina.

He lifted his bag and it was light as he slung it onto his shoulder. He stepped out in the direction of the Alturas and on the hard, flat surface of Main Street he understood what it might be like for the sailor to come off the sea. Here the land did not rise to his step and his steps no longer felt in sync with his movement.

One of Dott's girls from the red-light district saw him and whistled. She wore a long taffeta skirt and blouse and carried a parasol. He stole a glance to both of his sides to make sure it was for him and then he waved to her and she curtsied right in the middle of the street to him and smiled. A man driving a two-horse team yelled from his post for her to conduct her business indoors and then shook his head at Walter.

The girl nodded her good day to Walter and kept walking, but he could feel her all the while gazing at him. You home to sign up for the draft, Walter? she yelled from across the street.

No, graduation.

He watched her for how she moved, swaying her hips and swinging her skirt hem as she walked. Seeing that Walter watched, she turned her head so he could not look her in the eye. As he quickened his step he barely missed bumping into another woman stepping out from the post office door. He apologized, and with a scorned look on her face she told him to watch where he stepped.

Ma'am.

Don't ma'am me, she said and looked like she would go on, but the child she had in tow, whimpering with the grip she kept on him, let out a shrill cry, and the woman, tired and spent, swung around and boxed the boy on the ears. He wailed louder.

It was but two blocks to the corner of First Avenue and Main Street. He walked into the hotel and through to the restaurant. The Chinese man recognized him and pointed to an empty table right by the bar. The restaurant was empty and Walter shook his head and said he would not be eating, but thank you anyway.

The Chinese man gave him a look of knowing and smiled and said, You are meeting someone here.

No, Walter said.

Yes? I thought so.

No.

You are meeting the girl.

What girl?

The girl. She is in town. You come to see her.

What girl are you talking about? Walter said.

The girl you see earlier.

The Chinese man poured a shot of whiskey into a glass cup and pointed at it. Have yourself a drink. It is on me, he said, smiling and nodding and dipping his shoulders in deference.

Walter felt overwhelmed by the man's gestures of politeness and found himself nodding back and bowing slightly too, as if to keep up, though he didn't understand why he did, other than it seemed the polite thing to do.

I'm Walter Pascoe, he finally said, when he began to feel uneasy with so much nodding.

I know who you are, he said. I'm Fats. He held out his hand and one eye looked him back, while the other one, glass, turned around in its socket.

She will be very happy to see you.

Walter sat down at the bar and felt his pulse begin to race at the thought that Fats really was right and Trina was upstairs. He took large swallows of the drink and felt it burn as it ran down his throat and then go warm like a stoved ball.

Fats chatted away. He knew Walter's father and liked him very much. He asked him questions about herding and the going price of wool, which Walter said he last heard was at fifty-two and a half cents but it had been a while.

Going to be tough on the poor devils have to buy clothes, Fats said.

Probably right.

Fats smiled and nodded his head up and down. Yes, yes, I know I'm right.

113

Hear news now and then when someone brings it, but that's it, Walter said.

Yes. Maybe. You are right.

Walter was ready to be gone, but he swallowed the last of his drink before telling Fats he'd best be leaving.

You leaving?

Yes.

But the girl. The girl.

What about her?

You came to see her. She waits for you.

I don't think so.

No, not the case. He shook his head once and then began nodding it up and down as he had before, his one eye bobbing and his lips spread wide with smile. He poured another drink for Walter in a fresh glass. Yes. Yes, she does. She waits for you upstairs and again his right eye trailed up the stairs and his left stayed behind.

Another drink for you, Fats said.

Walter didn't know which of Fats's eyes to look into and tried to look evenly between the two but finally settled on a place on his forehead in between his eyebrows. Walter pointed toward the main stairway that separated the bar and dining room from the parlor.

He kept nodding. She broke her foot.

When?

A week ago. Drink your drink.

The warmth had traveled up his stomach and throat.

Fats told Walter how a doctor from Long Beach was in town looking after his land interests. The brake on his carriage was not up, and when his horses were spooked, Trina was run over and her leg was broken.

Did he take care of her foot?

No, no. I don't know any better than you, he said, putting his hand to his eye. He held it over it for a few minutes, began rubbing it, and then placed his thumb and index finger on opposite sides of the eye and popped it out, catching it in his other hand. He stared at it for a minute and then began twirling it in his hand, like a die he was about to throw.

Is that better?

Is what better?

114

Better without the eye?

Yeah, sure, Walter said, not knowing what was proper. He was becoming anxious now and finally sure Fats was talking the truth. He took the glass in his hand, leaned his head back, and swallowed the rest of it. He was getting nervous and the drink in his stomach made him feel warm and more at ease.

He's not a doctor of people, M.W. They call him doctor, but he must learn something else. I take the girl to Dr. Fox in the Fox building myself.

Is she all right?

I did it right. I took her to Dr Fox in town and now she rest here. Go on. Yes?

Walter asked him where he might find her and Fats told him, up the stairs, the last room on the right. Walter nodded and went to the stair landing and turned his head back once to look at Fats, who was still twirling his eye in the palm of his hand. Then he climbed the stairs and did not take time to stop but knocked first before realizing he had not planned for it to be like this. But then he couldn't say just what he planned and he knocked again.

Who is it? she asked.

Walter. Walter Pascoe.

There was silence.

I saw you downstairs. In the bar a while ago with your father.

I remember.

Can I come in?

Come in, she said.

In the back of the room her shadow climbed up the wall, her body shapeless in the layers of blanket and sheet. She shifted, motionless, watching him as he entered.

Mounted on the red-tinted walls were three framed oil paintings and there was a cheap varnished dresser on the far wall and above it a wavy mirror that bent the room. The one window was drawn up with olive curtains. The sun parted down the middle of them like a seam and the filtered light blew gently through the room. Her coat hung on a hanger by the door and a dress was draped over a chair.

He reached for the wall with one hand and stroked the undressed planks of wood, and the room was electric. He stood there in the midst of

115

what might just as well have been an afternoon storm on the plain, where everything you go to touch touches you back with its own force. He touched the wood on the wall again with his hand and felt how smooth it was and then without thinking to he patted it hard and there was the flat tone of something being smacked.

That might've hurt, she said. Are you all right?

His hand went warm from where he'd hit it and then that warmth seemed to run the length of him, as if stretched by a pulley, and he decided it was the drink siphoning through him. Her figure was curved out of the bed in a long arc and the only skin of her he could see was her neck coming out of her nightgown and her face, even her hands were tucked away. Her skin was white and pale with an orange rose glow about her cheeks and her hair was down and fallen around her shoulders.

I'm fine, he said. I heard about your leg.

It's not so bad as it looks, she said, looking toward the door where the chair was.

They say it will heal?

Soon enough, I'm sure. Do you want to sit down, she asked. Her eyes sparkled and flashed and when she smiled her soft chin pointed.

Will you be here much longer?

A while, I guess. She explained to him how the doctor with the carriage was paying for the room and had told her she might stay as long as she wanted.

As long as you want? Walter said.

She looked back at him slightly embarrassed. Not like that, she said.

Like what? Walter asked.

I mean it's just that he made it clear I wasn't putting him out any. I remind him of his daughter back home in California.

He thought to tell her how pretty she looked and wanted to tell her so to prove to himself he could. But he stood with his feet square and heavy beneath him.

There was noise sounding from below, music in muffled bursts seeping through the room, like chatter. And then there was the sound of feet scouring the floor, the clatter of boots on wood, the wrestle of a stuck metal door, and finally a door creaked open. A man and a woman in the room next to them spoke, and Trina and Walter looked to where the sound came from. Then the voices sank and were hushed and Walter and Trina stopped listening for them.

Walter, how'd you get here? she said and lifted her head and looked directly at him, her eyes turned calm and deep.

I rode.

She smiled and her head bent and he knew that wasn't what she'd meant.

You know, I tried to catch you one more time before you rode off that day, she said.

No, I didn't know.

Of course I knew you were gone.

The man in the hall raised his voice and told the woman to hurry and then their voices sank to raspy mutterings.

Frank and Joe have a way of making people do things they wouldn't, but you did seem pretty ready to be gone off. You were off Main Street by the time I was through the bar door again. You might have looked back.

I'm sorry I didn't, he said.

With her cheeks turning a darker shade of pink she scooted herself up higher in the bed. She was in a long white cotton eyelet nightgown and a satin ribbon, loosely tied, was fallen across her neck. The gown slipped over her shoulder and she propped herself on her elbows to stop it. She slid her legs out from the covers and began to ease herself up.

He went toward her and handed the crutches to her as she bent down for them. Finally standing, she looked down at herself as if to make sure all the parts were in fact intact and then slowly, in a lame twirl, she hobbled in a circle on her crutches, showing off her nightgown.

Can you believe it? Even the nightgown for God's sake.

It looks good on you. It fell over the curve of her breasts and swept about her body as if someone had floated a silk cloud around her. He couldn't take his eyes from her, and he didn't try to.

You look so pretty, he said slowly, and then he looked to her face to see if he'd embarrassed her.

But she just stared back at him, her white neck and face glowing and her lips still and barely parted. Then she didn't seem able to stay straight-faced any longer and she let out a short laugh and put her hand to her mouth. They didn't say anything for a while and then with what might

117

have been habit or nervousness she began twirling the ribbon on her nightgown again and her sleeve slid up her arm so that he could see the white of her arm. Still he did not move toward her.

I like it, he said.

Thank you. She kept twirling the ribbon, her face growing more serious. What I said earlier, she said.

Yeah.

I mean to tell you Frank Ivy isn't my father. I know better than to be what they'd make me.

Walter wondered why she should tell him and what all he was to infer from what she said. I didn't know, Walter said.

My mother left my father in Boston, said she saw one too many taverns she didn't want to call home. She said he acted like he thought he was some kind of blue blood.

What's that? Walter asked.

English nobility, I guess.

Oh.

I know it doesn't mean anything much, but sometimes around Christmas he sends me a book and he writes me a note in the front of it reminding me not to forget who I am. He doesn't say who I am, so I guess that's something I'm supposed to figure out for myself. I just wanted you to know Frank's not my father.

Okay.

I just didn't want you to think something else.

Like what? Walter said.

Maybe that I was selling myself or something. Joe Moran made it sound like that and I guess you could think that, with me staying here.

You said earlier why the doctor was putting you up.

But you could've thought something else.

I guess I could've.

It's not just that I remind the doctor of his daughter. She got lost to the pox when she was seven. It's why he's so willing to put me up. You know, she's gone.

Any hardness he had seen across her face that day in the bar two months back seemed to have vanished. He wanted to go to her and take her hand and then hold her, and as he stood there watching her lips frozen, he became intoxicated in his own longing. He waited for some part of her to step toward him and for that to be a sign for him to go to her, but she did not move.

He had never known this kind of want, and his legs felt to be held up only by bone, as if the muscles in his body had all been cut. His ears were ringing and he wondered if he were perhaps drunk. She seemed less real and more alive than she'd been in any dream he'd had and he could not bring himself to move.

I could go now and let you rest?

She paused. You came in this morning?

Yes.

You haven't lost your mare again, have you?

You might say she lost me, he said, the drink talking through him, easing him up farther and making him feel loose and as if he had holes in his feet.

Back in Hailey is she?

No. I had to put her down. She broke her leg a few weeks back.

Where were you?

I was moving down into Deer Creek off Panther Gulch. We were coming off a steep ridge and the weather was real bad. A thunderstorm was moving across us and we were being pelted down by rain. Rosina, my mare, spooked, and then we started sliding down this ravine. She ended up rolling. Broke her leg.

I'm sorry to hear it.

Walter felt the silence coming on like it always did when people spoke of loss and said their dues but then didn't know where to go with it. He wished the Rosina horse hadn't come up. He reached out for the wall. Some say you can feel the age of wood on your fingertips simply by touching it, he said.

You saying you know the age of the tree that wood siding on those walls came from? she said, lowering her voice in amazement.

No, I'm not saying anything like that. Just that some people don't even count the age rings of the stump the wood was treed on. They can just tell.

But you don't know?

No.

Oh, she said, and she sounded like she were disappointed, as if he'd somehow let her down.

He wanted to go to her, but he felt drunk in his step, weak in leg. The room was stale with smoke and the smell of polished furniture and when he breathed he tasted alcohol lingering in the back of his mouth. He stammered for words so he wouldn't have to leave.

Trina, I wanted to tell you.

Not now, don't say anything just yet, and she looked like she would go to him with her hand up to cover his mouth, but instead she brushed her hands across her lips like she were parting a secret.

He didn't know what she expected him to say or what she didn't want to hear.

I thought you might not come, she said.

He looked at her. Will you stay here tonight?

She was quiet again, motionless. Yes.

I leave in a few days.

Maybe I'll see you before then, she said without waiting for him to respond. You ever seen pink soap with flowers inside it?

She hobbled to the bathroom and brought back a tiny bar of soap wrapped in a pale lavender tissue and unwrapped it. She held it to her face and shut her eyes and then held it under his nose. They both looked at it, and since there seemed nothing else to say about it, she wrapped it back up and hobbled back to the bathroom to replace it. Then the room was a hushed quiet and inescapable like warmth or a temperature. Standing back beside her bed, she swung her hand gently at her side. He reached for her wrist and held it. I'm going to leave now, he said.

She looked surprised, and with his hand still on her wrist she gently lowered herself to sit on the bed, almost as if to sigh. The mattress shifted and the springs squeaked and he let up on her hand. She smiled and drew her slipping gown up again and Walter left her.

It was a short walk to his house from the Alturas, about six blocks up. He breathed deeply the whole way home, memorizing his breath, thinking there had to be a sort of memory in air. When he breathed just right he swore he could smell the exact same scent he had walking into her room and he could see everything the way it was, the folds of the green velvet curtains, the bed that rested her, the way it did not sink or fold into her, and the nightstand at her bed with the book on it.

Chapter 11

A T F I R S T H I S mother didn't see him, and Walter watched her reading on the front porch. When she finally saw him her head lifted and her hands shook some as he climbed the stairs to the front door.

So good to have you home, she whispered voiceless, tears coming to her eyes.

He bent down and kissed her lightly above her brow before taking a seat in the wooden swing beside her. He pushed off with his feet to set the swing in motion and then let his feet scuffle lightly on the porch floor while his knees bent and straightened. Then he put his arm around his mother. The chain creaked and the wood of the swing squeaked as it settled under his weight. She leaned her head back so that it rested on his arm. Her hair was white and wisps of it fell loose from the bun and tickled his arm.

Think we might have some lemonade?

Of course I have lemonade. I mixed up a pitcher this morning and some sugar cookies.

You doing all right? he asked, knowing what would come.

I do not look all right?

That's not what I was meaning. Just wondering how you been feeling.

I am feeling as fine as I ever feel and that's something.

She held up her right hand and patted it on her head and then at the same time took her left hand to her stomach and began rubbing it in circles on her belly.

I still have coordination, she said. I just remember some people never learn to do this, patting and rubbing at the same time. I'll do just fine.

Walter nodded and tried patting his own head and rubbing his stomach and then pretended to be confused and dropped both his hands and shrugged his shoulders.

I'm starved. I'll get the cookies.

You make your way. I'm right behind you.

He told her not to get up, but to stay. Then he rose and went to the wooden screen door, carved with birds his father had seen in the valley. He added carvings every time he identified a new one in the area and he had yet to cover the door. The birds were detailed and even their wings were finely etched to demark individual feathers.

He brought out lemonade for both of them, an extra glass of milk for himself and a plate of sugar cookies on a tin tray. Walter set the tray on his mother's lap and then pulled off his boots and propped his feet up on the porch rail to let the air run over them. They sat sipping lemonade and dipping their cookies and the afternoon crept up on them.

What is it like out there for you? she said.

You've been there, Mother.

It is different for everybody. Does it suit you?

Suppose it does. John's all right.

He is, isn't he?

We get along real well and we're faring all right this season.

Not so many herders can say as much, she said, folding her hands in her skirt. It is bad enough with such a hard winter. Your father says they're suspending the sale of all wool until they know how much the government's going to need for the boys. Do you think John has heard what is going on with the prices?

I don't think so. He hasn't said anything, not that that means much.

He keeps to himself, doesn't he?

Now and then. Any word about when they'll start selling again?

I couldn't say, but even once they resume selling there is still talk of fixing the price of wool. The boys from around here are already being sent out of town.

I didn't know.

It's worse elsewhere. The word from Washington is that we ought to admit Oriental labor into the United States. Otherwise they say they won't be able to keep the important industries running at full speed. Farm labor is being regarded as the worst hit, and you know the gardens the Chinese keep here in town. They're the best vegetables to be had.

What about after the war?

I guess they'd go home then. It's just during the continuance of war we'll need all of them.

That's probably the worst of it. They'll be ones who want to stay.

Did you see the muffin in the tin next to the sink?

No, you just said there were sugar cookies.

She brought a cloth napkin to her mouth and wiped the sugar cookie crumbs from her lips. Then she set her hand on Walter's knee and patted him. You run along. I don't want you to feel like you have to sit here with me all afternoon. You have better things to do.

She had a way of making herself out to be some burden to all of them, as if he sat with her strictly out of obligation, and it always annoyed Walter, but it wasn't something that got discussed because she'd tell him it wasn't worth discussing.

I had my muffin this morning, but I just realized you might have had one now as afternoon tea, she said.

He didn't think his mother could afford to have cakes about the house, but he knew she had made them on the special occasion of him coming home. He told her he'd save his stomach for supper and have one later. He wasn't hungry, for all he could think of was Trina and how long he'd have to wait to go to her again.

We'll be eating early tonight, she said, picking up her glass of lemonade. She could barely lift it to her lips without spilling some. Her bones stood out from her skin and for the first time he saw her for how thin and frail she was. She set the glass back down, her arm trembling the whole way. He wanted to take the glass and set it down for her, but he knew it would only hurt her feelings.

He waited until after they finished the cookies and his mother had opened her book again and Walter said he thought he'd go upstairs and wash before supper. He walked to the base of the stairs, and, with his socks and boots in hand, he felt the floorboards loose beneath his bare feet. The wood shifted and creaked under him, but it was smoother and more level than he remembered. He had to think hard as to how the grains of wood once ran under his feet when the house was new and just built. The boards were a sort of lifeline and they weathered along with all of them and he wasn't sure he knew how the wood was supposed to feel, now as compared to then, but it somehow seemed important to know. So he tried to feel the grains in the wood and decided he still could. The banister wobbled slightly under his hand and creaked and he admitted that the house had aged somehow.

Laid out on his bed, he found a pair of navy trousers and a starched cotton shirt for graduation. He sat at the foot of his bed and then leaned back onto his elbows. The afternoon had plunged in earlier, and now the light of the sun edged its way back down the wood floors closer and closer to the window where it would finally vanish with the day. But for now the room was still lit and the white curtains were bright and like some windswept sail with the window raised high the wind filled them.

He stayed at the edge of his bed thinking which of his classmates would have turned eighteen that year and who his mother was talking about when she said some of the boys had already gone. He didn't feel particularly good or bad about their going, only more estranged from them than he thought. For he knew so little of the war he could almost assume his life had somehow run right around it, skirting and evading it altogether.

After a while he got up and bathed and dressed for supper, and before long his mother was calling, saying dinner was set. When he walked in on the dining room it was placed with silver candlesticks and salt and pepper shakers and a white tablecloth she had hand-stitched with daisies in all four corners.

Your father said there was no sense in me setting the silver. He said I might make you feel like you were a guest in your own home.

I feel like I'm home, Mother.

His father sat at the table straight-faced, his dark hair perfectly parted down the side and combed. He looked serious in his starched white shirt and gray vest and Walter thought he looked more dressed for company than his mother could ever look, even if she were to set her finest silver and crystal bowls. But his face softened at the corners of his mouth and he seemed pleased to have him there even though he couldn't say so. He sat perfectly erect with his elbows resting lightly on the table.

I told her all the fancy china wasn't going to make you any hungrier than you already are, he said, placing his napkin on his lap. I said you'd just be glad to have a good meal.

I'm starving, Walter said, taking his seat across from his father at the table and spreading the cloth napkin on his lap. I could smell it upstairs. And though he hadn't been the least bit hungry, Walter found his hunger returned once seated at the table.

The serving of the meal was a production insofar as George tried to help Ann, which only made her more flustered. He offered to carry the dinner kettle in for her, and she told him she was fine and that the least she could do was set a proper meal on the table. He carried it and set it on a large wood butcher block on the near end of the table where she could easily serve them and pass their plates.

Walter could smell the thick sauce of some stew or meat gravy. He thought how he had grown to expect mouthwatering servings of meat and gravies that stayed in his mouth long after meals were through. The kind that hung on in the mouth and nose like smoke and burnt logs long after a fire is put out.

Your father can say his piece about how I set this table, but in good faith and good spirit let this food nourish us all, and give us strength for all time, so long as we can receive it with an open heart. Amen, she said, flashing her eyes at George as she began to ladle stew into a bowl.

George stared into his plate.

His mother had not said a prayer at the dinner table in years. George had never agreed with Ann about any sort of divine or spiritual life they might share. He never spoke of God or a higher being or the likes. He could commiserate and sympathize with people in pain in his resolved, enduring way. But he could find no explanation for the fluxes and disparities between human experiences, why some suffered and others thrived. He refused to pray.

Walter remembered a time back when they had held hands and bowed their heads around the table and his mother had said dinner prayer. It lasted for what seemed like a year or two. He imagined it was around the time when his mother began to invest herself as a Christian Scientist and was secretly envisioning them all converting.

It ended one night when his mother said a prayer, mentioning all of their health and asking for courage so she might heal and be wholesome again. It was a day her paralysis was acting up and she'd taken a fall out in the back pasture and her chest was aching from what they all knew was most likely a broken rib. She would not see a doctor. George had asked her if she'd think about taking a train to California for some professional advice. She flew into a rage and told George he ought to know better and understand that her body was not her own.

He remembered his father in a fit of frustration rising to his feet, clutching the table end as if he might flip it, and then in the end pounding both his fists on the table. He told her her condition was what it was and that it was only going to get worse. She began to weep into her hands and asked him if he'd only pray for her.

He told her he'd pray for her forever if she'd ever go to California with him to see a real doctor. She left the table and Walter never remembered another word mentioned about prayer, or a doctor in California for that matter.

Ann passed George the bowl and her arm shook so that Walter reached up to grab the bowl and pass it over to his father. She looked down at him quickly, but Walter shrugged it off as if to say he didn't think she'd be able to reach that far, and though she stood biting her lip, he was relieved when she said nothing.

With his bowl before him, George lifted it to his face and smelled it. Then he dipped his little finger in it and licked the stew from it and they all watched as his face puckered. Ann dropped the wooden ladle back into the stew and dove her hand in to retrieve it, scorching the end of her fingers. She blew on them and wiped them on her apron and by the time Walter had a wet towel for her she had served them all.

Walter sat down and no one spoke. His father's spoon clanked against his bowl as he went to stirring the steaming stew. He waited some time before taking his first bite, hovering over the stew, as if trying to make out all of the ingredients.

Finally George asked if she'd used wine in the stew.

She stopped eating and asked Walter to pass the butter. Slowly she spread a thick layer of butter up and down a slice of bread. I used port.

George slid his bowl away from him and folded his hands on the table. Ann, the town's on rations.

She didn't say anything.

126

You want to try running the store with people thinking we're living like we are tonight.

Tonight, George, that's all. One night.

Ann, they start bantering with me and begging me to sell on credit. One night, one year, it doesn't matter. I can't have people thinking I'm getting rich off them.

I know, Ann said.

Walter watched his father wriggle slightly in his chair and heard his boots scuffle on the wood floor as he tried to be still. There was the pounding of chair legs edging out from the table when his mother brought out a platter of roasted carrots and tiny onions topped with butter. Walter's own legs had begun to rattle under the table as he was stirred by thoughts of seeing Trina later that evening, so he was startled when he looked up and his father was not going to the kitchen but leaving the room.

Ann shook her head and Walter watched his father go back into the bedroom. It was later in the meal and Walter was cutting away at his meat and had just taken another serving of carrots when his father reappeared.

He took a seat in the rocking chair and pulled a silver flask from his boot and sipped at it and then replaced it in his boot. Then he began to talk to Walter and it was like he'd never left them at all, only like he'd moved from the dinner table to the rocker.

His father told Walter he was quieter than usual and Walter said it was nothing and no one pried to ask what the nothing was or if it was anything at all. Ann simply looked at George and told him Walter was probably tired. Then his father asked when he'd have to be back and Walter told him the day after next.

George stared out the window for a time, and Walter and his mother ate in that nervous quiet until George told them both how the field out back ought to be turned and some grass seed spread. Again his mother dropped her fork and scrambled to have it back in her fingers. Walter looked from his mother to his father, taking in the awkwardness he had so heartily ignored and tried to convince himself it hadn't always been so.

Do you feel like tilling the back pasture? George said, looking at no one in particular.

Walter said that would be fine and George nodded and waited for them to finish their supper. After they'd eaten, Walter rose to clear the dinner plates and Ann stood as well.

Why don't you just stay seated? George said from his chair.

I won't be putting either of you out.

You're not putting anybody out, George said. Then he told her not to bother with the dishes that night, that he would take care of them when he finished with the evening chores. When she told him it wasn't a problem, his voice rose slightly, Ann, let me get the dishes. Please.

She stood and went to the kitchen and by the time they would come back in the dishes would be tended to.

George went out the back door and Walter followed. A wind had kicked up and clouds were gathered and heavy to the west where the sky was the color of deep blue water.

There may be some dry lightning this evening, George said.

They tossed grain to the chickens and some for the sheep. George broke open a new bale of grass hay and threw a flake to his two mares and the cow. Then he pumped water into a metal pail and gave it to the horses and came back with another one and filled it as well. He told Walter to go ahead and toss a bit of the grain on top of the horse's hay, telling him their coats hadn't been quite as shiny this season.

Standing there Walter could feel his food settling and his stomach turning and clenching a bit with all that he had eaten. It was still warm despite the wind and changing weather.

You'd think the war had hit them as well, his father said. They were a matching team of red sorrel thoroughbreds his father drove the carriage with and Walter didn't think they looked any worse than he'd remembered.

Didn't shed out proper this season. Their haunches still got winter hair. I curried them out last weekend, but it doesn't seem to have done a damn thing. He pointed to the mare with her head lifted to them. She's the worst. She'd been drawn up in the flank off and on all summer. Sometimes I think she's got the colic and I stand out here and walk her for hours. She's never tried to lie down on me.

But you seen her pawing like she's gonna lie down?

No, not even that. Just a hunch. She starts dropping her neck down while she's standing and I seen her strike at the dirt and I can't ever see if

128

it's a fly she's after, or like you said, she's pawing to go down. Damned if I know. Your mother thinks I'm half crazy. She's seen me walking that mare long after the light's gone. I tell her we can't afford to lose her. If I had to find myself another one, what would folks in town say then. They think were proud as it is, and I'm always waiting for it to come down on us that we're uppity to boot, he said. Then what? I say. Then what? Of course, I don't say that to your mother.

You never said you cared what other people thought before.

It wasn't ever like this before.

So what are you saying? Walter said, easing the gate to the pasture shut and walking toward his father.

The war, Walter. It's changing everybody. I'm not the only mercantile in this valley. Lost a few to Lane's in Ketchum. You'd think a war would make a people more loyal to their own, but it makes 'em desperate.

Not many that would travel that far.

I'm never sure what they'll do, and maybe I ought to know better, but I'm telling you, I plain don't know. But in any case, I just stay out long enough to convince myself the mare is not twisted up with the cramps. I wait to make sure she shits, that she's not going to die on me.

She looks all right.

I taught you to know better than to trust what you see.

Yeah, Walter said. Just that everybody's got it worse than everybody else now.

Not what I meant.

I know, Walter said. Not really what I meant either.

His father slid his hands in his pockets. They started with the draft notices. You hear?

Yeah. I sort of guessed it was J.D. and Brett when Mother said some had already gone. You think Mother wants me to sign on?

Walter, your mother would never say that.

Yeah, but is that what she thinks or wants?

There's no telling, he said, placing a hand on the back of Walter's neck. His hands were cold and he squeezed more firmly than Walter expected. Matter of time. Have you thought about enlisting?

Walter nodded, and then his father bowed his head and nodded too and they both looked locked within themselves. Walter started to say something, but his lips didn't quite get the sound off right. His father raised his head suddenly, almost as if he were wanting to hear something coming far off on the wind that neither of them would recognize.

You say something?

Nothing.

Thought I heard something.

I don't think so.

Good. Well, all right, his father seemed to say, all in the same breath as he headed toward the back door of the house, his shoulders stiff, his back rigid, and his hands still at his sides as his legs swung in obeyance.

George would not tell Walter he'd be proud of him one way or the other but just let it go at that and as Walter walked he wasn't quite sure himself as to where his commitment lay. And perhaps on any other given day he would have enlisted and read his father's silence as a kind of grave expectation. But tonight it wasn't that he didn't care what his father had to say, only that it did not register with any immediacy, for twisted so wholly around his mind was the prospect of having Trina. She seemed to occupy the whole of him so that he could not weigh his father's silence for what it was or wasn't.

Back inside again, his father sat by the fire and pulled out his flask for another sip. His feet were stretched out and as if he'd somehow read Walter's mind he told him he'd understand if he wanted to get to bed and rest and be ready for graduation the next day.

Walter said he thought he would and again he climbed the stairs and made his way to his room and heaved himself on the bed and lay there in the darkness. He left his clothes on and much later he heard a light knock on the door, his mother checking on him. He did not open his eyes. She tiptoed in and he could feel her standing over him. She whispered something, and he slowly opened his eyes, but her back was already to him, tiptoeing out of the room.

His bones sunk into the mattress that hollowed beneath him and he pulled the bed quilts tightly around him. He lay there for some time, he couldn't say exactly how long, though it felt like hours. When he sat up he feared he had waited too long, but then he saw the moon large and round and lighting the land more full of itself, and convinced himself morning was hours away.

He reached for his boots, a book from his shelf, and left trying to make his way softly down the stairs.

On the front porch he sat down on the stairs. The screen door rattled and there was the whipping and whirling of wind moving from no particular direction. He pulled his boots up and walked to the Alturas with the wind blowing his shirt flat against his chest.

The doors were open. Walter recognized one of Friedman's store clerks at the bar counter and three other men were gathered in the bar playing cards and laughing over drinks. He left them alone and they took no notice of him. Fats was behind the counter, but he did not look toward Walter. He wore a patch over his eye.

Walter went to her room and knocked lightly only once so as not to disturb the surrounding rooms. The man and the woman next door were not to be heard, but at the end of the hall a tall man came from his room and walked toward Walter. Walter turned the knob and found it unlocked, so he stepped inside and said her name.

Yes? Who is it? she said, a slight hesitation in her voice.

He told her who it was and her voice softened and she ushered him in.

I had to see you.

Are you all right? she asked.

I'm fine. I'm sorry. I woke you?

That's all right, I don't mind. I was just surprised, that's all.

I didn't mean to surprise you?

No, not in a bad way.

It's just that there isn't that much time. I've got to go back out soon. I wanted to see you. I thought I'd bring you a book. He felt a need for explanation, and at the same time he felt himself to be out of words, and the ones he knew seemed without meaning. He could not see her from the doorway and so he walked to her bed and stood over her and she looked up at him. He started to say something else, and she shook her head and smiled and laughed lightly.

Walter, I feel almost like a cripple cooped in this place. You really think I'm going to ask my only visitor to explain himself? Sit with me.

I wanted to stay longer this afternoon.

She nodded. In the dim of light given by the moon peering through the window she was soft-limbed and yet rapt and triumphant and possessed within herself as she stared at him playfully. Is it bad and windy outside just now?

Not so bad.

You're here for graduation then? she said, patting the bed with her hand.

That's not really why I came back, but yes, it's tomorrow.

Why did you come back? she said, her eyes rising boldly to meet his and her voice lowering.

Same reason I came this afternoon and same reason I'm here tonight. He stood weighted on both feet as if he were holding the floor level under him and at any moment she could throw the whole room end over end. He said it matter-of-factly and she nodded and told him she thought she understood.

She said she hoped it would be for that reason. Were you scared coming here? she asked.

Were you scared I might come?

I wanted you to come. Now your turn, you never answered me.

I thought my legs might fall off when I walked in here this afternoon. That's if you really have to know.

She laughed. That'd be two of us then. You're better now.

I look it, don't I?

Yeah, you do, she said. You looked fine this afternoon too, though, she said and smiled warmly.

I'm a lot better now.

She slid her pillow higher up her back and folded the blankets back to her waist. What'll it be like, graduation? she asked.

A line of us up front. A speech about the value of education, our duties as citizens, that sort of thing.

Something about the duty you all have to serve your country?

There might be.

And I expect that scene might just move you.

How's that?

I think you'll want to be a war boy, Walter.

He loved the way she said his name and looked at him like he were something she was trying to put a name to but couldn't define. Her nightgown was bunched around her shoulders and layers of fabric folded at her chest, having slipped up while she was sleeping, and he couldn't help imagining her bare legs beneath the covers.

She told him she hoped she might be able to go watch, and at first he thought she meant to watch him go to war and he gave her a puzzled look.

Like a queen all fancied up I'll come. I've got the gown and everything, she said, twirling the bow of her nightgown around her neck on her finger. Then I might be your girl and I could tell you not to ever go to war.

You'd be my girl.

I might do, she said, flashing her eyes and tilting her head in consideration.

He watched her eyes for how they moved and sparkled when she spoke. The shadow of a line creased just below her brow, the way it bent and deepened when she said certain words, the contour of her white neck shadowed against the pillow. And why would you tell me not to go? he asked.

The same reasons you probably know for yourself.

Tell them to me then, he said.

She became upright and her face removed as she told him of how a year ago she was out trapping south of the valley near the Craters of the Moon, where the land might just as well have been shell eaten for how sized it was with eaten holes of lava rock and wind-bitten brush. She said they'd been getting news about a war in Europe through the papers, and as she sat there and looked at the land, she thought, that's how the earth could look. That's the picture I put with the war when I read about it, that desert. I know it sounds kind of funny, she said, interrupting herself. I mean, I don't have a story about watching one man kill another to tell you how war will not end war. But I looked at how desolate and emptied and pitted-out that land looked, and I thought that's what we might all become. The war will take the best of you.

When she finished it was like she was returned to herself and she looked at him and blushed and smiled as if to apologize for straying.

You think about the war often? he asked. He wondered at her thinking so much about it and began to feel sad and lonely and somehow displaced for he could not conjure up strong feelings one way or the other for the war. He thought only that if he were called, he would go.

It seems like it sometimes. How about you?

Not like you. But I think just the opposite sometimes. The madness of not going. I think you could go just about insane. And what you might call the horrible madness of it all I think might be the enthusiasm for something that is deep and born out of holy conviction. He had no idea where what he'd just said had come from or whether it was from his heart. He looked about her room and asked if she'd read any of the books on her nightstand and at first she looked offended.

Walter, I read, you know. How do you think I know about the war? My mother doesn't tell me for she rarely comes to town. And then there's Frank – He's a man who can't read.

I didn't mean it like that, he said. He was near her bed and he set his hand down on her face. He ran his finger down her cheek and then straight up her forehead and touched her hair. It had been everything he could do not to touch her until now. He sat down on the edge of her bed and when he lifted his hand from her hair, she shut her eyes, and then he ran the back of his hand over her eyelids. Not everyone goes, you know, he said.

Her head turned and he could not tell if she was shaking her head in disagreement or not. She whispered and asked him if he might take off his boots. He pulled them from the heel and set them a foot in front of his feet and stayed seated, not sure what she was expecting from him. For a moment he felt young, awkward, and clumsy and he wanted to tell her so. Something told him not to, and the feeling passed, and he sat there for what seemed a long time touching her fingertips and palming them.

They began to hear thunder far off in a dull roar. She sat up and pulled the curtains as a great flash of lightning lit the sky, making her shoulders rise. She gently patted the space beside her in the bed with her hand, telling him it was okay to lie down next to her. I love a good storm. Nervously she said, Do you want to lie here and watch it with me?

There was no rain to be heard. The spectacle before them would be merely luminary. He held her hand tightly, and they lay on their backs waiting for the next flash of light to flood the room, and then there was a roll of thunder, a moment of silence, and lightning breaking and zigzagging across the sky and everything lit by the white light was closer at hand.

She rolled on her side so they were face to face. Then she shut her eyes and ran her toes down the front of his shin and his whole leg shivered and he couldn't help moving tighter against her. She wrapped her leg around his and the dry and quiet storm of bright light outside the window slowed but did not cease.

Walter slid his hand down her face and into the scooped neck of her gown and down the ridge of her breast. Her body caved toward him, and with her leg she pulled him near and he kissed her. He kissed her on the mouth and down the length of her arms that tapered out of the short capped sleeves of her nightgown. He could feel goose bumps rise along her shoulders, but the room was not cold. He ran the palms of his hands quickly up and down her arms to warm them. She opened her eyes and laughed and he couldn't help laughing with her. Then he put his fingertips to her eyes and slid them shut. He ran his lips along her belly and stopped there and stared at how white the flesh was and how bright it was even in the gold darkness. She pulled at his shoulders, encouraging him up to take her lips again, and he did so willingly.

They no longer listened for the sound of the sky. Now and then he would feel her body jump at the dinning claps of thunder and it was as if some part of the sound were racing through her bones. He kept trying to get closer and closer to her and he could feel the whole of her chest quivering and his own chest shuddering as if it would tear free of itself. And he thought if he could only pull her closer there wouldn't be space for their separateness. He reached for her hands and then her hair and he was grasping for anything because it was all he could do to be inside her.

She whispered, It's okay, and he knew what she meant.

His hands felt useless in that minute and he could not think to move, but somehow he did and she moved quickly over him. She unbuttoned him and slid his pants down about his knees and started to crawl on top of him. But he seized her and rolled her onto her back easily and came down into her.

She began to moan and her face looked almost pained and he became aware of the awkwardness of his own body and how heavy he must be on top of her. He shifted his weight more to one side and then the other, still not knowing if he was making it any better.

He asked her if it hurt and she stroked the side of his face and then ran one of her fingers over the top of his ear and said, No, not at all.

He was on top of her, feeling the whole of him slipping into her and burying her. She cried out once and then he put his hand to her mouth and let her bite down so her sound would not be heard.

Later he could hear his own breath and feel the sweat of his chest against hers and see her eyes that had been shut for some time. She brought her head down to rest on the pillow and he brought his face to hers. They lay on their sides until their bodies grew cool and her breathing grew shallow and he thought it suddenly to be like his dreams and he found himself squeezing her tightly about the ribs, forcing her air out, just so he could feel her chest rise and swell, taking breath once more.

Then she took his hand in hers and held it between her legs where she was wet. With the storm passed and lightning far off on the horizon, he slept a fitful and deep sleep full of all disquiet living things. He woke some hours later and it was still and all was quiet and he knew he should be gone. Before he could say anything she took his hand to her breast and held it there and he felt the heat mounded and put his lips to her.

She said, You'll come back soon, won't you?

He asked her if she could imagine him not being able to come back, and she smiled at this and as it seemed to make her peaceful and content, she shut her eyes for a while and her jaw looked soft like a baby's that has not yet learned to clench in fear or want.

She opened them once more before he left to look him in the eye and tell him not to leave her ever again, after this once.

Well, then, you'd have to agree to run away with me.

I will, she said. When I can, I'll come to you, she said, looking down at her leg. Or else you could just stay right here with me, she said and laughed before pulling him over her once more so that she could feel the weight of him around her.

He asked her where she'd want to go if they were to run.

She said that part didn't matter. She said she'd come find him as soon as she was able and finally her eyes fell shut and she did not open them again, as if she'd somehow managed to seal a promise with him and opening them might break it.

He stayed beside her. The horizon was not yet aglow, but even the hills through the window were silhouetted and angled like the point of a solemn man's jaw. He slid his arm from beneath her and put his lips to her ear.

I will see you again?

You say everything like a question.

He looked at her soft eyelids and ran the tips of his fingers over one eye and then over the bridge of her nose, on over to the other eye, all the while waiting for her to open her eyes.

Do I? he said.

Another question.

And her voice rose out of that same shallow breath he heard before sleep, so it seemed sleep had not changed her. This place, this room, these confines had withdrawn her even from herself, and as Trina was there and his arms were about her, he was uncertain as to whether he held her. For it seemed that something larger than themselves kept them together, and her voice, soft, was sequestered maybe by the walls so that the place breathed in and out. And then he slept again.

Sometime in the early dark of morning he woke and thought to go. Wind stood on the curtains and lifted the fabric from the window and then gave way and the curtains settled and grew strong in their straightness. The whole room was without shadow and the wood on the walls had a soft amber glow to it. He did not wait for morning but it came and he rose with it and felt deeply the sense he was leaving something behind.

Chapter 12

TRINA STAYED ON at the Alturas mending her leg longer than she needed. Fats said the doctor would put her up as long as she wished. So she stayed, not because the doctor let her, not because it was hard to leave the comforts of that room of burnished wood and lace and clean bed quilts, but because it was as if she would leave something of Walter behind in the going. She and Walter were there and there was a piece of both of them in that room.

Two months after Walter had gone, Ann knocked on the door of her room, not unlike Walter did the first time, with hesitation, and her fist landed only once, almost as if she were hoping Trina wouldn't hear her. When Trina came to the door, Ann passed her the envelope, her hand trembling. She was buttoned to the collar and perfectly starched and pressed. Freckles ran across her nose and cheeks. Trina thought she wore them well and found her braver and less grave somehow for having them.

The seal was broken, but Trina did not pull the letter out to read it. She nodded and said, Okay, not sure what she was consenting to, but Ann kept looking at the envelope, waiting for her to take out the letter.

When still she did not remove the letter, Ann began shaking her head. A mother cannot bear such news to her only son, she said.

A moment later she was shaking her head telling Trina only mothers can bear such news and know how it will be received. There were tears at the corners of her face and, humiliated, she reached to wipe at them.

You must take it, Ann said. Please.

I'm not sure that would be right.

Take it, please.

He's been drafted, hasn't he?

I'm in no condition. His father shouldn't be away from the store more than a day.

Trina shook her head, still not sure why they had chosen her to go, and Ann seemed to know what she was thinking.

Walter's father agrees.

You're sure about this then, ma'am?

Ann went on to tell her that ever since the supper, that evening after graduation, she and her husband knew that Trina and Walter would amount to something.

Trina felt caught and didn't know how to respond. Thank you, she said but then could think of nothing else to say that wouldn't come across too forward. She waited, still not convinced Ann was certain of her own doing. She still felt it was in Ann to take it back, the letter and all. For in her telling of how she believed Trina and Walter would be together, her face had not stayed steady. It was as if she spoke to convince herself, as much as anyone else, as to what lay ahead.

She could feel Ann weighing her up and resizing her. It was almost as if she were deciding she might have made a mistake the first time in her judgment of Trina's character. She thought to give Ann a chance to take it all back, knowing how it was when people changed their minds and how even the gravest decisions can be rescinded. She started to extend the envelope toward her and it seemed the gesture Ann was looking for. Still, Trina did not know how to make it all right for the both of them. She extended her hand and thought to give Ann a hug, but when she did Ann did not reach around her. Her body caved away from Trina's, limp. She shook her head and Trina felt a certain distance stretching between them. Trina had seen her weak and it shamed Ann. She had come up on her too fast, or maybe each of them had come up on the other too fast, but sometimes those things aren't made up.

Ann seemed anxious then to be gone and told Trina she was sweet and kind to be doing what she was doing. Trina could see she was trying to overcome herself, trying to overcome her body at odds with itself. She watched her stiffen, lift her chin just a bit, and then turn her wristwatch one full turn around her wrist and that seemed to give her some sense of resolve.

I'll be going now, Ann said.

*

140

She planned to arrive in John's camp the next evening, sometime around supper. Walter wouldn't be expecting her. She rode carrying Ann's envelope with its letter of immeasurable weight. She felt unequipped to bear Walter such news and it was everything she could do to keep thoughts of his departure far off, out of her mind. She concentrated on the trail. She tried to imagine the look he'd have on his face when she arrived, how he'd approach her, all that she might say to him. With the coming of such thoughts her legs squeezed the paint on, more than she knew she should in such steep terrain, but she couldn't help it. She wanted to be there and with him more than anything.

It was only when she thought about how Walter's mother had asked her to take the letter to him that her legs softened and she eased back on the paint.

Trina reached Petite Lake the next day before dusk. There, she watered the paint horse and ate the biscuit and ham and apple cake Ann had packed and she thought about the rest of the ride awaiting her. She decided she could make Alice Lake the next day with two good hours of flat light before her. Then she could make Stanley the following evening.

She rode through trees and sagebrush to the west side of Petit Lake and then on the lakes far side she followed a trail blazed by sheepherders. The trail broke into a series of switchbacks and, climbing higher, she ascended into new landscape. The sagebrush and trees gave way to firs and forest and Trina ducked her head and bent over the paint's neck to avoid branches and low-hanging limbs.

All the while her legs brushed against grouse whortleberry and chokecherry bushes grown thick along the trail. She had the sense she was breaking path and the land was being entered for the first time as she traversed switchbacks between canyon, cliff, creek, knoll, and pond. Foremost in her mind was the thought she had not passed far enough, fast enough.

By the time she arrived at Alice Lake the sun was down. She hobbled the paint and got a fire going to heat a pot of coffee. She took dried elk meat from her leather haversack and decided that would hold her over. In her bedroll that night she was restless and imagined that Walter lay beside her. She'd wake up and think they were in the Alturas and then she'd go over and over their few days together there.

He had managed to come to her four more times before going back to the herd. Each time their lovemaking had been more satisfying and each time it had been harder to let him go. They'd clung to one another, whispering things they'd never said to anyone before about love and the world and the way they'd been brought together.

She thought about the day he told her he had to head back out to the herd and she wondered if he'd thought to be mad at her later for the names she'd called him. They'd just finished making love and she had her head buried in his chest where she could feel how fast his heart beat and she began tapping her palm on his skin like a metronome.

It's faster this time, she'd said.

My heart?

Yes. It's fast, but not quite as sure as mine. She told him no one in the world could know or feel as good as she felt. When she lifted her head from his chest to read his expression, he smiled at her and shook his head and told her she could kid herself if it pleased her. He set his hand on her head and began stroking her hair. Trina, I leave this evening, he said.

Stay with me.

I'm still with you.

That's not fair, she said, sitting up. With as much seriousness as she could muster behind a smile she could not hide from him, she told him he was brutish and loutish and petulant and ill-bred and any other number of words she could think of to suggest she thought horrible of him for leaving her. If you ever really leave me for good I'll rip your heart out with my bare hands, she said, sitting on his chest. You believe me?

He laughed and grabbed her by the shoulders and pulled her to him once more. Almost, he said. When their faces were so close they could feel each other's breath, he asked her if she was done calling him names.

No, I'm not, she said.

He laughed and folded his arms behind his head. Very well. Go on, then.

She bent her head and kissed him and told him that was all she had to say. There'd been no specific plans made as to when they'd see each other again, so she knew there was no way he could be expecting her.

When it grew light the next morning everything rose around her. Across the upper end of the blue-green lake paraded a row of dragon peaks, one of them with two heads like a serpent torn against itself, bent on looking in opposite directions, the other peaks chiseled and yet crude like an unfinished Indian arrowhead. Lodgepole pines were scattered around the lake and stood tall on the granite peninsula rising out of the water. Two mountain bluebirds camped on a limb above her bounced from branch to branch before taking flight. They traveled close to the water, diving down with wings that seemed frozen and failed, but as if brought back to life their wings were found and they were up again, flapping against the air and rising and nearer still to a new landing post.

She got up and all she could think was to be riding and still nearer to Walter. She dressed downward head to toe, as was her ritual, putting on her hat, which was wide brimmed and more like a sombrero. Then she wrapped a large neckerchief, its opposite ends knotted in front of her neck and the rest billowing down the back. In high winds she turned the scarf around and brought it up over her nose to keep the dust from her face and eyes. She pulled on a shirt and a leather vest, which she left unbuttoned, as a Mexican cowboy she met at the fur market in Owinza two years ago, the same one whom she bought her sombrero from, told her she was sure to catch cold and rheumatism if she kept the leather vest she was wearing buttoned.

She didn't know what to make of him with his short mustache and dark eyes and unwavering hands he kept still at his sides, as if moving them too might change his luck. She didn't think much of superstition, but she unbuttoned her vest there in front of him that day and it had been unbuttoned ever since.

She took him as something of an omen bearer. He did not scare her, but in a life where death can strike without warning, predilections are better heeded than ignored. And so her dressing came to be patterned and regimented. After her vest, she pulled up her trousers over the long johns she slept in. Then she pulled on her boots that were attached with spurs that never came off.

Trina mounted the paint and circled the lake and passed the two shallow ponds a quarter of a mile below Alice Lake where she met up with the trail again. The water came aglow against the soft orange backdrop of a granite outcrop just broken by sun.

She could think of nothing but Walter, how it'd be when she got there, how she'd tell him what she carried, and what Walter would say once he had his draft notice in hand and all was laid out before him. She thought about how Walter would bear the news of his draft with self-collection and he'd take it as something matter-of-fact and as something of duty because he would know no other way. And she didn't blame him, couldn't blame him, for as much as she despised the concept of war, she loved everything that made him who he was.

She had yet to tell him she loved him and regretted she had not. On the final evening when Walter was to head back to meet John, he invited her to an early supper, saying he wanted her to meet his parents. Trina said she'd be there and she sort of meant it to mean forever.

Of course he didn't know this, and after dinner when she stood beside him as he prepared to mount up, he told her she had this way about her. He couldn't put his finger on it, he said, but he motioned toward the trees with the back of his hand and told her she seemed to have this way of knowing things about to come, sort of like how swallows, any bird really, knows a storm. The way they all go hush in the trees and the leaves hang from their branches like limp wings. And then suddenly the birds are calling and flapping and bustling their feathers and cawing back and forth and the whole tree is set astir and the leaves and everything alive are echoing back and forth because the force of a storm is at hand.

She reached for his hand and squeezed it. Are you calling me some sort of soothsayer or witch? What do I know is about to come, Walter Pascoe? she asked.

You don't believe me, he said, shaking his head, a smile across his face.

I want to, she said. Makes me sound pretty damn mysterious.

He took both of her hands and bent toward her like he would kiss her quickly on the cheek and be gone. Wait for me, he whispered into her ear. I'll be back down.

When he left, her slender body seemed to convulse with agitation. Her insides felt like ice, and all over she felt tortured knowing any amount of time she had to be away from him would be too long.

Now Trina rode to keep up with air brushing cool across her face, thinking to herself that she had known nothing of what could happen to them and most of all she was certain she had never planned on sending him off to war.

She kept a good pace and the paint didn't need to be pushed. Surefooted, he was at home on the trail that soon turned from packed dirt to shale. If she gave him his head he'd take all the rein and gallop up steep inclines like a goat who runs absent the possibility of falling headfirst. Not only did he move fearless but also tireless. He could run through this land with its strips of granite outcrop as if it were the desert from which his breed originated. His small hooves were hard and after days of long travel on sharp-edged stones he showed no signs of bruising.

Even today as his veins surfaced on his neck, wet with sweat, his rhythm did not slow. Now and then, she checked him in her hand to shorten his stride and save his energy. But he spared nothing. He kept pushing onward as if he knew not of hill or flat or sand or rock, but that it was earthen ground and tried and therefore passable. The cadence of his stride went uninterrupted and she realized all might be fordable with the desert in your blood.

It was as she planned. She arrived in the coming of night when the trail turned shady. She leaned forward in the saddle, easing her weight off the paint pushing up the last narrow draw. She could feel both of them doing their part to be up the graded incline, the last one before the Stanley basin forged wide. Then they were up and the valley unfolded before them like a long rug sent loose and running. Strewn across the meadow were sheep and on the west side of the valley she could make out a herder's wagon.

Chapter 13

T RINA RODE DOWN the draw into the high grass and there
Walter saw her and made his way toward her. John watched Walter
walk, and he trailed behind, almost as if he knew she would bear them
bad news. When she stood mounted in front of them, Walter asked if she
were trapping with Frank.

John was near enough to hear and smiled and rolled his eyes playfully.
She look like a girl on a trapping job, Walter?

Trina laughed.

Everything okay down below? John said.

It's all right.

All right?

Yeah.

Just making sure, John said. He waved his hand in the air and pointed
at his sheep wagon. I take it you'll see she gets some grub if she hasn't
already eaten. I'm calling it a day. Annette's already done the same.

Once John was inside the sheepwagon, Walter grabbed Trina's
haversack in one hand and stepped in close as she dismounted.

I'm glad to see you, he said, taking her in his arms.

Me too, she said. Feels like all I've been doing is waiting till now, she said,
bending her head to his shoulder. The paint started to graze behind her.

Let's get him hobbled, Walter said.

No more horse chases?

No, he said, that's not what I had in mind.

She smiled and when she turned around to grab the paint's reins her
back was to him and he slipped his arm around her waist and pressed his
body to her backside.

147

I missed you, he whispered, resting his chin to her shoulder.

I know. It isn't the same with you up here and me being down there.

You're here now, Walter said.

She couldn't see his face, but she felt his jaw relax on her shoulder and then he leaned the side of his head against hers.

Walter set up a lean-to away from the wagon. It was near the creek bed and when the light grew faint they could hear the frogs' deep echo and the gurgling of the water falling over rocks. He told her how it was being settled up in Stanley and how good it was to be bombarded by stars every night. He pointed to the constellations and held her finger to the sky to try to show her where he looked. For minutes they were quiet, looking straight up into the black night.

Trina asked him if it were just Walter and John alone at it now. Walter said it seemed that way some days with Annette sleeping so much. He tried to tell her the ways Annette had changed since she'd become pregnant, but then he knew the difference was nothing Trina would be able to see, not knowing her well before. You'll see her up in the morning, Walter said. She'll be up to greet you first thing.

All the while they lay awake late that night talking, Trina was struck dumb by what she was supposed to say to Walter. It had something to do with how well he'd serve his country and it included some reassurance as to how the war would be over soon and that she'd wait for him. She had every intention to tell him as much, but when she lay down next to him and his breath whistled warm against her back, in the hollow of her neck, she felt a certain softening and lack of conviction. She let him sleep.

As she grew tired she thought for a moment that she felt the ground beneath her shift as it might do at the start of an earthquake. It was her own body collapsing in that space between wakefulness and sleep and she caught herself giving slightly to the ground.

That night she clasped his arms to her chest and he held her tightly and they didn't move except to wake and draw closer to one another. She remembered taking his hand to her mouth and kissing it and then him reaching inside her shirt to hold his hand on her warm skin. Occasionally she would fall into short periods of sleep, but then he would stir and she would touch him and try to quiet his sleep. Then she would lie there breathing him in and feeling what it was like to be near him for a whole night.

The next morning she rose and he stirred beside her and draped his arm around her waist and cupped her breast in his hand. As she started to turn over to face him he held her tightly and whispered in her ear. He told her she had some force about her. He said that something about her he had put a name to. She had gravity to her. He said he had come to feel her like a sandstorm, come from far off, built up over miles and miles of travel. And again, she didn't have it in her to tell him what she carried.

She wanted so much to have him all to her own. Last night had seemed one of those nights where only the noise of the sky could startle them out of their own wakefulness with one another. Before then she had never been sure if he fully trusted her, if he really knew her. She sensed only that he wanted her enough to forget what he did and didn't know about her. Sometimes that was enough.

It was like that the first night he came to her in the Alturas. She knew it was his first time when he slid in next to her and put his hand on her shoulder, scared she'd roll over and away and past him. He knew something of the way people and bodies can be consumed and exhausted in one another's clutch. Trina sensed he wanted the all of her but didn't know how much to hold. He surrounded her, but afterward, when their bodies were finally given over to one another, he let go of her like a hand flung free, a trap snapped wide open and breathing. She never ran, or felt the sudden need to be free, but it seemed a test he was bent on trying, setting her free.

She leaned up on her elbow and could feel a river rock against her hip.

I got to get up and pee, she said.

Oh, he said and squeezed her tight before relaxing his hand on her belly. Go. I'll wait for you, he said, as he drifted back into sleep.

She rose out of the bedroll they'd wedged themselves into for the night and felt the grass wet with dew under her hands as she pushed herself up and standing. She went off into the meadow a ways and squatted behind a few sheep. When she finished she didn't go back to Walter. She went to camp and laid a fire and took an iron kettle and filled it with grounds to start the morning coffee.

It wasn't long before John was up. He was polite enough, but he asked if she weren't some sort of bear the way she clambered the pots and pans.

Just thought I'd get breakfast going, is all, she said. I'll stop if you like, but I thought Annette might like the help, with her more tired and all.

Thought you knew where everything was, did you? John said, scrunching his brow and smiling.

No, just figured it's the same on every sheepwagon I've ever been around.

Annette propped the door open just wide enough to put her face out. I'm just getting myself straightened, and then I'll be out proper-like to say good morning to you, Trina. And my God, John, if this girl here wants to make me breakfast I won't be the first to stop her, nor should you. Trina, you go right ahead.

Trina laughed. Thanks for your permission, ma'am.

Annette shut the door.

And you've seen your share of sheepwagons? John said.

For God's sake, John, let up on her. You'll embarrass her.

I've seen a few.

That right? he said, curling his lips

It's just that every wagon's got a grub box and that's not too hard to find. It never gets too much more complicated than that.

That's right, Annette yelled from inside. They like to make it seem more difficult than it is, but some of us is just born knowing how to make do.

John smiled at what Annette said and told Trina that some potatoes and eggs would be all right by him. She joked with him about lamb chops being the best thing in the word to eat with a fried egg and he told her she could go clipping the tails off all the foxes in the world but to leave his sheep alone.

Annette stepped out of the sheepwagon and looked at Trina and smiled warmly. You're just as pretty as I remembered you. She went to Trina and gave her a hug like she'd known her for years. Then she put her hand on Trina's shoulders and told her not to worry about John. Don't mind him, he just gets a little prickly-like, she said. Then she turned her face to John, Don't you?

John hollered toward the lean-to and told Walter he better come out and help him defend himself as he was outnumbered, and shortly Walter joined them.

John sat eating his eggs. How long you plan to stay, Trina?

John Wright, what other kinds of question you aim to be asking this morning? Annette said.

I'll be getting on, Trina said.

No need to go rushing off. Then suddenly John leaned forward and spat and said, Christ, there's a shell in my eggs. You're fired. And then he leaned back and laughed hard. Annette, these might be right up there with yours.

Walter took another spoonful of eggs and told Trina they were real good.

You would say that now, wouldn't you, Walter? Annette said. Trina, they're real fine.

John, who had finished all his eggs in a few large mouthfuls, nodded, took another sip of coffee. You're welcome here, he said. We pretty much stay put from here on out. Move them to fresh grass, but this is as high as we go. You're welcome as long as you like. Know it pleases Walter just fine.

You've still got your share of work cut out, Trina said. I won't be around getting in the way.

John nodded. No, the work never quits. Got that right.

I imagine they won't have much trouble finding work for you. That's if you want it, Annette said. You think about it. I'm heading down to the stream to freshen up, so I'll see you two later, I'm sure.

Once the plates were scraped clean, John wandered off to feed the dogs without telling them he was going off and it was just Trina and Walter by the fire. Her heart began to race and she could feel her face go flush. He stood with his foot banked up against a rock that made up the fire ring. He grew still and she saw the muscle in his forearm go long and taut. He took up stirring the dead fire, where the Dutch oven was now cooling, with a stick. He leaned his head toward her and smiled at her and she could feel him studying her.

You'll bury the oven stirring like that, she said lightly.

He nodded.

Walter.

Yeah.

I got to tell you something.

He stopped stirring.

You've been drafted, Walter.

Still he did not stir the fire. He regarded her with a far off forlorned look of wonder, as if she delivered notes to the families of the deceased, and a coldness crept into the corners of his eyes. You came up here just to tell me that.

I wanted to see you, you know that.

He looked at her hard. Jesus, I thought maybe you just came on your own, he said.

She started to stand, but he held his hand out motioning for her to stay seated.

He took all the sound out of the place and the awkwardness she had so feared drove at them. He nodded again and relaxed his grip on the stick and let it fall to the ground. I was going to go sometime, anyway. When do I go?

And suddenly she knew another side to him that was far off and irretrievable and that wouldn't pretend to be there for her just to make things seem easier than they were.

She went to her saddlebag and pulled out the envelope, neatly torn at its seal.

So, she knows? he said when he saw the broken seal.

Your mother gave it to me four days ago saying I knew the high country as well as any man she could send and she thought it gave me a good excuse to come see you.

He read over it and then refolded it and tucked it in his back pocket.

They say I report to Fort Lewis in Washington. The second week of August.

That's it? I mean that's all it says? she said, wanting something more. Pretty much.

She could think of nothing else to say so she kept on burning the distance between them with her silence until he couldn't answer her. For the first time she noticed he couldn't look her in the eye. Then she was talking, asking him things, just to hear her voice and his voice sound together, just to be sure he was still there. All the while feeling deeply how she was already trying to bring him back.

You think your parents will want to have you near town before you go?

He shook his head. I'll stay with John until it's time.

It was the second week of July. Trina nodded, because she knew she had no choice but to understand.

Chapter 14

M IDDAY THEY MOVED the sheep a quarter mile west, and
by early afternoon it was warm and the sheep were bedding down
and the dogs were going lazy. John told Walter to go fish and have
himself some fun. Annette was napping and he said he was going to have
himself a nap and that the sheep would stay put.

Walter and Trina rode through green fields stretched like promises
and edged with rocks and sloping banks, heading roughly toward a strip
of the Salmon River rid high on both sides by canyon. They took their
time, and now and then the horses dipped their heads for a mouthful of
grass as they marched on with no real aim or direction offered by their
riders, but always closing in on them was the day. The light was soft,
bleeding the air dry and empty so that belief and imagination could not
get away from themselves. She tried not to dwell on the morning's
conversation and he quietly resolved in his mind he would not labor over
the war or mention it again before her. Inside him was some intuition that
it would only breed a strange kind of hate and jealousy between them, for
the war was something that could not be helped or prevented.

In the middle of a field where the grass was blazed yellow with sun,
Walter suddenly stopped and dismounted and began walking. Trina did
the same.

Grasshoppers were thick in the tall grass and they clung to the weeds
already gone to seed. Walter caught them and held them in his fist.
What I got in my hand could take a whole wheat field out in a season,
he said.

Trina nodded. He came up beside her like he was going to put his arm
around her, and when she leaned into him, he dropped one down the

back of her blouse. She pulled back, but he already had hold of her by both her arms. She'd been hemmed in by the deep silence settled between them and quiet ever since they set out fishing, but she couldn't help laughing now. She told him to get it out, quick.

You don't like grasshoppers? he said, not letting her loose.

What's got into you? she said, wriggling to be free.

He slid his hands under her blouse and up her back and then stopped on her shoulder blades. She felt him finger a grasshopper off, but his hands stayed and his fingers touched down on her spine like drops of water, and then he smoothed his hand flat on her back. He looked at her for a long time.

I can't stop thinking about you, he said.

No? she said.

He dropped down on his knees and his arms slid down the length of her back side and then he pushed her skirt up to her waist to stare at her bare legs. You know I never stop thinking, he said.

About me?

You.

She dropped down on her knees. He unbuttoned her blouse and his face went to her chest and his lips followed a line across her breasts as if a trail had been left for him there. She let him follow that trail across the whole of her body until she was trembling all over with feverish hope. His eyes shining and his lips parted for her as he caressed her with his hands until she became so overcome she could not think whether she touched him back. They became buried in a sea of green grass with their movements led by the desperate impulse to have but a few oblivious moments where they could enjoy each other at last, alone without the sense things were closing in on them.

Please, Walter, she said, running her fingers through his hair.

He came to her face and made like he would bend down and kiss her, but he stayed staring into her eyes with his lips just brushing the tops of hers and then his face softened because he knew what she wanted. He lifted his chest from hers and the hot air, stale and empty, rushed in between them, furious and buzzing. His white chest rose above her and as she waited for him, her insides pulsed and raced. Then he came down on her almost too quick and too hard, thrusting deep inside her, and she cried out his name. He put his lips to hers quickly and kissed her hard, so she felt as if she could not scream, could not breathe. And then she felt the sensation of being lifted off the ground, like what it would be to fly, and he was inside her, going through her.

After, as they lay warming their bare chests in the sun, she could still feel the blood in her lips and taste the sweet of him like clover and tea in her mouth. She felt hot with him as if he were all over her still. She didn't want to let him go. She rolled over to her side so her back was to him and then reached for his arm, which she draped around her. He held her there pressed against him' until the sun ducked behind a cloud and the goose bumps began to rise on her skin.

You're cold, he said.

I love you, Trina said, and it came out louder than she thought it would and was urgent and like something said in anger.

He bent his lips close to her ear. I love you, he whispered. You know that, don't you? he said.

Yes, she said, but say it again. She wanted to hear him say that forever, tickling her ear the way it did, like warm wind. And she knew then she could lay there for however long that was to hear him say it, but that sort of time doesn't stay.

And it didn't. His arms were coming off her and as he sat up, he said, Let's go catch some dinner.

Walter stopped at a bend in the river where the water rushed around a pile of boulders. The water was green and clear and willows were interspersed among the high grasses. He said there was bound to be at least a dozen trout hiding out under the falls, near the shade of the rocks. The rocks were big and gray and lined with white quartz.

Trina took off her boots and socks and found a boulder mounded out in the shape of a stair where she could sit and dangle her feet, feel the river run through her, and let the cold go to her head. It was good to be away from the sheep, the responsibility Walter had to them, and the relentless pacing blue heeler waiting on Walter and John's every move. Here it was like they waited for no one and no one relied on them. They were alone in the world and it was peaceful and almost carefree. She'd picked up a few grasshoppers of her own along the way and when she loosened her grip on them they rustled like straw or dried grass come to life. She thought she could hear them and their tangled legs and wings that sounded of pages of very thin paper being rifled through.

Walter had brought a few tied flies from the mercantile with him. He took one off his hat, but he said she should keep the grasshoppers as bait if she decided she wanted to give it a try. After a while she set a few loose on the rock. One she kept in the palm of her left hand and the other she held gently between her thumb and index finger. She thought about how she used to pluck the legs and wings off grasshoppers when she was a child. At the age of six she had it in her head that plucking a grasshopper was somewhat like plucking a chicken.

The first chicken she'd been given as a child to pluck wasn't quite dead. Her mother tossed it to her, but its wings were still flapping and its legs still running. She watched her mother chop the chicken's head off on a wooden block, saw its legs keep running, trying to get away, its wing fluttering, and wondered what her mother would do to quiet the thing. Her mother did nothing but throw it in Trina's lap. She remembered screaming and her mother saying, What's wrong with you child, you never seen a chicken with its head cut off? Go on and pluck it. You act like you've never been around a dead animal. And Trina had seen her share of dead animals and helped skin them too, but she sat there horrified by it. She'd just never seen how long a bird could hold on even with its neck wrung and severed.

Her mother told her to go start plucking grasshoppers' legs and wings. That's good practice, she'd said. You'll see just how slow some things die and you'll toughen up.

Walter yelled to her, asked her how come if she had her shoes off she wasn't going to go ahead and wade in.

The water looks cold.

You've got your feet in it now.

Yeah, and it's cold.

It's not so bad. You can go all the way across it'd be the same as where you're sitting now. I think you'll catch more over there than on your side.

I sort of like my side.

For fishing or for sitting?

Maybe a little of both, she said.

He laughed and cast his line back out following his fly downriver. Still say you should come over here.

Yeah, Trina said. She looked down and realized she had picked the wings and legs off the grasshopper without really paying attention. And she knew the insect would topple if she set it down on the rocks, for its wings balanced it and leveled it to the world. One grasshopper she had let go was still seated at the corner of the rock and she slid her hand toward it, to watch it jump and find cover in the rock and nearby scrub. Instead, it veered from her hand, landed in the water, and was quickly taken under by a rising rainbow trout.

The legless insect she still had left in her hand she tossed to the river. It fell off toward Walter and that seemed more natural than the fact water currents run down and not upstream. Everything seemed to gravitate toward him, and even staying on the rock watching him seemed an act of resistance. She promised herself she would never forget his day. Then she thought about how the things you most wanted to remember, the things you promised yourself you wouldn't forget, frequently managed to escape you, and the things you didn't give two shakes whether you remembered or forgot haunted you like bad dreams you couldn't quit.

She sat and wondered if she was better not coming back here to visit him before his leave in August. She knew it would make it more difficult for both of them to say good-bye. For today she could sit and pretend they had forever and that the only cares in the world were their own, but already the sense of today was compressed into something shorter than it was. It had all begun to end since her arrival into Stanley, and it would go on like that, day into night, and it would all seem forthcoming. It was something unexplainable, and she was not paranoid, only attuned to loss as if it were always impending and ringing with echoes the way a fever does with aches and chills.

Fish were rolling over in the water around him, striking at the hatch of mayflies. They rose and fell, tripping on the wind, their lacy wings giving away their frailty and something of the inevitability of their short life spanning a few hours that might or might not grow into days. There was something to the brevity of their life, the fact they were without mouth, the fact they flew without eyes, the fact their adult life did not include eating and breath. They were seeing everything for the very first time and then they'd be gone without ever knowing how short their stay was really meant to be.

Walter started to wade through the stream to hand Trina his rod, but she shook her head.

Come on out, the mayflies are on.

I'm watching them.

That's not the same, he said, casting farther and deeper into a dark shady hole on the far side of the bank where the water was dappled with the ripples of trout feeding.

Give me a minute here, Trina said.

Did you see the size on that one? he said. What do you need a minute for?

To make my feet go cold.

They're all over. They'll go cold quick enough if you wade in. Come stand behind me and I'll lead you across.

Across the great divide.

Wherever you like.

She stayed on the boulder and after a while she moved her toes and could not feel them. It seemed like a way of forgetting the months, possibly years that lay ahead without him. The cold did not make her go dull and forgetful. It had a way of drilling the day into her and she wasn't trying so much to forget, as to become like the cold, like flowing metal.

One day, Trina, he yelled across to her.

One day you'll what? she said.

I'm going to build a cabin down on Silver Creek where the grasses change colors with the seasons. We're going to sleep in a featherbed and watch geese part the sky in migrating arrows.

That sounds nice, Walter.

We'll have horses and a big dog and a barn cat. He asked her if she liked apples and she said she did and he told her there would be apple trees surrounding the house.

You've thought about all of this?

Yes, he said, before spotting a mountain sheep bounding onto a rock ledge. It looked down at them and Walter turned slowly so as not to startle it and then pointed slowly up to it, not sure if Trina had seen it. It was white and had large horns protruding from its head. It shook its head at them, determined to provoke them, as if they were something it could butt out of this world even from up high. Then it bounded off, effortlessly scaling rocks and ledges until it was high up and beyond their sight.

Walter kept staring at the upper ledges of the canyon. Not watching his line, a fish rose, struck at his fly, and rolled over folding into the water, leaving Walter's line alone. He shook his head and she heard him utter, Damn, under his breath.

Damn it all, she said.

He turned his head and looked at her and then cast his line back out. It fell soft on the water before trailing under the surface to tease another fish and it wasn't much longer before Walter had two rainbows and two brown trout netted. She was still sitting on the rock waiting for him.

He smiled at her and told her his bottom would fall asleep if he did that much sitting.

Maybe mine is.

Well, then, its probably a good thing we're leaving when we are, he said, wading out of the stream, wrapping his free arm around her and lifting her off the ground. You never know, it might just fall asleep and never wake up, and then what would I do?

That happens, you think?

Suppose it could.

Maybe someday I'll just have to make a point of sitting for as long as I can in one place.

Or you could ask me in a year or so.

When's that? Are you making a proposal of some kind I don't know about? she said, smiling and turning her face up to his.

Trina, I'm going to war.

Trina's head was bent down, watching the placement of her feet on the river rocks.

In some trench in France. I think that's where they'll send me.

She stopped and he had to stop or let go of her hand.

Don't ever say that. Don't ever joke about that. That's not funny. Not in the least.

Hey, I was kidding.

It's not something I want to kid about, falling asleep, that is, she said.

He squeezed her hand hard and told her he was sorry and leaned over and kissed the top of her head. Why don't you stay here with me? he asked.

She told him she couldn't because her mother was expecting her and they'd need the furs she brought in to help them through the winter.

He nodded and they walked out of the canyon the way they came and occasionally they looked down at their hands holding and didn't say anything. When they got to the canyon opening where they left the horses, they mounted. With Walter looking out somewhere in between his horse's ears, Trina found herself fumbling with the rawhide reins, rubbing them between her thumb and index finger as if she were warming a set of fingers left out in the cold, stiff frozen fingers she might stir blood back into.

It was her fingers that gave way first as she looked down and saw them chafed and red and raw. She replaced her hands on the saddle horn and did not bother to neck rein the paint for he moved beside Walter's horse and needed no guidance.

She rode beside Walter until they were back in camp and put up for the night and sleeping and until their arms finally slid off of one another and it was morning and she was supposed to be leaving.

I have to go. My mother will be waiting for me, Trina said.

Stay, just until I leave, he whispered. Please, it won't be long.

They did this for days and every night she would tell herself that it would be their last, but when morning came she'd have lost all will to leave him. She kept putting off her departure, and for three weeks they slept together at night under the black hull of sky, making love over and over. When it was time for Walter to report, they rode out of Stanley together, guided by the flat light of the stars and a round moon.

Chapter 15

THEY WALKED TOGETHER a last time on a day in late
August when the grass was burned to the color of oatmeal. Trina met
Walter in the mercantile late one afternoon and they left through the
backdoor without the notice of Walter's father. They crossed Main Street
and traveled west on First Avenue until the road was no more. She didn't
ask Walter where they were going and he didn't say. They spoke very
little.

Even as they neared the Big Wood, where Walter held back willow
and low-hanging aspen branches so that she might pass, she simply
nodded thank you to him. They had bore themselves silent under the
expectation of their imminent separation from one another. And with
neither of them wanting to be seen the coward by the other, they walked
in a mighty silence biding time, the way truth does waiting for naysayers.
They could not know it then, but they were making vows of loyalty for a
lifetime in their walking, winding crooked on their way to the river. They
could not speak, for to speak would be to undermine that which was
already planned and laid for them.

Leading her down to the river he watched her arms swing at her sides
and her long fingers, pale in the light, touching the air and he thought
how he would do anything for her. It seemed the easiest conclusion he'd
come to in life. He turned around and stole a glance at her eyes. He
thought back to how, when he first met her, they haunted him as some
unknown or unsaid truth or promise.

He felt as though today her eyes might reveal all he was to know of her
and that he would discover who she was for all time. But as he waited for
her to impress herself on him, she waited for him to rush up on her and

take her down in the grass and tell her to forget about the war, that it would not last, that it wasn't so, that it had ended that very day. She thought herself silly, even foolish, for there was no such consolation to be had or found or even dreamed.

When they approached a stretch of the river that broke to gravel bar, a killdeer bounced alongside of them not twenty feet out, tormented and bobbing, trying to lure the two of them into a game of prey, faking a broken wing. All the while she tried to draw them from her nest. She scrambled back in the direction from which Walter and Trina came, but they did not follow. Realizing she did not stop them, she flew back in front of them again, trailing still in another direction, broken-winged. They paid her no attention.

It wasn't until they came back off from the river and lay down side by side in the high grass that Trina told Walter it seemed late in the season for the bird to be nesting and protecting young.

Walter rolled on his back and raised his hand high and Trina did not know if he even heard her. If he did, he paid her no attention. He raised his hand to the sky and his arm ran parallel with the grass and dangled on the air. With his hand up he seemed to reach beyond himself. But when she asked him what he was doing, he told her he was just shading his eyes.

He might as well have been shading Trina's eyes or leading her blindfolded into a kind of sleep. For, she thinks, he has stolen my senses, shut my sight, drowned my spirit, and drawn my breath. The world recedes and then almost disappears in these moments holding his hands with the grass riding above them. She lies there without seeing the form of the individual blades of grass but sensing something of a pattern in which they are becoming entwined and enveloped.

She holds her own hand up then and weaves her fingers in his and he turns his head to the side so he looks her in the eye. She feels like he is handing over the world. And she waits almost expecting a covey of quail to rustle in the grass around them, spy them, and then explode into the air, waking her. Grass blows in around her face and he begins to weave it over her cheeks and eyes as if it were her hair. She raises her knee and her skirt slides up her leg exposing her white skin to the air and sun.

His eyes do not stay and she does not have time to tell him what all she needs to say. The moment passes like a tide moving out and then back in,

162

so that the swollen pressure that drew her out in the first place and made her think to tell all there was to tell, the boundless deep of that which might have been revealed, was already contracting, gravitating back within itself. She lowered her leg flat.

From that day forward she'd wonder if she should have told him then she knew she was pregnant. She'd ask herself whether she even knew. She worried herself over and over. Countless times after Walter was gone she'd admit to herself how inescapable was the feeling of life being born inside her.

But that day she told herself she was foolish for thinking herself with child, for what an awful mistake it would be to be wrong. She drew inside herself. She could not bear to tell Walter of a child. For now, the dream of a baby would forsake only her and he would not have to go to war with the thought of leaving the two of them. She lay there next to him in the quiet. She imagined her body growing outward, spreading her abdomen wide like a river. And it seemed her insides pulsated with a new kind of blood not yet born of purpose. Even if she did know she was pregnant, it wouldn't make either of their waits any easier, and this seemed more clear than anything. Telling him might only make him more cautious. And she had the sense it was not caution that brought men back from wars.

He would carry himself off to war and she would carry something of the both of them with her each day, without him. It seemed like a silent responsibility. They both had responsibilities with the war coming, things they wouldn't say aloud.

He asked her if she could sing.

I hum on occasion, she said.

Hum me a tune, any one that comes to mind.

All she could think of were war tunes, the ones the ladies sang at the platforms when their boys went off, all about being brave and strong. She told him she couldn't think of any.

He started humming a song she didn't know, but she imitated him all the same and it seemed to work. Her hand lay across his chest and he played her wrist with the tips of his fingers and it tingled as if he touched her bones. Then her whole body trembled under his touch like a long, reverberating cord that ached to be touched and resounded.

She knew she would cry and not be able to stop unless he took her right then. She couldn't take it any longer. She grabbed his hand and squeezed it and then let up.

He could feel her shuddering, that nervous, desperate sort of want that can devour a body. They looked at one another and he did not have to ask her if she wanted him. They needed each other that afternoon, not so much out of tenderness as desperation. The both of them urgent to be inside one another, if only this one last time. And so they made love as if it were the last time, as if it were the world's last celebration of life itself.

They turned and twisted in what became a wrath of hate, for time was getting away from them. They clung to one another, pulling back what was already out of reach, tormenting themselves trying to possess what could never be attained in this lifetime, the consummation of two bodies forever in concert. And like the serpent that never resigns itself to luck, but always deception, they went on and on escaping one another, eluding their ending. The finality of a day, a life, the exhaustion of a body that finally does give itself over. And still not over, they fell into long spells of quietness in between their lovemaking in which it seemed they couldn't be still enough. They did not move for they seemed bent on trying to hear. As if they might hear their own flesh and blood rushing between their bodies.

They fell asleep in the grass and when she woke a hat was set on the top of her face, shading the sun.

You started to look hot.

And what's that look like? she whispered.

Like you're squinting in your sleep. Your eyes sort of pinched together.

I've been sleeping for a while?

A while. You're cheeks were getting pretty red.

She felt the heat mounded there, as if blankets had been layered on top of them to break a fever.

It's past supper?

Yes. You hungry?

No.

I'm not either.

I want you one last time, she said.

They walked hand in hand out of the field and back to the dirt road. As they came nearer to town, the road glistened in the sun as if it were bound together by thousands of silk threads, plied on one another layer after layer. The layers gave under their feet like loose cotton and then the wind was on the whole mass, lifting it higher like a bedsheet caught on a wind. The dried barbed heads of cheatgrass were taking flight, lofting higher and higher above the road. It was only in late July and on into August that the grass became so tangled and free within itself.

It's beautiful, she said.

I'd say it might be one of the more glorious sights I've seen if I didn't know what the hell it was.

I know.

There isn't anything more nasty or fatal than that stuff out there this time of year, Walter said.

Not so bad as coyotes.

Worse. Cheatgrass buries so deep inside a dog's ear it won't matter if a coyote or a cougar runs through the herd. The dog won't hear a damn thing. Deaf dog might just as well be a dead dog out there herding.

Walter?

What?

You plan on coming back here when you're through?

Where do you think I'm going?

Cheatgrass is all broken up, she said, raising her hand up with it, watching it dismember in the wind before them.

It was scattered across the road in balls now, like very dry snow someone tries to throw.

Look at that, she said. Can hardly imagine it was ever all together.

Walter nodded.

I was just asking.

I know. No place else I'd plan to be, though.

But maybe one day you'll be setting your sights higher. What if this place isn't home one day?

She just wanted him to give her something, tell her something that would keep him with her for as long as it took him to go away and be gone. She wanted something to occupy the largeness of his absence. But there was nothing. Without thinking to she ran her hands over her belly and smoothed her dress down the front of her and then she knew she wanted the baby large and big, growing inside her, filling her up, taking him up. She was so afraid telling him would leave her hollow.

I'll be back, he said. We'll work it out. Don't worry.

And for the moment it took to turn oneself around and imagine waving and then being gone, she believed him.

There's not a place much higher than this one, he said. It'd just be a higher reach to the sky from anywhere else.

That's what I think, she said and let her face soften.

Back in town they stopped at the Alturas where Trina was staying until Walter's departure. When Walter had taken money from his pocket to pay Fats, he shook his head and told Walter it was not necessary for the doctor had already paid for Trina to stay more days than she had when her foot was broke.

You'll be there tomorrow? Walter asked.

Not long now, she said.

He bent and kissed her.

She simply nodded and said again, Not long.

She just had to hear her own voice aloud because so much of what was said those days in between his going was in what was not said. She had to remind herself that words have sound that resonates and carries long after thought has gone. Sometimes thoughts heard aloud do make things real and the echo left can make all the promises said just a bit more real.

Chapter 16

S H E R O S E E A R L Y the next morning and left the Alturas and went to Ling's for a biscuit and jam and a cup of coffee. When she was through and paid up she went into his bathroom and examined herself before the mirror. Her shirt was wrinkled at the collar and was missing a button. She tried to smooth her hands down her blouse, which didn't do a thing for its wrinkles, and she looked down at her stomach and felt herself to be large, though she knew she showed only to herself.

She left Ling's quickly and rode to Friedman's general store. She bought one of the blue work dresses they had hanging in the back of the shop with the money she had got off the fox furs she sold the week before. Then she asked if there was a place she could try it on. Mr. Friedman pointed to the back of the store and told her to go in the first door on her left.

It was a water closet and it smelled of mildew and metal. She put on the dress, bagged her blouse and jeans, and left her boots on her feet. The dress was loose and did not gather tightly around her waist and she felt better in it. At a mirror in the store, she stopped and took out her comb and made a straight part in her hair. Then she paid Mr. Friedman and left the store quickly.

She felt herself awkward and a different weight centering her on her feet. Her mouth was dry like bone left in the sun. She picked up a pebble. She ran it in between her fingers. Then she put it in her mouth and sucked on it the whole way to the station. She tried to feel her mouth wet and imagined she was drinking water out of a pump in the ground. There was no water to be found, and she felt herself dried out and wondered if she'd be able to speak.

He was waiting for her. He stood on the platform with no more than a gunnysack slung over his shoulder. He told her to hurry in a sweet way and he was smiling and his arms opened wide for her.

Your parents?

They'll be down any minute, but they said they'd give us some time alone.

Good of them, Trina said.

He wrapped his free arm around her shoulder. There were other people gathered on the platform. Foremen with hay and grain to ship off. A herding outfit lined up, ready to load a car with baled wool. There was a family dressed up and heading out of town and their trunks were at their sides. Walter seemed to take no notice of them.

He leaned down and kissed Trina. She was caught off guard but her lips softened to his and they held on like that for what she felt was a long time.

He would not let go of her that morning.

When his lips parted from hers he rested his hand in the small of her back. He pressed it there.

I like it when you do that.

He pulled her in closer to him.

You watch your back. Will you? he said.

I will, she said hanging on his words. Then she laughed and it sounded like she was crying and there was some of that there too.

Look who's talking, she said. You watch your back, Walter.

Those mountains can move on you, he said.

She heard the sound of a tobacco tin kicked off the platform, its final clink in the rocks beside the track and it was empty and hollow.

I will, he said, leaning down and brushing his lips along her neck. Her lips fell on his forehead. Then she leaned her head on the side of his shoulder and all she could see was the grid of the track, the steel rails and the wood ties. Row after row. Stacked and placed with such symmetry.

Walter recognized the Simmons, a family of cattle ranchers. Mr. Simmons was nervously eyeing his pocket watch and saying his cattle should have already come. He said the train was late and began to pace while his wife tried to grab his hand and keep him still.

The toll fee up to Stanley been raised for spring, one of the sheep foreman said to a younger man standing there with him.

What's next? she asked. Her eyes were still fixed on the track.

I'll be in Washington.

Maybe you'll stay there and won't even have to see the war, she said, and it came off too easy and fast and because it did she felt she'd somehow jinxed it to be so. I'll pray for that, she said, and the first tears came. And whatever happens, she started to say and stopped.

I'll write to you, I promise, he said. I'm already missing you, he said, and his lips didn't look like they were moving but rather frozen still.

It was the way he spoke, and she had never really noticed until then, but he talked a little tight-lipped like he had to watch how much he gave away in words. He spoke like someone reciting a prayer, not quite sure where the words had come from and how much of them were his own, if any.

Look behind you now and then. You'll see things get moved around on you, they don't quite stay the same.

She shook her head for she wanted him to stop. Is this the time for this, Walter? I'll stay the same and I'll be right here all the while so you'll always know where to find me.

Do that for me.

She was biting her lower lip. She felt the blood and color seeping from them until they were white and there was nothing left to them. It dawned on her then that she might not make it without him. She knew she'd love him for the rest of her life and the knowledge was that simple. He wasn't someone she'd ever get over and she was certain of this, certain they were meant to be together, and if asked to explain how this came to be so, she would have blushed and said she knew it the first day she saw him. If someone had tried to convince her that love did not always last forever, it would have been like someone trying to tell her the color red was actually the color blue. Life had given him to her and she had fallen for him.

Her face began to collapse and she could feel it begin to shudder, the way bodies do giving over to long sobs. She'd avoided his actual departure up until now, not really believing in it, holding out that somehow they might escape this war together.

But he really was leaving her. He slipped his arm from around her back. He took her hand and started to walk down the platform with her because they had to keep moving. They couldn't be still, for it was like admitting defeat.

She felt it in her elbow. All the blood in her body, all that was in her lip had collected there in her elbow. She didn't think the blood would make it out to her hand. It was going limp and cold, and she didn't know how much longer her hand would stay clasped.

Things change on you. That's all I'm saying.

Who are you talking to Walter?

Both of us, I guess.

Her mouth tasted of dust. It tasted of a sandstorm arrived. It lifted all around them, under their step, and then settled in rippled pools behind them, following in the wake of their tracks.

What if you just weren't to look back, and then you weren't to feel like you'd ever left anything behind. What if we weren't to have regrets, she said.

Not like that, Trina, he said quickly.

Her chest collapsed against itself and rose, only to fall again as she tried to catch her breath and hold back the coming sobs.

He quickly turned her around with his hands on her shoulders. He kissed her again and it was like he breathed running metal through her and she felt cold and hot at the same time. Then he looked at her, as if he was trying to memorize her, trying to get enough of her. She pushed her body into his and leaned her head back. The tears rolled down her cheeks, but she did not take her eyes from him and she made no move to wipe them away. She no longer saw or heard anything, just the fullness of a space about to go empty. They were out of time.

I want to tell you, he started to say and then he shook his head.

Tell me, she pleaded, gripping his elbows and giving them a good squeeze. Keep talking, please.

Things, they just happen. It'll be all right, and he seemed to say this more to ease himself than her.

She couldn't push him any farther because he was thinking larger than himself. He waved his hand in the air like it was an idea. He kissed her again hard now and it was almost painful.

Please don't go, Walter.

He held her and her head pressed against his chest. She breathed in the last of him.

I have to.

170

I know. She reached into the pocket of her dress and pulled from it a pocket watch on a silver chain. He stared at her in amazement like she had done something he could not believe. To hold you steady even in the bad times, she said. She looked up and thought she saw his eyes go wet in the corners, but it might have been the sun reflecting off of them. The sun blazed yellow, breaking on the rails, making them glisten like thin ribbons of water. A stream of steel for as long as the eye could trail. She clung on to him with her life and with her arms wrapped tightly around him, she sobbed into his chest.

I wasn't going to cry. I'm sorry, she managed to get out.

Don't be.

I can't bear this.

He held her tight. Yes you can.

Take me with you.

I'll be back. With a good-bye like this, he said, his voice fathering, I couldn't not come back. His head was resting on top of hers again and he stroked her hair and whispered in her ear.

I love you so much.

Then his parents were behind him, breaking them up. Trina stayed by Walter's side and kept her hand on his arm. His mother's hands trembled, having already given up to this day long before. Her lips teetered on his cheeks and landed softly. You do what I always done and told you to do. Just like you've done so far. You'll be all right.

Then Ann was dabbing her eyes and shaking her head and moving back a few steps. My boy. My boy. My only son, she said. You take care of yourself. We love you.

Walter's father started to shake his son's hand and then opened his arms wide and held him there. He gave him one firm pat on the back and then he was pushing them apart.

Trina felt them all breaking in the waiting. She was ready to see him off then and still not any more prepared for his going. At nine o'clock Walter boarded the caboose of the mixed passenger-and-freight train. He leaned out the window and waved to her and yelled back to Trina that he loved her. Then it was over. His train was whistling and bellowing smoke and chugging down the tracks to Fort Lewis.

Chapter 17

THE DAY WALTER and Trina were saying good-bye the organ player at the Alturas was shot. The bullet traveled through his back and into the pipe organ player.

When Trina arrived to pick up her things people were gathered in front of the hotel. Dr. Fox was sitting on a bench out front with bloodstains spread on his shirt and up his sleeves.

Trina came to the front of the hotel and inside she could hear crying and sniffling and the voices of men she couldn't distinguish. Dr. Fox held up his hand before she went through the door.

Don't bother, Miss Ivy. Stay where you're at. No need to go messing around in there.

I'm not messing around, Doc. I'm just here to get my things.

All the same better to stay out for now.

What happened?

Somebody got Jack Shipton.

Jack Shipton was a hermit who lived high up in Ohio Gulch who came down to play his fiddle in Hailey on the full moons. He'd bring his own three-legged stool with him wherever he went. Even when he came to town he kept to himself and didn't talk to anyone. He'd find himself a corner in the saloon and just start playing. In between songs he did shots of bourbon and by morning he was always laid up in a heap outside the saloon door. By late morning he could be seen crawling out of town with his fiddle under one arm and his stool under the other.

Trina had run into him a few times up in his area and he'd always shooed her away. She kept her rifle in her arms when he was around.

He'd run at her with his fiddle bow, saying he liked to be left alone if he caught her setting traps by his place.

Somebody must've saw who?

Not this time.

Nobody was there?

The doctor told her how he was playing the "Irish Washerwoman" over and over on his three-legged stool until Fats finally told him he'd heard just about enough. He asked him to play something else. Shipton walked over and sat himself down at the piano and started playing the "Blue Danube" and the next thing Fats heard was a gun going off. He was in the back making himself something to eat before the dinner crowd and he came and found Jack knocked out. He was floored on his back flat. Through the back. They got him in the windpipe. Way I heard it, Joe Moran was stumbling around drunk, talking about women, and it was like he didn't even hear the shot. Figures.

They think Moran might have done it?

It could have been anyone. People have been spotting Shipton at the post office picking letters, cutting seals, opening small money. That doesn't go over so well. But then again, Moran's fast with a pistol. It's no good for either of us wasting our breath speculating. I just don't know.

Seen Frank today?

I haven't. Is everything all right? Your leg good and healed?

I'm all right, she said. Fine thanks. And what's Donnely doing here? she said.

I guess Dott happened to be seeing a gentleman here this week. Donnely heard the gun fired. He's been standing outside of here ever since it happened, making sure Dott's all right. She hasn't been out all afternoon. The doctor laughed. I think she's in there trying to calm down one of her girls who was down on the first floor, in a room right behind the piano when the gun went off.

She wasn't hurt, was she?

Oh, she's sobbing it up a bit in there the way those girls will. She said she saw the bullet sail right over their heads. Dott's trying to talk some sense into her.

Trina nodded. Just going to gather my things and say good-bye to Fats.

I'm not sure that's a good idea.

It'll be fine, she said. She was insistent on getting her things and leaving town. Arriving weeks late to her mother and Frank's camp in East Fork, she wasn't sure what difference an hour or even days would make in explaining herself at this point. All she knew was that with Walter gone she couldn't sit still for too long without coming undone.

The doctor tilted his hat toward her and nodded good day.

She went in and Fats was mopping the floor and when he saw Trina he shook his head.

No place for the lady.

She nodded, but she wasn't bothered by the blood. She kept looking up the stairs as if Walter would come down them.

You wait for somebody? If not, you best go, Miss Trina.

You all right? she asked.

He explained in his broken English that he'd been better but how all would settle down soon.

Who do you think shot him?

Don't know.

There wasn't anyone else here?

No know, Trina. That's all I say. Piano ruined forever. Hole shot right though it.

The front of the piano and the ivory keys were stained red in places.

You run along. Not so good luck here right now, Fats said.

Luck changes, she said.

Yes, he said still nodding. Not so quick always.

The ride up to East Fork felt long and everything she saw reminded her of Walter. Even though the paint kept his usual stride, his body was wet with sweat and she could feel it breathing up through her saddle. And as the day was cooling off and the heat should have warmed her, it made her feel sick and hot. Her stomach ached and she sat hunched over trying to lessen the cramps twisting inside her. All the while the motion of the horse seemed to make them worse.

She came into camp just after supper and with all her sadness she had not thought of an explanation for them as to why she'd been gone for several weeks. Joe Moran was at the fire shuffling a hand of cards in his lap and a flask was at his side. He had that far off look about him.

He told Trina she was late.

I was kept in town longer than I thought, she said.

The camp smelled of whiskey and burned game meat.

Of course you been kept longer than you thought, a month longer. Don't think you can lie with me. Frank's already told me how you left with no word. Wearing his shotgun chaps, he sat with his legs splayed wide, raking his fingers through his hair. A leg doesn't take that long to fix itself.

I took care of some things in town.

Your own things or someone else's?

My own, she said, feeling her speech become clipped and terse.

And aren't you proud? I saw how that doctor put you up. He kept you there all this time?

She didn't say anything.

I see how it is. I talk to you and you don't talk back. How the hell's that working?

Her mother stuck her head out of the tent. For god's sake. Leave her alone. You got any sense about you? None. Can't you remember what it was to be in love once. Then her head was gone and she pulled the flap down on her tent and it rustled. All Trina could smell was meat gone black and charred and she could taste it on the top of her mouth. She wished her mother hadn't gone back into the tent. But it was always a retreat of some sort, into the bottle or into the tent.

There had been a time when it wasn't so. Her mother had raised eyes with her looks, her dark hair and sullen dignity. But over the years she had been flattened by wind and rain that weathered even the strongest. And children who should have made her large and proud left her empty and barren. She could carry no more.

Been a while? Joe Moran yelled over his shoulder to her.

Since what? she bellowed back with her head still inside.

Since love or getting any.

Speak for yourself. And whose fault's that? She laughed like someone were tickling her and her voice cracked. Not mine. Then she was silent.

Her mother didn't surprise her anymore. She felt like nothing about any of them surprised her anymore. She'd been setting up her own tent away from all of them, her younger brothers and sisters, for the last couple of years. It gave her the most time to herself.

Meat's burning, she said.

I can tell how my meat is and ain't, he growled.

She started to walk away.

I don't have to take that, he said.

Jack Shipton got shot today, she said.

Up the gulch?

In the Alturas.

What the hell was he doing there?

Playing his fiddle.

And he got shot. Dumb cocksucker. What was he doing, playing that damn washerwoman song too many times?

Something like that.

I'll be. Screwy, he is.

He was sitting at the piano. Bullet went right though the back of him and into the piano.

She couldn't stand any longer, for her stomach kept cramping up and she longed to be lying on her side. And the more her insides hurt, the more she longed for Walter and for his arms to be around her. There was no way for her to get away from Joe Moran so quickly, and so she sat down opposite him at the fire. She was tired and worn out, but she had to wait Joe Moran out a bit, see to it that he was passed out just so she was sure he wouldn't try to come to her in the night.

You said he was fiddling. Get your story right, he said, more spittle than usual flying from his lips. Shipton don't play the piano. He pulled at his chin.

Guess he decided he'd give it a try. Played the fiddle all afternoon and then moved to the piano, and that's where they got him.

They?

Well, I don't know who. Nobody saw.

Played cards with Frank earlier in the day. Shipton showed up as we were leaving. I told Frank that Shipton was a dirty, lousy son of a bitch who never washes. Frank started feeling his own head itch the way I went on and described the lice sifting through that man's head. I really had him going, Joe Moran said, laughing.

177

Then Joe Moran scratched at his head and looked at his fingers as if he were picking lice off of them in the firelight. Instead he started wedging his fingernails in between his teeth as a toothpick.

Trina groaned under her breath and bent farther over her knees, clutching at her side as the pain grew worse.

White and just like a miniature earthworm, damn lice. He held his thumb and forefinger in the air so barely a crack of light could run through them. Small, but nasty buggers, lice are.

Trina stared at him.

I told Frank somebody ought to shoot Shipton dead before the whole valley's turned lousy.

You got 'em?

Got the lice? No I ain't got 'em.

You're scratching your head, Trina said.

Doesn't mean I got 'em. You pestering me?

No.

It means that son of a bitch makes me itch. Like I said before, it's the very reason somebody did us a favor shooting him.

She watched him over the firelight and saw his eyes red with drink and the way they looked to throb in the smoke of the fire. He wiped at them with the back of his arm.

Probably, somebody just had it with Shipton, Joe Moran said, pulling his meat out of the tin pan with his fingers. He bit into it and held onto it in his hand as he ripped off a piece. Goddamn, it's hot, he said, blowing and puffing with his mouth open and the meat already in his mouth. Wasn't me. I didn't leave Shipton sore.

Fine, she said, taking the out.

Wait a minute, he said, slapping his hat to his knee with a sudden fit of energy. You're not with that Pascoe boy are you?

Leave me alone, she said.

You watch yourself, young lady. Don't go making yourself prouder than you is, he said, holding his burnt shred of meat in his fist and waving it. I'll go and show you who's proud, he said, gargling his words, his head wobbling back as he fought to keep it upright.

She turned around as if to make her way to her own tent. Her back was to him in her walking, but he yelled at her anyway. Well, just don't you go and get yourself in the middle of trouble or it's not only you who's in for trouble. All of us, he said blabbering on. Frank already told me about Walter. He's not too pleased about that boy and you.

So he's not, she said, but she didn't think he heard her. She didn't care.

Well, go on. Then in another sudden burst of energy, he started up again. Go talk to your mother. Go see if she needs any food. I'm done yelling in at her. I try to take care after her when Frank goes wandering after animals, and what do I get, not a thing of respect. You take care of her needs tonight, since I sure as hell ain't. He laughed and pointed toward the tent and whispered, You go see for yourself what that good-for-nothing mother of yours is up to.

Trina looked back at him.

He smiled and then laughed again. What'd I tell you. Go on, he said waving his arm.

She walked toward the tent and it rustled like her mother was straightening things around inside. She stooped to her knees and lifted the flap to the warm glow of light coming from within. From where she kneeled she could see the large arching shadows rising and falling on the back wall of the canvas tent. She barely missed setting her hand down on the oil lantern as she crawled inside the door, still not seeing what there was to see.

He was large and his white back rose in front of her like a plank set for her to walk across. His skin was pale and almost pink in the light and dotted with black moles she couldn't take her eyes from. And underneath him was her mother. Her ankles stared out at her, wrapped up as they were around his body.

The man grunted as he rode her up and down, as if she were a wild horse. He kept raising his body off her to reposition himself, only to plunge down a minute later. As he heaved his weight down on her, he grunted, and her mother let out a short cry and then she began to moan too.

She did not want to see what she saw, but then it was too late not to see. Squatted behind them, she did not register whether she was horrified or mesmerized, only realized she stayed, transfixed and paralyzed by the bodies tangled up like agitated animals. His white ass moving round and round and her mother's legs spread so that her knees flapped against his sides.

Mother, she said.

Her mother lifted her head and then went to lift her upper body to see who was coming in on them, but the man came down on her hard and she flung to the ground and made no sound.

Joe, can't you leave us the fuck alone? he yelled.

And then the baby started to cry. She was wrapped in a rug on the far side of the tent wall. Her fists came out of the blanket and flailed in the air. Trina looked at her, but there was no way around them.

He turned his head around and saw it was Trina. Frank smiled at her. He kept his eyes on her. Then he began to thrust harder and harder into her mother.

Like mother, like daughter. Bitches like a good ride, he sputtered, and spittle flew from his mouth down onto her mother's knee and then he groaned, as if this short spell of exertion was already wearing him out. He lowered himself back down on her mother.

Sorry, sweetie, Trina's mother said, laughing and grunting and giving herself back over to Frank completely. She was drunk and there was no fight in her, only submission.

Get the lazy bitch out of here, Frank said. Then he turned his head back around once more to stare at Trina with that dumb tooth-faced grin.

She scrambled to her feet and ran from the tent. She could hear Joe Moran laughing and she ran harder. When she got to her tent she could hear the rustling of brush and stones being kicked over.

She lifted the gun from her pack and cradled it tightly across her forearms.

Sweetie, I can see the shadow of what you're holding. You got some idea in your head?

What's it matter? she said.

You think you're just going to walk away from all of us, do you? I'm going to surprise you Trina. You get out of here and go somewhere you'll be taken care of. That's all I've come to say, he said, and then she could hear him staggering off.

She did not undress. She packed her bedroll and her belongings and waited for the night to go quiet and everyone to fall asleep. They'd search for her when they came sober because they'd want the extra money her furs brought. She listened to the crickets, but she did not sleep. The sky came to buzz and she thought it to be the sky's way of droning on and on in dark forgetfulness. But she couldn't rid herself of Frank's white back, how sheer it was in the lantern light, like a pale fire. It was everything she could do not to see the line along his spine stretched and strung long.

She tried to hum Walter's tune in the dark. In the thicket she heard a rustling and thought she could distinguish Frank's gait. She put both hands on her rifle and held it up to the dark. She knew she'd fire. Then it was still again and she figured he had wandered off back to her mother's tent.

When she no longer smelled the smoke and cinders of the fire, she rose. She bagged her tent, bedroll, and a few extra changes of clothes, saddled the paint, and left Frank and the rest of them.

Chapter 18

T HE DAY WAS steel gray and the sun pierced its way across the silver sky in streaks, flattening the land so it did not seem a long ride to be off the gulch and in the valley. She moved in the still haze as one does through a dense fog, with blind ambition and no real certainty. And as the town spread before her like a village of matchbox houses, dotting the lanscape, she could make out Walter's house, the pasture with the two mares, and the roof of the chicken coop.

Her arrival was coming on her too fast and she wished it were still earlier or later as she looked down to see the crops of ice melting before her. Puddles of water pooled and gathered in tiny bogs and rivets so that mud splashed up the paint's fetlocks as he clopped along. In some steep places it was slick and he went to drop his haunches and halt, but the ground kept moving with him, sliding him down.

As they neared she became more uneasy as to how she could explain to Ann how things were. She feared what they would say, even more what Ann wouldn't say. Her coming pressed in on her and the air reined in, heavy like water, for there was nothing to be said. It was November and she was at least six months along and there was no longer anything to hide.

She knocked on the door and no one came. She knocked again, harder, and felt her knuckles sting and burn down to the bone. A voice sounded from within.

Who's there?

It's Trina Ivy, she said to the door.

Trina had hid in the hills from Frank and Joe Moran for three months, but the weather was turning bitter and this seemed the only way. She stood there knowing she still had time to leave, but Ann had told her on the train platform it made sense that she stay with them. Ann told her she wouldn't be bothering anything. Before they parted Ann told Trina she'd like to be able to expect her at least when the weather turned to snow.

Come in, she heard.

Trina turned on the doorknob, but it seemed to catch and remained shut.

It should be open, Ann said faintly.

She pushed again.

Give the knob a good turn.

It gave and opened in on the main room. Ann was seated in the corner with a blanket spread across her body and pulled up to her chin. Bandages were piled in her lap, none of which were rolled. Her eyes did not meet Trina's for a long time. She strained a smile and forced a thin arm from the blankets, but still she did not look at Trina. Finally, she raised her hand in the direction of another chair. Trina moved to take a seat on a leather cowhide chair with big wooden armrests.

How have you been? Dr. Fox told me you're not feeling so well, Trina said.

Ann was dying and her cheeks were hollowed and the skin around her eyes was yellowed. The air was stale with her bedridden body and fouled by musty laundry, aging water, and the sweet sulfur smell of bluing liquid they used for whitening clothes.

How would he know how I have been? Ann asked.

Not quite sure. It's just what he told me.

He doesn't know, she said wearily. I have been all right. Might take me a little longer this time, getting on my feet again. I'll get there and be strong. She strained to turn her neck and look at Trina.

Yes, you will.

Trina looked about the room.

There were lace curtains on the front windows and a pink and blue patchwork quilt hung on the far wall of the living room. The walls were of wood and had no wallpaper. There was a lamp near Ann's bedside, but there were no wall hangings, fans, pottery, or fancy carpets adorning the place. A fireplace screen with some kind of bird on it shielded Ann from the direct heat of the flames. The house was tidy and uncluttered, but she could tell it had not been properly washed in some time. A layer of dust stood on the end table, above which pictures hung. There was one of Walter standing by a creek with a fishing rod in one hand and a trout in the other.

It was taken of them down on Silver Creek, Ann said.

They're real nice, Trina said.

I'm glad you came. Your face looks thin though, she said.

Trina looked down at her stomach bulging in front of her. She could feel her blood racing and her cheeks burning red, waiting for what would come next. Tears came to her eyes and she couldn't hold them in. I'm not going to apologize for how I am, Trina said.

Ann held her hand to her mouth and she began to cry. I wouldn't expect you to, she said. Ann held out her hand, motioning Trina to come to her side.

Trina grasped Ann's hands, which were dry and did not feel so much like skin as wood, for there was no trace of heat or cold to be detected in them. Ann could not grip Trina's hands and so their hands merely rested in one another's as they wept.

Ann collected herself first. You shouldn't be so thin, you know, she managed.

I get enough.

You are too thin. You'll be good staying here. It will be real nice for all of us. Ann seemed to nod and then eased her head back on the pillow. Her head shook some and it was hard to tell what sort of gesture she was trying to make or if she was trying to make one at all. There was exhaustion all about her and while she made every effort in the world to be alert and in good spirits, the strain on her body was evident.

You'll roll these for me, won't you, dear?

Of course, Trina said, removing the bandages from Ann's lap.

No, no. Not now. You can do it later. Get your belongings inside and yourself settled up in Walter's room. There'll be time.

She told her it was the only room at the top of the stairs and Trina turned to go.

When she got to the archway of Walter's door she stood there for a while. She ran her hands over her belly and could feel the baby moving inside her. His twin bed was against the wall covered with a blue quilt.

The floor was made of wood and a small rocking chair was set in the far corner. There was a painting of some mountains and sheep above the bed. She assumed she'd find traces of him everywhere and was surprised to realize the room might have been anyone's. She tried to smell him from where she stood and could not and the same ache she'd felt in her chest when she woke that morning returned.

She went to his bureau and ran her hands over its surface which, aside from a few books, was empty too. Walter's room was not unlike the rest of the house and while she could think of no reason why it ought to be different, it disappointed her that it was not. She'd expected with George owning the mercantile the house would have been adorned with a few more luxuries and ornaments of their prosperity, but there were none to be found. The house was settling quickly into her as something that felt unlived in and sparse.

She rested her head down on Walter's pillow and smelled the faint odor of musk and cedar and hay. Tears burned as they ran down her cheeks. She shuddered and let a tremble run through the length of her body and pinched her wrist to be sure she was not asleep. Then she lay there still staring at the ceiling.

Ann called up to her to ask if everything was in order. Trina said it was, and she did not hear Ann for some time as she went about arranging her few things in the room. Her clothes and jacket she folded into the dresser.

When she went downstairs again she rolled Ann's bandages and was asked to deliver them to the Red Cross meeting held at the town hall that night. With Trina settled in the house Ann became restful and slept through the afternoon while Trina prepared a stew of potatoes, carrots, and pork.

When George arrived home he welcomed her warmly and told her he was glad she'd come. He did not say anything about her being pregnant, but when they'd all finished their first serving he told her she ought to take another helping.

I'm fine, thanks, she said.

You probably are, but it's not just you I'm thinking about.

She blushed as he held out his hand for her bowl. He did not say another word about the baby coming or when it would be due. He asked her what types of furs she'd been trapping. She explained how she'd had some luck with mink and beaver and that prices were fair as there'd been a run of ads promoting fur neckpieces.

Ann listened and when Trina finished her second helping and it was clear she would not have more, Ann asked for another helping for herself. George started to rise as if he needed to see her bowl for himself to believe it. Then he smiled and settled back into his chair.

She hasn't eaten like this for weeks, George said.

The next morning Trina rose early to mend the fence George had said needed repair before winter. The barometer had dropped and overnight the mountains had received a fresh coat of snow and the contrast between the black and the white was startling. The white not only recolored the rocks and trees but resized them in massive spectrum, for the white seemed to bounce off everything and make it larger and taller.

She pulled the wire tight, stretched it, and then tied it around the wood post before cutting it. Even with leather gloves on, her hands burned from the constant pressure and tension of the work. Mending fence was one of those simple tasks that had to be done no matter what, and she took pleasure in routine. She breathed in the cold air, felt it run the length of her lungs, and was warmed by the thought of the life she carried.

Now and again Trina leaned into a wood post for a minute to catch her breath and take in the sights around her. Chickadees darted between trees and scavenged the ground for seed or bits of grain missed by the horses. They moved with a speed and lightness becoming of those species that truly live and fly as if their wings will never quite keep up with them.

Trina worked on through the morning, the cold burning her with a sense of purpose, and the white of her breath blown out like exhaust off a fire smoking itself out, making her feel put to use and satisfied. She could make good time by herself, and while the wires dug deep in her hands and left them blistered, chafed, and numb, the work did her good.

She came off the fences at noon to tend to Ann and do some chores about the house. There was laundry to be done and she figured if she could get a fresh round of clothes and linens throughout the house, she might be able to freshen the place. She put the soiled clothes in a boiling kettle to soak and then went to check on the pot of simmering potatoes and onions she had started in the morning.

Ann had warned Trina how George would not have them abusing their good fortune and standing in the community by taking home goods that would not be found in other households. Potatoes and onions were two supplies he did not bother to ration and so she put both to use. She added logs to the stove and warmed her hands by it for a few minutes and then went back to stir the soup.

Dear, is it potato soup you're making? Ann asked from her bed where she lay on her back.

Trina told her it was.

Fine, Ann said, almost as if she were let down but yet not surprised.

Trina sat bedside next to Ann and spooned the watery soup down her throat.

Your skin looks a little hot, Ann said, in between a spoonful.

I've been out for the morning.

You watch yourself that you don't get too heated.

I've been out in the cold, got a little color in my cheeks, that's all, Trina said. She spooned another bite into Ann's mouth and the woman stared at her. Her eyes were bright, like glass, like ice frozen through and through, and they did not leave Trina's. It was Trina who looked away first, down into the soup she finished spooning.

He's written you nearly every week. I didn't think you'd really come.

Trina looked at her incredulously.

He misses you, Ann said, dropping her eyes. He asked if you might take the Union Pacific up to Washington and stay with him a few days. He said he had a feeling they'd be sending him off to France soon. He doesn't seem to know about the baby.

No, I didn't tell him.

Well, he misses you all the same. I just didn't expect you'd come be with us. I thought you might be too ashamed, not that you should be. Ann paused and looked at her hands.

Trina waited speechless, a dull throbbing ringing around her temples.

I read all of them. I couldn't help it. I'm sorry.

May I have them? Trina said.

They're in the end table drawer, Ann said. Her voice was tired, as if it ached. Have you written him?

Yes, but I had nowhere to send them.

Ann lifted her thin arm toward the table. Take them. And I don't want any more soup.

Trina took the bowl and went to the kitchen and poured it in the evening soup kettle and did not wait to hear Ann scold her for not eating.

She went to her room with the letters and sat at a chair to begin writing Walter. She told him she'd just arrived to live with his parents and that's why her letters were so late in coming. She told him how they'd made her welcome and that she was settling in fine. She did not tell him his mother was dying. She told him John and Annette were living in town for the winter and that lamb prices had been decent at market. She told him how town folk said Annette had that notorious pregnant glow about her and that John seemed proud. Again, she could not bring herself to tell him she was pregnant and allow him to go off to war worrying about a baby.

She told him she'd be in his arms now if she could. In the end she told him how these were sad times. She said it wasn't the same watching days come up without him. She said, I love you. She signed the letter and dated it November 11, 1917.

Her letter would be dated exactly one year before the armistice was signed. Before the war was over Walter would be sent by fast train across the continent to Camp Lee, Virginia, to complete his officers' training program. Then they'd send his company to France as infantry replacements. He'd be a foot soldier and rise in rank as he took Germany on in the front lines. He'd fight like there wasn't a tomorrow.

She began lacing up her boots to go back outside when she heard a crash downstairs. The house was so quiet, especially when George wasn't around. The noise startled her and she ran for the stairs. But as she came down the stairs she thought she caught the image of some figure moving outside the near window.

She heard a low groan and saw Ann fallen to the floor with her elbows pushing off the floor, trying to lift herself and then Ann was still, crumpled up, with her head to the wood floor.

Wait. I'll help you, Trina said. She ran to her side and with both her hands under Ann's arms she began easing the frail body onto the bed. Ann had tears in her eyes and she tried to mutter something under her breath and then resigned her strength over to Trina.

Ann was light now and her bones stretched against her skin and it seemed it wouldn't take much for her bones to rip out.

I was trying to get out of this bed, she said.

Let me help you, Trina said.

Well, I'm not trying to get anybody's help. I never have, she said. There was a fierceness about her Trina did not expect. I'm fine, and the last thing I need is babying over like I'm some baby bird. God gave me this body, but it doesn't mean he wanted me to go complacent within it.

Trina tried to quiet Ann and patted her shoulder and told her she'd help her sit up when she needed to.

I only get weaker sitting around like this. I'm tired of being sitting all day. I got to be up. She put her hands to the mattress, as if she would try again to lift herself. She shut her eyes and went again to support her body with her arms, as she tried to move into a sitting position. Her arms gave way and her body collapsed and her shoulders crumpled into the bed. The room was dark and, with the sun tucked behind the clouds, dusk seemed to be coming on them, though it was early afternoon.

Ann opened her eyes and stared with those empty eyes that looked as if they had lost something.

I am sorry, Trina said.

You needn't be, Ann said.

It wasn't right of me not to come and tell you sooner. I was embarrassed.

Hush. You don't have to tell me.

Sometimes I think I'd just rather it was said.

It's already been said. A stillness had come over Ann and it was as if for once even her paralysis was tired and her body was quiet with its own exertion.

Trina sat by her side and watched Ann until she thought she heard a tap at the glass. Something lurched inside her and her shoulders raised.

Ann saw the startled look in Trina's eye and told her to hush. We've got little sparrows bumping into that window. You looked like you had the fear of God in you, young lady.

Trina forced a smile and then under the pretense of getting back to work she stood and went toward the window where a new pile of bandages were set. She scooped them up in her arms and quickly scanned the yard. It appeared to be empty, so she went back to sit by Ann and roll bandages.

After a while Trina reached over for Ann's hand and squeezed it. You felt a good share of what this earth has to offer, ma'am.

Ann shook her head. And some days I've seen too much, though I'm not supposed to be thinking like so.

Suddenly tears began to well in Ann's eyes again. I miss him so. I just wish he could be here.

Trina kissed her hand. Me too.

I'm scared for him, Trina. I know he will see more than either of us will ever see of this life. He'll have men falling in front of him and behind him. He'll hear sounds that he won't recognize. They'll be smells not of this world. And I know I'm supposed to believe that's a good thing and that his spirit will triumph.

No one says it has to be a good thing.

She was choked up and she forced the words out like a confession long in the making. Trina, I'm so scared my boy will come back unrecognizable to this world. He won't know what's his anymore. I have this sense war will do that to him, make him lost and forgetful.

He'll make it, ma'am. There isn't any other way.

There were no streaks of light parting across the room to throw shadows and so they sat alone but for the sound of their own voices. Then there was the distinct sound of a knock at the back door echoing through the hollow wooden room and Trina was filled with terror, for she could not help thinking they had finally come for her.

Ann, be quiet for a minute. Please.

Trina, you got to try not to worry like you do at every noise. You can't go on living thinking every sound is Walter. It will just make it worse for you and make the waiting longer.

Trina rose and did not hear what Ann said. She walked quietly toward the back window and stooped low so she could not be seen moving to the window. When she was at the door, she cracked it open and no one was there. Then she flung it wide open and peered around for any movement in the trees or around the pasture. It was all flat light for as far as she could see. She saw nothing.

When Trina returned, Ann picked up where she left off. She was smoothing the bedsheets with her hands and her lips were trembling.

I tried to raise him proper, but I'm not sure there's anything that could have prepared him for that kind of ground. It is what's on that ground, Trina, what comes off it, what goes down with it. There'll be things out there going to be buried alive for all time. She wrinkled her brow and her whole face seemed to furrow as if she were there seeing and smelling all of it. I can't say I gave him anything to prepare him for all that.

Not sure there was anything you could have given him, Trina said, not wanting Ann to say more.

I might have taught him to pray to a God. We didn't raise him with any proper God. George and I couldn't agree on one.

I'm not sure one has to have a God to know how to pray.

But to believe, Ann said. There's a difference, and I'm not sure he knows it. Ann reached her hand out and rested it on Trina's belly. And as her hand neared Trina's the trembling resumed, the paralysis coming back after its brief rest. Her fingertips fluttered on Trina's belly like baby bird wings testing the air for flight.

I wanted to see this baby, she stuttered.

Trina felt herself go red and she kept staring down at Ann's hand.

You may not believe me, but when you walked in that door and I saw how big you were, I was proud. I wanted this baby so much. I knew Walter'd go on and keep living in this baby of yours.

He'll be back. We'll all be together.

But if he doesn't.

Trina cut her off. He will.

I got up and tried myself today, Trina, and I'm not going to make it. You saw me.

Don't talk like that. You'll make it.

She shook her head. I'm letting go now, Trina. Not of you, or Walter, or George, or this little baby inside you, but of this body. I won't say it has outdone me, but it can't keep me anymore.

Trina rested her head down beside Ann's and kissed her cheek.

Ann you'll be all right. You said so yourself earlier.

Not with any faith.

That doesn't matter, Ann. She told Ann to wait while she went for

George. You hold on, she said and went to leave Ann's side, but Ann held her with her hand as firmly as she could.

I don't want you going out there, not today. There's something startling you out there. I can't believe it's much of anything, but I've never seen you quite like this. You mind me and stay here with me. We'll just wait here. I need you here right now.

Trina sat close to Ann whose eyes now flitted across the ceiling, and held her hand, and when the woman's legs began to tremble, she went and ran her hands down Ann's shins trying to soothe them. When Ann said she was cold, Trina took a blanket from the foot of her own bed and got a heavier pair of socks from her bureau. As she went to replace Ann's socks, she couldn't help staring at her feet, which had already gone black. Her skin about her ankles was graying and slightly purple as the blood was going from them. She held her feet in her hands stared at the purple veins streaked over the top of her feet and massaged them until they were no longer cold.

That's nice, Ann said, with her eyes falling shut. She fought to keep them open. You understand George and I have said our good-byes. It's only you and this baby I had left. You'll say good-bye to Walter for me one day. You tell him how I was saying my good-byes to him through the both of you, one day in November. It'll be like he had two messengers this way.

Walter would return in October, when the ground was going wet. Some boys would return home as early as April. They would all be on different trains and the town would still come to greet each one of them, as if each soldier deserved his own coming home. Bonfires would rage on Main Street to celebrate the armistice. Trains would whistle all the way into town, screaming through the silence that had been with everyone for so long.

Ann?

I said hush.

Please, wait.

Let me be. I've done and said all I needed to say.

She shut her eyes and slept and did not wake.

In the coming days Trina would try to write Walter about his mother's death. She would tell him she was sorry and that she couldn't begin to imagine how hard it would be for him. She would try to describe death in such a way as to make it veiled and somehow more peaceful. She would try to tell him about his mother's strength, her great courage and her proud and dignified sensibility. She would mail the letter two days after the memorial service, when the town was blanketed with fresh snow. She would walk to the post office and stare at the deep imprints her boots made across the white landscape and she would look behind her now and again.

Chapter 19

I N J A N U A R Y , W H I L E the boys, born into men, were walking across the mustard fields of Lyon, the Wood River valley was white with snow and barren and traveled by few. Christmas passed quietly in the house on Croy Street. John and Annette shared it with George and Trina and all pretended to be closer than they were, and all became closer for their effort. Trina and Annette were both large with child, and they shared stories and feelings and hopes and together anticipated their babies' arrivals.

They drank eggnog, lit a Yule log, sung Christmas cheer at the church on Main Street, and hung in there together, calling it hard times for all. During Christmas, Trina, who had taken on Ann's duties with the Red Cross, wrapped double the number of bandages she was assigned and tied each with red yarn she got from George. It was the smallest gesture of Christmas cheer Trina could send Walter's way.

Annette's baby came in January. An eight-pound boy with blond hair that stood on end and he seemed to occupy all of their lives. Trina cooked for them those first few days while Annette got her strength back and she held the baby and cooed and talked to him as if he were her own. She had knit booties for her own baby and in doing so she did an extra pair for Annette's boy, Ben.

When she wasn't visiting Annette's baby Trina was doing everything she could to help with the war effort. She read now, more than ever about it. George brought her home magazines and newspapers from the store and she kept up with the women's auxiliary notices about how to be an efficient home manager. The housework didn't bother her in the final stages of her pregnancy, all work was now in preparation for her baby.

Still, she lived in fear and kept watch in town and around the house for signs of Frank and Joe. And she listened for the baby to pound its fists inside of her, and the long periods in which the baby did not stir she would grow worried and restless.

One night when she and George sat down to supper, they did hear a knock at the window. It was George who rose to go check on the sound. He peered out, shook his head, and said it was nothing, maybe a bird run into the door.

He sat back down and for the first time in weeks George seemed to want to talk. He told her how Cliff Bolles had come into the shop and ordered a Texas stock saddle, one of the nicest kind on the market, with a carved square skirt with double riggings. Then on top of that he bought a pair of angora chaps, saying he would be going on a long ride soon.

He started to barter with me, George said. I told him there wasn't that kind of room on either of the things he was buying. He told me how I wouldn't regret my decision and that when it came time for me to replace my mares, he'd set me up with a sweet deal. He explained it was hard times for everybody, but that he really needed a good saddle because his cantle was breaking down on his old one.

Did you tell him you weren't planning on your mares dying anytime soon?

No. I just said I was never going to be a dealer or a trader. Cliff just smiled a big-toothed grin and shook my hand and told me, Fair enough.

Walter told me John isn't too fond of him, Trina said, swirling her spoon through the pork stew, trying to cool it. She wondered if Walter would buy a horse from Cliff when he got home, or if there'd be some other dealer.

Oh, I think it's more complicated than that. Nobody knows what to make of that man, because he gets out clean every time. There's only a few out there like him, but they make a trade of it and survive longer than the rest of us even dream.

He glanced up at Trina and she smiled, because she came from one of those families, though he couldn't know it. Trappers were traders and their own breed of dealers but of the same blood in that they knew how to survive and endure. They knew how to live wearing the very coat they just claimed to have sold. Somehow they always made out as if they'd never traded a thing.

They finished their stew in the hushed quiet of a crackling fire and she took his bowl and went and rinsed it off along with her own. The two of them shared this kind of quiet existence and he asked for nothing and seemed grateful for anything she gave him. It occurred to her he was only waiting for Walter to come home, as Ann would have wished, and then he too would die. Life had little meaning to him now and the glimmer he used to have in his eyes was put out like a fire. It was as if he gave himself over with Ann's death and any kindness people granted him now was simply generosity for the ill and beguiled.

Though he had talked more than usual tonight, his face was sunken and she could tell he was tired. As soon as he finished eating he went near the fire and sat down in the rawhide rocker and began reading. She went and sat near him and asked him to read aloud to her. She stopped him in the middle of his reading to ask him whether he thought this really would be the war to end all wars. He stumbled over an answer and then tried to go back and reread the passage before as if the answer could be found there, but there was nothing and finally he snapped the cover shut.

He told her that war was a religion and that he'd never known a religion to die quick. He told her war was a life and not a death. He explained how people, not war, were the great abstraction, for they were infinite in number and inarticulate in their suffering. And he said it was a whole lot of restless suffering in need of direction that brought men together to fight. He took a deep breath.

And when they fall in war there is a kind of blessedness almost like a baptism? she asked.

They say blessedness can be found, he said, out of his dark sunken eyes.

But you said war is a life, not a death?

I say it because maintaining a war and a life require faith and a will to go on living. Death does not require any commitment on the part of the people. He told her how he'd read that Napoleon lowered the height of the French by two inches. War took the fit and left them the unfit. It stole strong fathers, husbands, sons, and brothers and left the epileptic, the consumptive, the inebriate, to ignoble a new generation. He said that was

Napoleon's mark on a generation but that he was no different from any of the great leaders calling on the best of men for a noble cause.

She asked him if he believed bloodletting could change a man's spirits.

No more likely than you can drive the evil thoughts of a man out by blows.

Then there is no purity to be found? she asked. She told him to go on and he shook his head.

Evils cure themselves eventually. I do not despair of humanity, he said, recovering himself upright and straightbacked in his chair. I only despair that we do not live long enough to see it figure itself out. His eyes watered and he wiped the corners of them and then he reopened the book and resumed reading out loud.

She sat there caught up in the quiet rumble of his words rolling over the pages, and she stopped listening for meaning and heard only his sound. She held her hand to her stomach and imagined the steady hum it might sound like to her baby falling asleep under the motion of the rocker and its grandfather's voice. She looked down and smiled, knowing it wouldn't be long.

Soon after he started reading again George began to fall asleep and Trina let him do so, and went about cleaning up the house and heated snow in the copper boiler for the dirty clothes to soak in overnight. Then she woke him gently and told him it was late and he ought to get some rest.

In the morning when she woke he had already left for the mercantile. She went out to feed and grain the animals. There were three feet of snow covering the land and the whole place seemed huge. Under trees where the shadows were deep the snow was flat and flecked with bright quartz like whites. Across the field the white stretched and sprawled and there were so many bold and sloping lines where benches and foothills ran together and mountains grew up to the sky. The mountain peaks were silhouetted against a blue sky so as to look serrated and chiseled with a knife. Clouds were piled up on the western horizon and a storm would likely roll through later in the day.

The animals warmed by the morning sun were lazy and walked slowly about their pens. The horses did not go kicking at one another fighting for the first grain bucket; rather they stationed themselves peacefully before their troughs. She took eggs from the chicken pen and threw them handfuls of corn. The work went quickly and in no time she was back in the house taking off her scarf and hat.

George came home for lunch that day and they sat at the table eating leftover onion soup. When George stood to go he set an envelope on the table.

You got a letter from Walter today, he said.

Trina's hands were reaching out before she even gave it a thought.

Patience. Patience, he said, and the lower half of his face softened and a smile broke.

George.

I know. I know. He started to hand it to her and then pulled it back quickly.

George.

He extended it and then snatched it back.

I got to see it, please, George.

It isn't going cold.

She looked at him smiling.

I just have to have my bit of fun. I got one too. Rare, two letters would come on the same day. What are the chances of that? He smoothed the letter on his chest with his hand. I think it's more than a page. Longer than mine.

She knew better than to pester him anymore. George? You going to give it to me now.

Yes, I am, he said.

She scooted out from her chair and moved up the stairs as quickly as she could now, with the letter in her hand.

She piled her blanket over her lap and sat on her bed.

December 21, 1917

Dear Trina,

It's nearing Christmastime and all I can think of is home, chopping a tree with Dad, hauling it behind the two mares, and then coming home to a hot meal Mom made up. And then there's you, and I keep imagining where you are in all of this, since we haven't done December before. I think you're with Dad and me, picking out a tree. You hold my hand as we walk. Of course we have gloves on, but it doesn't feel like it. Your skin is hot on mine and our fingers lock, the way you always make them, holding on the way you do.

I see your face all the time. I see it when I shouldn't. When the high explosives boom, the earth shudders, and I think it's giving under our feet, I reach for you and I am holding the both of us up or maybe you are. I'm not quite sure. I run far from the other men, because there is such a tendency to flock together here, the way sheep do. And you're dead that way, because disasters aren't isolated incidents. They aren't selective. They take you all. And it's not so much you're running from them as from each other.

I listen for the roar of the big coal boxes falling behind me and then the piping high-pitch whistle of the low-spreading daisy cutters. And I leap and jump haphazardly and dive down again for shelter, and by chance I'm spared. The wounded are shot down like hares by the airmen.

I'm sorry. I should not write of such things. But, Trina, all I see are the fields of home. The grass all gone wheat color. I see the field by Picabo. I see the six-line wire fence me and a bunch of guys rigged up. You know two summers back we ran the jackrabbits as hard as we could by horse. They were eating the crops so there was a bounty up for their skins. We pushed them by the hundreds, maybe thousands, down the valley into the barbed-wire fence just north of Gannett. They ran straight at it blind and furious only to lose their heads or their limbs. Some of them lost it all and we did not even bother skinning them they were so wrecked. What the wire didn't do, we did with our wooden clubs, batting their heads until they lay in piles. A bounty of dead pelts.

And yet those dead rabbits were badges, tokens of a sort. We weren't done with them after all. We picked them up and skinned them and got money off them and felt ourselves proud boys for weeks. And I still see the pads of their feet kicking up at us, bits of sage and dust as they bounded faster and faster, getting away from us, only nearing closer and closer to the front line. And there was an innocence to it all.

I lost my main man yesterday. Dean McCurry came with me from

Virginia. The planes came low and I thought he was covered and we rolled into separate trenches. Same goes for him, he doesn't believe in huddling up like sitting ducks. We could hear the planes and we spread. It was his turn. I heard the sound like a thousand rifle shots come on a tin roof at one time. I don't know where this metal sound comes from. It looks like a rainstorm on very dry land, with all sorts of craters surfacing in the wake of the barrage.

I won't say more, I promise. I love you. I keep seeing your belly in the dark. That pearl-colored flesh rises to my fingers. I think of your skin soft and your eyes full of promises and I keep telling myself yours are big enough to carry the dreams of both of us. I'm tired now and morning will come quick. I'll seal this letter now. Otherwise, I'll think it too dark, come light, and I won't send it. And then it will be an even longer wait for you to hear one of the only things I hold with lasting conviction now – our love. Trina, I love you.

Tell Dad I'm thinking of him too. I hope you are all making out well. Toast for me Christmas Day and after. I'll be home as soon as I can.

Love always,
Walter

The letter left her sad and lonely and she held her stomach and whispered to the baby inside, telling how they'd be fine and how its father would be home soon. Then she read the letter again, this time out loud, so the baby might hear its father's words and be comforted. After a while she got up and went downstairs and packed some bread and cheese in a satchel and put on her snowshoes with the thought of walking to Annette's.

The sun was hidden behind the clouds and the light was flat and gray. Burdened and weighted out of their fullness, the trees were heaped with snow. Two horses hooked to a cart were tied out in front of the Alturas and the horses pawed the ice-floored road, antsy to be moving. She went to the mercantile and found George alone. He raised his eyebrows and walked to her quickly. It was as if he expected the worst and his face was tight and his stare long and hard.

Are you all right?

I'm okay, she said. She went to his counter and sat down on a stool.

I thought something might've happened or you heard something. He looked relieved and rested his arm around her.

You're looking a little beat, he said.

A little tired maybe.

You thought about walking over to Annette's place. Might do you good. Seeing the baby might cheer you up. What do you think?

She said she was on her way there and he patted his hand on her back.

There now. Get yourself some fresh air. Hold Ben. The baby, it'll be soon now, Trina. I can't imagine you'll have to wait much longer.

She agreed and bundled her scarf around her neck to go back outside. As she was leaving, Bolles was coming in. He kicked the snow off his boots just outside the door and came in rubbing his hands together.

I'll be. Cold front moving in if I don't say. Barometer dropping, George?

It is.

Trina.

Mr. Bolles, she said, and they both tipped their heads to one another.

Any day now? Is that right?

Believe so.

You're looking real good.

Thanks, she said and went to move around him and out of the store.

You wouldn't be seeing Annette or John any time soon?

I'm going there now.

Tell John I got a good crew lined up for his spring shearing.

I didn't know it was already that time.

Can't be too early planning that stuff. John's going to use the lambing shed this year. He's finally broke down and is doing it under a roof this year. Finally found himself without a hired hand, he said, glancing down. You understand, with Walter gone and that Baptie not worth drudging out of the woodwork.

I understand.

You'll tell him?

I'll tell him.

It'll save me a trip. Tell him they're good and fast, a crew of boys from Mackay I got for him.

George interrupted and asked what the shearer's union had prices fixed at for the coming spring.

Say it might hit thirteen cents a head. I reckon these boys might do it for a bit less with some moonshine thrown in at the end of a working day.

Doesn't mean it's any less out of the pocket.

Probably right.

Bolles started stroking his mustache, talking about the gas lines these men powered their shears off of. These boys will shear ninety to a hundred in a day. The best of them will turn one over every three, four minutes.

Sounds like it will work out, Trina said.

Course nothing going to look good compared to the season John had last year. He made good money. Grain prices going to be worse this year. People thought they had it bad last year.

They sure did, George said.

Well, they ain't seen nothing yet. Though it wouldn't be the first time I'd seen John weave silk out of straw. Hell, he did it last year, and I ought to be waiting on that man to turn things even better this year.

Could do, could do, George said.

Don't mean to pry at you-all none. You got any word from Walter?

Just last week, George said.

That's good. He faring it out?

About as well as the rest, I suppose.

Bolles looked toward Trina. Can't be easy.

He'll be home soon as he can.

He got any sense when that might be? Say anything different than the news we hear?

Not so much, not really, she said. I got to be moving on.

Very well. Have a good day. Stay out of the cold, it'll nip you.

She told him to do the same.

When she arrived at Annette's the place was warm and she unbundled her things and set them near the door. The two women sat down by the stove and Annette set the baby in Trina's lap while she got up to make coffee. Trina told Annette how while she was walking there'd been a sharp pain that cut across her stomach like she were being cinched with wire.

I got panicked for a moment thinking the baby might be coming.

Annette smiled and said, Well, thank the lord that wasn't the case. Nothing to be making light of. She reached for Trina's hand. Don't go walking alone in this cold.

I had to get out of the house.

No matter. You call me and I'll come get you. What happens if your water breeks and all? You can't be taking those kind of risks, not with that baby.

I know it, Trina said.

She went on lecturing Trina on how she knew how much she loved Walter and how she had a piece of him inside her and she best remember that. He's going to love that baby like he loves you. I seen him, how crazy he goes over you. You take care of that baby as if it were him you were taking care of. She squeezed Trina's hand even tighter. I know you're hearing me. Promise me that, Trina.

I promise, she said, handing Ben back.

Annette took the baby from Trina's lap and raised him to her breast to nurse.

Trina asked if John was just out for a bit, and Annette said he'd left that morning for Jerome. They had to push the sheep farther south and put the rams in with the ewes for breeding. They had no idea when this round of storms might subside so he went down to help the hired hand move them.

He and I'll be all right, she said. But it's you I worry about, being alone.

She told Trina how she thought it would be nice to have the extra company since John was often forced to go be with the sheep. She said, It being any day now, you shouldn't be staying with George who won't be much help and might not even be home.

Trina kept listening, almost wanting there to be more, feeling as if a strong burden were being lifted from her piece by piece.

We got the extra room fixed up for the baby, but Ben's in our room for now and you wouldn't be any problem. I know John would tell you the same if he were here, though he might not say it quite so friendly-like as me, but he'd mean the same.

Trina offered to help cook and said she could still do her share of the work.

We're not going to have you walking around like our slave girl.

Trina rocked in the rocker and felt the weight of her body settling and growing heavy in the chair and all over she was beginning to feel warm.

You doing all right otherwise? Annette asked.

Some days better than others.

You miss him something terrible-like, I imagine.

Trina nodded and bit her lip. Terrible. And this baby. I want it so bad, I can hardly wait for it.

Annette told her how she couldn't imagine a harder thing, being alone, but said if it were any consolation at all women had been doing it forever, waiting for men for one reason or another. He's off for a better reason than a lot of men.

What do you mean?

I mean he's doing the best he can not to let you down.

But you think he'll make it home?

Can't tell you that. But he will if he's able. I know that much about him.

You think he'd send a telegram or write when he knew he was coming home?

He might just up and surprise you.

That's what I been thinking.

Probably you better than anybody else gonna feel him coming home.

Annette?

What, sweetie?

I'm real scared.

I know you are.

Trina sat there and she kept rocking and Annette did nothing to fill the silence. And for the first time since Walter had left, Trina felt comforted. She didn't have to tell Annette what she feared and she knew she wouldn't ask.

I lay awake some nights wondering how quick I can get to your place or Dr. Fox's, Trina said. And then I wonder if there's ever that kind of time. I imagine where in the house I might have it and if it's possible for a baby to come out all on its own. I think I know it can. Animals done it for years. My own mother told me stories about her mother having a baby on a wagon. There wasn't another woman there. I know it can be done.

It can.

Trina crossed her arms around her chest. And I know I'll be so happy to have it. I want it so bad.

I know, Annette said. You just be patient-like and things will come as they're suppose to. That's what I always say. John says I get a bit too fatalistic, but I tell him what other way is there to be. He just looks at me and shakes his head and tells me to be whatever way I am, that I'm just right.

The warmth off the stove was making Trina's cheeks go flush and she was tired and began fighting drifting off to sleep. She traced the lines in the wooden arm of the chair, trying to stay awake, and thought back to that first day Walter showed up in her room at the Alturas. How he pretended to know the age of the wood walls. She flattened her hand and stroked the wood and knew she had no idea how old it was.

Annette held Ben's fist in hers and began to sing softly to him. Trina watched them and studied them as if they were something sacred, as if Annette possessed the only baby born unto the world.

You think George will be all right if I come stay with you?

He'll be just fine. John spoke with him yesterday before he left. He's all for it. We been worried for some time. George agreed but said we'd have to run it by you. He didn't want you feeling like it was him shoving you out the door.

But you think he'll be okay in the house alone?

Trina, he'll be fine. Might even be good for him. You two been through a lot together, it might be good for him to be left to his own thoughts for a while. It was arranged and Trina felt it really was for the best and after a while she fell asleep in her chair and when she woke it was afternoon. Annette offered to take her home in the cart, but Trina begged her to let her walk, saying it was a short distance, that the air would do her good.

Then from there on out you can take me everywhere, Trina said, until the baby's born.

Annette nodded. I can see how you two worked out so well. You look to be just about as stubborn as Walter is. Well, then, I guess George can drive you back here later this evening or tomorrow morning.

Chapter 20

S HE COULD SEE the door was ajar as she walked up the path. Thoughts fleeted through her mind and she considered the possibility she hadn't pulled the latch tight. She approached the door cautiously, wondering what animals might have entered, and stopped when she heard Frank's voice. A shiver ran through her and all the fear she'd penned up in her body for months began to race.

I had myself two good bear dogs in my life, Joe Moran was saying. A airedale and a hound.

A jar crashed to the floor and there was the sound of buttons scattering the wood floor.

That hound dog would go with his tail swishing the air back and forth, and I'd know he was on the scent of something good.

Hounds are dumber than an ass.

You would know.

Hell if I wouldn't.

That hound dog never tangled with not one porcupine or not one cougar whole time I had him. God damn, these Pascoes got their share of dried goods. You eat green beans, Frank?

Hell, no.

Trina could hear the glass of another broken jar shattering on the wood and then the sound of a can and then another can.

Me neither.

She eased herself onto the snow and began crawling around to the other side of the house, with her ear edged up close to the house to make sure they kept talking. She thought to stay low so they wouldn't see her figure through the windows. She could edge her way along the south side of the fence line and then hide in the aspen groves until they left, or she could try for town from the far end of the pasture.

She tried to hurry, but when she got to the corner of the house she could see two pack horses standing out back. She thought about setting them loose and running, but they'd most likely see her, and she knew she wouldn't be able to outrun them.

Then the front door flew wide open and Frank peered outside.

Called that airedale Skunk, Joe Moran yelled from inside, because he did have one problem. He could never keep himself clear of their spray. Frank?

Never had a dog of mine skunked ever, Frank said, stretching his arms up high in the air.

Trina made to crawl away quickly out of sight.

Lookie here. The bitch has come home, just as good as a dog, Frank said. Might have a better nose than that sorry red-skinned coon hound you accidentally shot in the ass, Joe.

I'll be damn, Joe said, coming into the doorway.

Trina crawled faster, but she couldn't keep her weight from breaking through the surface of the snow. She'd crawl and then, topheavy, her hands would sink, burying her front end to the elbows.

Frank laughed and Joe Moran came up behind her.

He grabbed her by the back of her coat. He lifted her up so she was standing and then grabbed her by the wrist. Her stomach bulged under her coat and she tried to cover it with her hands.

She's pregnant, Joe Moran said.

Son of a bitch. Will you look at this, Frank said, waving his hand in the air. All the time I believed it was that doctor putting her up.

The wind was picking up and her face burned. When she went to wipe her face Frank grabbed her hand and told her to keep her goddamn hands still.

She shook her arm free of him and started to kick him in the shin, but the snow slowed her and he easily dodged her kick. He laughed. She was scared, but there was nothing to do but fight them.

Frank called her a slut and dragged her past Joe Moran into the house, holding onto her wrist so tightly her hand went white and numb. She pleaded with him to ease up on her. He told her to stop her whimpering and slapped her across the face. Then he pushed her and she stumbled backward toward the dining room table where she caught herself on the back of a chair. Her face stung so that she held her hand to it. She tried not to cry.

Joe Moran was already back at the kitchen hutch dropping Ann's silver in a potato sack. Possessions he chose not to steal he threw to the floor. There were canned tomatoes, pickles, and smashed jars of green beans. There were teacups and their saucers.

This is my girl's home, Frank said. We finally found her. And you didn't think we would, did you, honey?

Her wrist smarted as if iced for a long time. They'd been drinking and reeked of it. You bastards, she said.

Silver prices are real high, Frank said speculatively. Market's been right there for a while.

Joe Moran came and stood behind Trina, stretching her hair out, running his fingers through it and then gathering it again in his hands.

Frank pointed to the silver Joe had just bagged and told him he ought to go start tying it on the pack horses.

You going to help me or just watch? Joe Moran said as he wandered out.

I've got a few things to finish up in here first, he said. Frank clutched Trina by the shoulders and shook her hard and told her not to be going anywhere. Then he turned his back to her. He went to the kitchen and was bent over pouring all of their flour and sugar across the floor. Trina reached for the chair behind her and lifted it over her head, and then she ran at him. The chair came down hard and he fell to his knees, groaning and reaching for his head. She brought it down on him again and his hands slid out from under him and his face went to the floor. He groaned and reached for his head where the blood was oozing out and turning his hair black. He called her a bitch and grumbled under his breath as he kicked his leg out at her, trying to knock her off her feet. When he rolled over blood dripped from his nose and from the corners of his mouth.

She could not get out of the kitchen before he stood and turned to face her, his head lolling and his hands red with the blood he swept from his head. Then his hand felt for his mouth, and he fingered his front tooth that was broken in half and licked the blood clean from it. I'll be, I think I broke my tooth.

Her courage was gone as quickly as it had come and she stood frozen with her arms at her sides. There was no getting around him. He looked at her and his face bent into a snarl that revealed anger and even pleasure. He reached for her hand and took her little finger and snapped it.

He dragged up his shirt sleeves and she could see the heavy muscles in his arms, and she cried out but he held onto her hand.

Then he struck her across the face. Her head shocked with pain and it was all she could do to stay on her feet. She put her hand to her face where it burned, but another blow was already coming at her. She turned her head and he got her in the jaw. Her teeth rattled together as her mouth was snapped shut. She cried out in pain and started to squat down onto her knees. She began to wet herself.

She's got herself a little weaker living the good life, he said, as if he were talking to someone else. Then he just sat over her looking at her as if she were some specimen in decay. He spat on her face, but she did not flinch.

She heard footsteps sounding outside, slowly, like the butt of a rifle pounding on dry, hard earth, and she thought his steps were walking over the top of her. Her stomach was clenching up in pain, and she flinched under the spasms and cried out. She held her fists tight together to contain the hurt, but it did no good.

She backed herself farther into the wall and bent her head down. Stay away from me, Frank, she pleaded. Then she could think no more and she cowered in the corner of the room holding one hand over her stomach and the other to her jaw. Then he was kicking her and she waited for it to be over so that the house might be empty again.

He pinned her hands to the floor, wrestling her to her back without much fight, for she didn't have much left in her.

You get off me, she screamed.

I'll get off you when I'm good and through, he said. He made like to straddle her, but she kneed him hard. She stared up at him into his black eyes that did not shimmer so much as they smoldered like beads of coal, sized up in the middle of his bloodshot eyes. Then his head was straining back. She shut her eyes and then he let out a yell and came off her.

Let's get the hell out here, Frank. It was Joe Moran's voice. You make yourself respectable sweetie, he said, standing over her. Then he booted her in the side, and it felt to go all the way through to her insides.

Trina tried to stand but didn't know if she had the bones inside her that would hold her.

Hope you know who's the daddy of that baby, Frank said, standing up. You might end up back with us yet if that baby don't come out like its daddy.

You want to take her? Joe Moran said.

Trina winced as she felt another blow of pain running through her stomach. She let out a short cry and clutched her stomach.

Frank stumbled forward a few steps, grabbing at his head and his tongue smoothing over his tooth. Frank shook his head. I've had just about enough of her.

Joe stood beside her once more and stretched her hair out in his hands and then bent and kissed it. He nodded and called her a sorry waste of a thing.

She collapsed as soon as they were out the door and lay there motionless for what felt like hours, soaking up the blows still pulsating through her body. She began to shake and tremble all over and she felt her face wet with sweat. Her insides felt as though they were wrenching against her.

Not my baby, she began to sob. Not my baby. She stared down at her finger and made to straighten it. It will be all right, she told herself, standing to her feet once more. She began cleaning the kitchen. I'm just fine, she said as she picked up the broken glass and bagged it. And when she bent down to wipe the canned tomatoes into a bag she paid no attention to the slivers of glass strewn across the floor. She found a broom and swept the area up and then mopped it.

Her face was swollen and her right eye barely opened, the skin around it already purple. The strain of lifting her head made her want to vomit and she lowered her head back down to be level with the floor.

George came home to find Trina on the floor scrubbing flour from the cracks in the wood with a toothbrush. She did not look up when he walked through the door.

My God, what are you doing? he said.

She reached for the broom with her head bent down. I'm so sorry. I wanted to have it clean by the time you got home.

What happened?

Frank and Joe came, she said, finally raising her head.

My God, who did this to you? He ran to her and put his arm around her shoulders and took the toothbrush from her hand.

She shook her head and she was all dead weight leaning into him and he didn't think she'd be able to stand.

You need to lie down. Can you get up?

He lifted her arm and set it around his neck and then slowly they stood. She leaned her head on his shoulder and, as he helped her ease herself down onto the cot, she clutched at his arm and wouldn't let go.

He kneeled beside her and she began to weep.

He told her it would be all right, and he patted her and held her while she cried.

Later he rose and told her he'd be back – he had to look around the place. He opened the drawers in the kitchen and then he went and opened the hutch and found it empty but for a tiny porcelain figurine of a bluebird. He went to another bureau and found it empty and he peered into the dry flour bin. All of the canned goods in the pantry were gone.

He went from room to room surveying the place as though he half expected to find them somewhere within the house. When he returned to her he bent down on his knees and put his hands to her shoulders and waited for her to lift her head. Their eyes met and he pulled her close to him and held her there. They held each other tightly and in between muffled sobs she told him how sorry she was for coming into his house. He tried to quiet her and stroked her head like she were a little girl, which only made her cry harder.

He told her it wasn't her fault and she managed to ask him whose fault it could be and he told her he didn't know, but it wasn't hers. He said it like he meant it and so she wouldn't have any doubts. He said the world wasn't fair and it probably wouldn't ever be, but he reminded her that she was strong and patient and that's what life took, a whole lot of patience for a few glimmering moments of beauty.

I didn't want them to do this to me, she whispered. Then she leaned her head into his shoulder and in a voice sounded so low as if to not let others hear, she whispered, George, what if they hurt my baby?

Then all of a sudden as if pulled from a long dull sleep, he started. He pulled back from her and put his hands on her shoulders. You're going to be all right. You keep telling yourself that, because I know how strong you are. You just hold on. Now, I'm going to help you pack some things and then we'll go over to Annette's place. She's expecting you. I'll get the doctor from there.

That night after she had seen the doctor, Annette sponged Trina's face with a cool cloth and wrapped a pack of snow in a towel to take down the swelling. She showed her to her room and tucked her in and told her to try to get some sleep. Trina heard them whispering in the main room for what seemed a long time as George tried to explain all of what he knew. She strained to hear him say something about her baby. Then she could hear Annette telling him everything would be fine and that Trina's face would heal in no time.

After a while she grew tired of trying to hear and she stared into the dark black gnarls swirled in the wood ceiling. Then in one of the knotholes she could see the eye of a storm, the dark spot where all the fine lines of the woodwork disappeared, all was black, dark, and deep, a single eye staring down at her like a wound still seeping. She gazed toward the window and it was snowing outside. Her eyes fell back to the dark wood holes spread about the room.

Walter came to her and she imagined him injured or shot. She saw him on a field with a gaping hole in his leg. And surrounding him were so many men dead he might be passed over as one of them. And his cry for help would not be sounded, only gurgled in the throat and drowned out by the firing squads overhead. She began to shake and felt herself burning, scalding with the fire of the land on which he lay. The dark earth aflame with so many men, so many arms reaching out through the thick air, desperately begging not to be left behind. In their turn, though they did not know it, they fanned the flames on with their hands, waving, crying out, sending the blazes sky high.

She raised her finger to cover the hole overhead. And she told herself he was sleeping sound and safe. The wound came seeping forth out of another hole to the left of her finger. And she saw his pants shredded and a knee cleaved open and gawking wide. She began to move her hands and squinted her eyes to shut them all out. Above her more than a dozen dark storm eyes peered down and in them lay the fallen craters of all things withering within their skin, within that shape called a body, that thing subject to going thin and worn and vacant.

She pulled the extra pillow on her bed against her chest and held it tight and stared ahead, trying to see and hear nothing. Her body was exhausted, but her mind would not rest. She sat up in bed and felt her feet on the wood floor. It was rough and the air rushed up her gown and she shivered and was dizzy. The baby did not move and she rubbed her hands over her stomach. In a walking that appeared not brought fully out of sleep, she traveled from bed to window and then slid back down between the sheets. It was not clear where wakefulness ended and sleep began.

She told herself, We are sleeping now. We are bound by one another. We are sleeping, she whispered to the life inside her. We will rest now and we will sleep. We are dreaming even now. And over and over she whispered these lines. We will sleep, we will sleep, we will rest until tomorrow. It must be quiet now. And the baby did not respond and she stayed in that half-sleep waiting for movement until she finally drifted off.

That night she dreamt up a horse trader. He was selling her a liver chestnut for when Walter returned from war. She dickered him on the price and he promised again the horse was sound and even-tempered. She paid for the horse and when she got it home she unfastened the halter and the horse shook its head, tossed its mane, and galloped in circles around the pen like a circus animal gone mad. When the pigs squealed in the adjacent pen, it galloped harder, and the clumps of dirt spun out from under its hooves. When she went to catch the horse, it reared and struck the air with its front hooves and could not be haltered. She stood at the fence line breathing a cold metal shock of air into her throat, fearing Walter's return home, not wanting his welcome ruined.

Then it was morning and she rose brave and profoundly calm at the first crack of light. The day was clear and fluid. Her body was a rack of pain and her belly was purpled from where they'd laid punches and kicks into her.

A foot of new snow had fallen in the storm overnight and it blanketed the ground a clean white. The temperature had dropped. It was always colder on the clear days of winter.

The baby was born two days later when the deciduous trees were bare and thin and colored only by absence. It was a girl and she entered the world quietly and left quietly and no one really expected it could be any other way. For a long time Annette could say nothing, she could only weep over the baby she held to her lips and kissed.

Trina did not cry, for she had lost her tears, but in a faint voice she'd asked Annette whether it was a boy or a girl. Annette told her it was a girl and Trina had nodded and shut her eyes as if that issuance offered some relief. Later Trina cradled the baby in her arms as she sat by candlelight, feeling the tension rising out of death, the way her body sought wholly a blessing from the hours and days she had left to come. The blessing was as it had always been, a will to keep on, and her blessing did not ask for a cause for survival, simply the means.

She looked at the baby and wondered how it became and how it had felt its way through life. She thought to ask it how it knew it could die, who gave it permission, and how was she to live with such suffering. The baby was limp in her arms, yet she felt its bones to be strong and thought how is this not the waste of precious bones. Everything felt backward, and she wondered how all humans were given bones of strength when it was the heart that seemed to lose spirit.

She blew out the candle beside her bed and slid deeper into her covers. Annette came to the bed and lifted the baby from her arms and Trina did not fight her.

Surrender was not like she'd imagined, not nearly as easy as she'd thought it to be, even a year before, five years before. Lessons had tested and taught her and not so much changed her as they had made her a little weaker, a little harder in her fight for what still would come. There was something cold about studying the necessities of the heart. But Trina did not study them so much as she was tried by them and in the end she was inseparable from the deed, the act, and the consequence.

Her existence was not unlike that of the herder who is tried by the herd he follows. Not so unlike the blacksmith who dodges the kicking hoof of the horse on which he attempts to put hot metal shoes. Not so unlike the work of tracking animals that trail off into nowhere in the white snow of

215

winter. Not so unlike the team of black Percheron horses that trot through the snow with clumps of ice balled on the back of their fetlocks and long icicles dangling off their muzzles. They move with grace in their heaviness. They are proud as they pull the wooden sled. They know not what they carry or what tracks they leave in their wake.

Trina could picture a sled and the pulling black Percherons. With time she knew she'd begin to find meaning in life, like the meaning that can be found in all burning fire. She'd wrestle on with the heat and stillness of a place to which she knew Walter would have to return. She would hold out and believe in all of it for as long as it would take, worshiping in sweat and cold their love and the memory of something held, if only faintly as a breath.

Chapter 21

THE TRAIN BUCKED as each car filled the chain of slack. They were headed west out of Norfolk, Virginia, where the houses steeped into the hills were wooden and boxlike and the roofs metal and silver slanted in the daylight. The train gathered speed on the outskirts of the city and lumbered on past factories, switchyards, schools, junkyards, and the dusty haze of mills.

Walter was seated in the dining car between Harold McPheters and K. D. Lindsay. Both men were from his troop and they'd been together for the duration of the war. There were other soldiers aboard the car, all of them going home: Arthur Gibson to Chicago, Illinois; Charles Farell to Bismarck, North Dakota; Bill Randall to St. Louis, Missouri; Joe Surebine to Tumbolt, Tennessee; Frank Gomez to Leavenworth, Kansas; John Astor to Laramie, Wyoming; John Mailer to Terminus, Utah; and Bob Bailey all the way cross-country to San Francisco, California. They'd all go as far as Chicago together and then they'd start to lose men as they boarded other lines, all heading in their respective directions.

Spread among the men were women in house dresses and tea dresses and chiffon and satin and there were men sprinkled among them who might have been traveling for business or pleasure, but the soldiers hardly registered them. The women were pretty and they didn't look like the women they'd seen in France.

War's been good to them, Astor said, speaking across the table to Bailey.

Walter thought Astor was right. The women were more bold and sure of themselves than he'd remembered women to be and he was surprised to think the war had maybe somehow changed them all. He could think of nothing else that might have and still he wondered how it could be so.

They're just better fed, Gibson said. He wore a sailor's cap and now and then he leaned his head way back to slide the cap farther up his forehead.

One sat in the front corner of the dining car near the potbellied stove. Her red hair piled on her head. Her skin was fair and she wore a brilliant green chiffon blouse with an immense cape collar that was low in front and had edges embroidered in black. It was dropped over thin yellow satin and it hung in loose folds to her narrow hips. At her waist was a belt of colored crystal. She wore a long panne velvet skirt.

Cat got your eye? Lindsay said, indicating the red-haired woman Walter was staring at. They'd all noticed her, the redhead in the green dress. Remember you're looking at her under oil lamps, Lindsay observed expertly. This sort of feeble lighting always makes them prettier than they are.

McPheters stood abruptly but made no move to leave the table and then just as abruptly he sat back down.

You all right? Lindsay said.

McPheters flicked at a button on his tunic and then folded his hands prayerfully and yet casually in his lap. He did not look like one given to pray.

You going to tell me she isn't pretty? Walter said, still staring at her.

Lindsay pretended to squint in her direction as if it was a strain on his eyes to discern the subtlety of her features.

She does appear to be traveling alone, he said. That tends to make them more pretty.

Is that an observation or a suggestion?

Maybe both, Lindsay said.

You got a girl at home, Pascoe? Bailey asked from an adjacent table.

Far as I know, Walter said.

You think she'll be waiting for you?

Walter shrugged. Two days before boarding the train Walter'd sent a telegram to Cliff Bolles telling him he'd be taking the train west. He told him to have a horse John would approve of at the platform in Shoshone waiting for him. He told him to mention his telegram to no one, not even John, and to come alone.

He wasn't sure why he'd been so exacting in his terms but remembered how he'd clung to the image of riding home from the war and surprising Trina and he'd visualized this scene over and over at night when he couldn't sleep.

She gone and got bored on you, has she? Sorry, man.

Lay off, Walter said.

Take it easy, Bailey said.

The men were weary and because they were heading home they felt like they ought to be in good spirits. Still, they were nervous and uneasy, and that gave them an added edge. Randall sat off by himself, cutting a deck of cards. He shuffled them and watched them fold together inside his hands and then he cut them again and resumed his shuffling without asking anyone if they wanted to play a hand of cards.

An older man in wool trousers with a cane rested in between his legs watched Randall relentlessly and smiled courteously whenever Randall looked up from his shuffling. In the man's old smile there was a gesture of respect and more empathy than could ever be found in an apology.

Just haven't told her I'm coming home, Walter said. He had not even told Lindsay of his plan to surprise Trina, yet he'd told Lindsay just about all there was to know about her.

Think you'll surprise her, do you? Bailey said. She might just surprise you. That's not always such a good idea. I heard about an artillery man who came in his front door and found another man banging his wife like a pig on their couch, his own goddamn couch. Big fat bastard he was, but there wasn't a goddamn thing he could do about it. You know what I mean?

Would you stop calling everybody artillery, Gibson said, raising his voice and drawing the attention of a woman across the dining car who suddenly took her child in hand and left the car. Not everybody's artillery, he said, leaning his head back, and this time his hat fell off behind him.

Another artillery came home and his wife was good and knocked up by some other feller.

Lindsay elbowed Walter and raised his eyebrows, indicating the woman in the back of the train Walter had noticed earlier. She was staring at him.

I would have shot the bastard, Farell said.

219

If he'd a knocked her up before he left, he wouldn't a had to worry about it, Bailey said. You thought a that? How many times does it take to knock a girl up if you're any good?

I swear I can knock 'em up the first time, but I'd do it to her three times just to be sure, Farell said.

So maybe Walter just doesn't know how good and knocked up his girl is, Gibson said.

Take it easy, Lindsay said. All of you.

Walter smiled at the woman in the green dress and she dropped her eyes to her folded hands.

What do you reckon we're going to gain by going home? Mailer said, pointing out the window with a sudden flourish of the hand. Then he pulled a pouch of tobacco and some rolling paper from a satchel.

Don't go and get all serious on us, Surebine said.

Bugger you all, Mailer said, sprinkling the tobacco onto the paper. I say we just about lost everything there was to lose going away, and I can't say or see what we're gaining by going home.

You saying patriotism is worn threadbare? To patriotism, Gomez said, raising his drink high and then taking another slosh off it.

The woman in the green dress stood and made to walk past them on the way to the smoker car, and silence traveled with her for they all watched her for how she moved. Randall stopped shuffling his cards and McPheters held onto the points of his shirt collar with both his hands.

Might we buy you a drink, ma'am? Bailey said, reaching for her elbow.

She looked toward Walter as she raised her elbow out of Bailey's reach. If he's buying, she said, and kept walking.

The air dangled the scent of perfume with her passing and Gomez scrunched his nose up down like a rabbit as Surebine sneered at him.

McPheters shifted his weight side to side, looking uncomfortable and then finally settling.

When you come back through, the drink's on me, Walter said, just before she reached the cabin door, and then surprisingly she turned around and blushed.

She left the cabin and Lindsay raised his eyebrows and told Walter he pulled that one off pretty smooth. Smooth, he repeated, as Bailey scoffed.

It was like Mailer hadn't seen the girl. He had three cigarettes rolled and was working on his forth. Gomez, having the odd habit of saying the meaningless, asked Mailer if he was rolling cigarettes for all of them.

What's it to you? You don't smoke, Mailer said.

Gomez told him he didn't but he just might if the tobacco was for him.

Bailey spoke up again. Pascoe, you didn't take me wrong back there? I'm not saying anything disrespectful about your girl. Hell, I quit writing my girl a month into this bloody war. I just done and gave up on her.

By late afternoon they were passing into groves of flowering elm trees losing orange and yellow leaves. The leaves were coming down so hard it was like a storm. The girl in the green dress came back through the cabin and Walter watched the way her dress swayed as she walked, stirring in him a dormant longing. But the longing was tempered and discharged of appetite and any sense of real pleasure. He wanted to want her, but she elicited a kind of emptiness and he could feel the insides of him clenching, a slight wave of panic running through some part of him aware of an incapacity that he could put no name to. When she sat down Walter smiled at her and she smiled back. Lindsay asked him what he was waiting for and Walter shrugged.

A candy butcher moved through the car with sandwiches, grapefruits, apples, and oranges. Bailey bought one of each and peeled his orange in front of all of them and ate it slowly, trying to tempt them.

It was nearing dinner and they were exhausted and hungry. They watched Mailer roll more tobacco.

You bastards never seen or tasted fruit like this, Bailey said

Farell told Bailey to fuck off, that he was the only fruit, and they all laughed. Then he lit a cigarette and smoked it.

Watch your mouths or you might get us all kicked off, Astor hissed.

He's not going to get us kicked off, Gibson said, sounding tired and annoyed. He leaned his head against the car wall behind him and pulled his cap over his eyes to make like he was taking a nap.

Astor's right, Lindsay said with a nod of his head as he thumbed through the day coach literature, explaining how the rail passed a law that said disorderly passengers using vile or profane language could be expelled from the train at any usual or unusual stopping place.

You saying we're being disorderly? Gibson said from under his cap.

Something like that, Lindsay said.

I'd like to see someone throw us off this fucking train, Farell said, bulging his lower lip with his tongue like he were packing chew.

What's better, the orange or the apple? Walter asked.

The men turned and looked at Walter. Something in his voice seemed to carry a challenge and to talk to Bailey at all was to ask for his calumny.

The grapefruit, Bailey said, with his usual civility. He held out a single wedge for Walter to try, and when Walter showed no interest in the offering, Bailey ate it himself.

George, Walter called, and when the candy butcher stood over him, Walter asked him to give the lady in the green dress a grapefruit and then he handed over his change.

Astor slammed both his fists down on the table and a woman seated near them wrapped her hand around her child's head instinctively and then, realizing where the sound came from, she gave the men a sour look.

Remarkable. A grapefruit, Astor said. I've never heard of such a thing.

Gibson sat up, flipping his cap back on his forehead. One of Mailer's dried up, skinny cigarettes would have been more enticing than a grapefruit.

From one fruit to another fruit, Farell said, moving his hand from Bailey to Walter as if fruitiness spread like a disease.

Lindsay shook his head and said, All right, don't say I didn't give you a chance when you're the one alone in your berth.

Walter laughed quietly under his breath and let it go.

As the train clattered over mountains their meal was served, cooked from scratch in the train's tiny kitchen. There was lamb pie, a dinner roll, and stewed apples for dessert. It came steamed with heat and the men blew at it but could not wait and forked it to their burning mouths. Then they took a drink off their beer to cool their mouths before forking in another bite.

McPheters ate carelessly and spilled a bite of lamb pie down his shirt front and Gomez asked how long it might be until he was to a launderer, and then he resumed eating. Lindsay leaned over Walter and tucked his napkin in McPheters's collar. He was careful with McPheters like he were someone old.

It was McPheters who was made to shoot his own brother. Patrick had been crawling on his belly for safety while shells were raining down, riddling the ground. He was trying to make it back into the trenches after a raid. The wounded were writhing like fish in a pond drying out, arms flapping. He crawled over some barbed wire, and McPheters thought he was a German and announced such and was ordered to shoot. McPheters fired and the next thing he knew Patrick was lifted in the air and then fluttered down. It wasn't until the next morning that they realized what McPheters had done. He'd never spoken of his brother since.

They ate quickly and said nothing and when Bailey was through he motioned the steward, a black man dressed in a starched white overcoat, over to them. Could you bring us all out another round? he said. They all nodded, confirming his request.

The steward counted them and left for the kitchen.

Thanks, George, Bailey called after him.

He's named George too? Gibson said.

Yeah, he's related to the other feller, Astor said. They're brothers.

You know him? Gomez said.

Nah.

So why'd you call him George?

It's what you call them, Farell said.

I didn't think they were brothers, Gomez said.

Halfway through their second round they thought to order thirds but were embarrassed at how hungry they were. People were smiling at them behind their napkins. Walter watched a boy across the dining car blow up his cheeks to make like he was fat and then he pretended to have a fork in his hand and began shoveling food to his mouth, imitating the men. His mother elbowed him and tried to scold him, but whenever she was not looking he resumed his pretend feasting. They all decided it was better to hold off, for they knew their stomachs would not bear such gluttony.

As night came in Ohio, the men went to their sleeping car and pulled down their bunked berths and closed their green curtains. Behind the curtains they slid out of their clothes and there was the rustle of curtains and the quick flashes of flesh slipped through the curtains. Bailey dangled his leg out on purpose and began to grunt as if he were with a woman. Farell started moaning too and the cabin was soon in chorus until Mailer told them he'd heard just about enough.

They laughed, for the men filled the entire sleeper and there were no

223

women to hear them. And then it was silent again and the men were left to think of their girls over the steady drone of the car creaking, almost whining its way along. The ones they'd made up to make nights more bearable, or the ones they'd carried with them from the beginning and over all their days of war and longing.

You going to go back to herding, Pascoe? Bailey asked from his berth below Walter's.

Reckon I will.

Hear it gets pretty lonely.

Not so bad.

Not what I hear.

What do you hear, Bailey? Walter said, tired and ready to be through with talk.

I hear you herders go crazy to get laid.

That's if you can't get laid in the first place, Walter said.

The men laughed.

When a sheepherder goes to the city, he's like a dog in heat, Bailey continued. If a girl stands still all the herder can think to do is fuck her, and if she runs all he wants to do is eat her ass.

Farell and Astor kept laughing and the rest of the men were quiet, pausing, waiting to see what Walter might do.

Walter had been Lindsay and McPheters's lieutenant and was one of the youngest to hold the position. The men recognized him for his instincts in how to understand the contours of the ground, the way it rose and settled, the way water cut the land and splayed it wide in places. He knew where to find shelter and had an ear for the character of shells, and he could tell beforehand where and when they would drop, how they would burst, and how to survive them.

Bailey hadn't known of these things, coming out of the shipyards. Unlike Walter, Bailey didn't know the way land could move and change and fold in on you. The sea might have taught him something of the unpredictable forces that can swallow men up, but it hadn't. For this Bailey had remained bitter, as if somehow the very land on which he was born had handed him a bad turn.

So how many girls you eaten out? Bailey said.

Then the men could hear McPheters turning over, his mattress squeaking, and then he was climbing down from his upper berth, his heavy barefoot weight settling to the floor and then his footsteps. McPheters drew back Bailey's curtain, towering over the prone man.

Forget it, McPheters said, evenly. Fucking let it go. The sleeper went dead quiet as they all waited for McPheters to end it right there. There was no telling what made men snap, but they'd seen it before. They could almost tell each other they'd made it and seen the worst of it and were finally home free, but something new was happening to them and McPheters was reminding them of it.

When Bailey would not relent McPheters slowly put his hands to Bailey's neck. Bailey couldn't stop him, and McPheters squeezed and Bailey sputtered, spit flying from his mouth as he fought for breath. And for McPheters it was no more than if he held a bird in his hands and was quietly ending its life. McPheters tensed across his back and shoulders, as he towered over Bailey watching his face redden, trapped in his hands.

Mac, Walter said. Mac, he said again.

Then McPheters eased up and Bailey choked in a deep breath of air.

If we weren't all heading where we were heading I might do you in right here, McPheters said.

I'm sorry, Bailey said, panting and still gasping for breath.

We all are, McPheters said.

I'm sorry, I didn't mean it like that.

None of us did.

There were tears coming out of Bailey's eyes and nobody could see them but McPheters, who daubed at them with the back of his hand.

Finally McPheters turned and went back to bed and no one said anything else. The men leaned out of their berths to blow out their oil lamps and the room darkened, lamp by lamp. Bailey's was the last to go. There were men who needed complete darkness to go to sleep and others who needed a light.

Bailey, you going to get your lamp blown out? Farell said.

He didn't answer.

I can't go to sleep with the light on, Farell said.

I can't sleep with it off, Bailey said.

We're night-lights, are we? said Surebine, who never spoke up about much of anything.

Let him be, McPheters said.

Then there was a breeze coming through the sleeper, lifting the green curtains. The smell of the men was thick and heavy. Randall had opened his window.

Do we really need it this cold? Astor asked.

Farell said he'd just as soon not freeze his ass off, if he could help it.

Gibson said as long as Randall didn't start shuffling his cards they shouldn't complain. And no one else wanted to try McPheters right then, so they let it be and went to sleep the best they could in that desert of silence, where the slightest of noise makes a man turn on himself for what he might have heard.

At three-thirty in the morning, Walter woke to the rattle of the cars clamoring over a bridge and he thought they were under machine gun fire. He woke them all when he fell from his upper berth and rolled onto the floor, landing with a thud like someone dropping for cover. Astor lit his oil lamp and the room came to a dull white glow. Walter held his hand over his eyes, seeing only a thin white light that he took for a magnesium flare.

Lindsay jumped from his bed and started to go to Walter. But Walter, telling them to get back, was stationing them all with his arms to their respective sides of the car. Bailey, who had scooted himself up in bed, lay down flat as if to make himself closer to the ground.

What the hell's going on? Randall said. He sat up with his Belgian Browning in hand.

No one answered Randall and all but Lindsay obeyed Walter's command to stay back. Then there was the unmistakable sound of McPheters climbing down from his berth again, freezing them, as they listened to his feet pad across the sleeper. He went uninterrupted until he kicked his feet into Bailey's canes that were leaned up against his berth. They clattered to the ground and McPheters kicked them to the side and went to stand over Lindsay and Walter.

Pascoe, Lindsay said, trying to kneel down eye level with Walter.

Maybe he's not with it, Gomez said. Mailer, give him one of your smokes.

He doesn't want one, Mailer mumbled, sounding half asleep.

You'll make him worse, Surebine said.

226

Mind your own fucking business, McPheters said.

McPheters hovered over Lindsay and Walter with his hands to his hips, and he kept watching the berths, as if he expected men to come from them. Walter was squatting with his chest to his knees. His face, beaded with sweat, was drawn tight and ashen, seeing whatever he was seeing. The sounds of the train clacking over the tracks coalesced into a harmony like that of concerted artillery firing and Walter drew his knees tighter to his chest.

Lindsay spoke to him softly and told him to take it easy.

He didn't see any of them, only his own temporary undoing. These episodes hadn't started until he'd come off the fields and suddenly found himself alone and without anything to hold together but himself. In his mind was the grating sound of shell explosions and fires blazing up and crackling in the air. He could see the land a bloody field and its inhabitants frozen in the most unlikely positions.

It'll be all right, Walter said aloud and then heard his voice and put his hands to his lips. He kept his fingers there to be sure he knew when he spoke and when he didn't.

Mailer stuck an arm out of his lower berth and reached for the floor. Out of his hand he let roll a cigarette, which made it halfway down the sleeper. McPheters bent over it and picked it up. Lindsay talked to Walter and kept trying to ease him down. He wiped the sweat from Walter's brow with a handkerchief and then he held it under Walter's nose and told him to blow. McPheters lit the cigarette and took a long draw off it, before offering it to Walter.

Now we're going to stand up, Lindsay said. That one was better than the last.

Walter exhaled, blowing out the smoke. You sure? he said.

Stand him up, McPheters said gruffly, taking one of Walter's arms, and they led Walter back to his berth. Walter sat upright on the bed with his knees still to his chest. Slowly, limb by limb, Lindsay, who was standing on the ladder, began to stretch out each of Walter's legs. He ran his hands down Walter's shins trying to calm the tremors running through him. Scooping his arm under Walter's head, he held him there in the crook of his arm for some time.

There was the sound of McPheters climbing back up to his berth and him rolling over once, his mattress settling under his weight. Someone in a berth below began a labored snore.

Walter began to think about the men shot under him. There was that one time when he'd arrived at the fork in the river. It was windy and there were too many shadows revealing too much and too little. Squatting in a shell hole, trying to get his bearings, Walter had motioned them forward and upstream, convincing himself they were within crawling distance of their trench. Those first to take his lead ran straight into the machine gun fire of an enemy trench. Those who had looked back at him to be certain of his direction had been spared. Lindsay and McPheters were among those few.

He'd heard Lindsay tell another infantryman before they got on the train that there'd been only one day he wished he hadn't been under Walter Pascoe and then he'd recounted the event. Walter shuddered and rolled out of Lindsay's arms to try to sleep. He could hear Lindsay saying, Not many men can boast as much – for only one day to have been under another's orders.

Chapter 22

I N   T H E   M O R N I N G, Walter said good-bye to Gibson, Randall, Surebine, Farell, and Gomez, who would be switching rails in Chicago.

Then in St. Paul, Walter, McPheters, Lindsay, Bailey, Astor, and Mailer boarded the North Coast Limited train. It was one of the first of its kind and the men were in awe of the luxury within which they found themselves. McPheters seemed to take pleasure in turning off light switches, waiting, then turning them back on as if to confirm such a phenomenon were possible.

Astor found a large leather chair by a steam heater and stretched his legs out and proclaimed he could spend the rest of his life on this passenger car. Mailer went to a mahogany card table and began to spread out his cigarette paper.

In sixty-two hours and thirty minutes the North Coast Limited would eclipse 2,056 miles. Lindsay and McPheters would ride the length of it to Seattle and they'd see Walter off along the way.

Aboard their new train, conversation was not had so easily. Fewer in number now, there was a heightened awareness that talk could become personal all too quickly. There were no longer the extra men to interrupt and change the subject and diffuse arising tension. Walter noted the newfound silence immediately and half hoped they'd go the second leg of the journey without much talk. It was to be so, but then it grew so that the silence was more deafening than any jabber they might have produced in an attempt not to talk about the war. And nights were worse yet, sitting through long enduring darkness and penetrating silence.

In the sleeper car their third evening, a hush settled over all the men, with each man going inside himself as he neared closer to home. No man could claim to have seen any more or less than the other, but every man claimed a way of dealing with it. Some men tried to sleep it off like too much bad drink. Others feared the sleep itself, for it had a way of dreaming up things they'd seen but had fought not to imagine.

It was Walter and McPheters who couldn't take sitting alone and awake in their berths any longer. They stirred and kept turning over until McPheters finally whispered to Walter that his stomach had the cramps from dinner.

Shouldn't have eaten the canned corn, Bailey said.

What do you got against canned corn? Astor asked.

It husks you from the inside out, Bailey said.

Well, that's you, Astor said. I've heard of green peppers ripping people up, but not canned corn.

But it has worked McPheters over pretty good, Bailey said.

There was the sound of McPheters climbing down from his berth and for a moment it crossed all of their minds that this time Bailey might be done for. Walter lay there and thought maybe Bailey was asking for more than he could take on purpose. That, or else he was dumber than Walter'd made him out to be.

I'll be in the smoker car, McPheters mumbled to Walter as he passed his berth. Walter was wide awake and told McPheters to hold on for a minute. Walter's army trousers were at the foot of his bed and he slipped them on quickly along with a T-shirt, and the two left the cabin. On their way out of the sleeper car, McPheters stooped over Lindsay's berth without drawing back the curtain and told him where they were going, but he did not stir.

The smoker was arranged like a cigar parlor with large round tables for cards and chess. It had red velvet curtains hung on brass curtain rods. There were no women inside it and only two other men sat at the bar counter and one old man, bone thin, sat in a chair against the car wall. Walter and McPheters took a table near a window and sat across from one another. They ordered drinks and Walter took a cigarette from his trouser and lit it and then offered another one to McPheters, and they smoked.

At some point Walter asked McPheters if he thought he'd be all right once he got home. Then he quickly tried to change his question and said, I mean what do you think you'll be up to?

McPheters did not so much laugh as he sounded out of his belly. Have I ever looked not all right?

Plenty of times, Walter said.

And I suppose you always looked all right?

Not what I was saying. I was just thinking about Patrick.

What about him?

Reckon it's not an easy break.

The river was no easy break either.

Yeah, and I'm not going home to be with their parents.

And I'm not going home to be with mine.

You're not? Walter said, surprised, for he'd always assumed that's where McPheters was going. He always told him about Washington and the orchards behind the family farm.

No, McPheters said.

Walter didn't ask him where he was going. He didn't feel like it was his right anymore. They all had lives to get on with now. A bourbon came for Walter and a whiskey for McPheters and Walter took his to his lips immediately while McPheters seemed to want to wait over his.

The bone-thin man sitting against the wall began a rasping cough in which he lowered his chin to his chest and let his knees splay apart as if the cough could run through him better that way. The two men seated at the bar looked over their shoulders at the old man and one stood his shirt collar up and pulled at it to try to make it as high as his mouth.

I think there might be a girl who just might be waiting for me in Seattle, though, McPheters said.

Who is she?

Can't really say, McPheters said, picking up his glass and turning it in circles in the palm of his other hand.

You mean you don't know her, never met her?

That's right.

And the orchards?

Oh, I was just a kid, he said, setting the glass down and still not taking a sip off it. God, I remember running through those things. Sprained my ankle running over all those rotten apples that fell down early, and I was big even then. Homesteaders put up a place in the orchard a few years back. You know how that works. It's theirs now.

Walter nodded as he put out his cigarette and drew out two more. It was clear McPheters wouldn't be talking about his parents and Walter decided it was probably for the better for the both of them.

George, another one? Walter said. Make that two. Walter didn't care how drunk they got. He thought he didn't care much about anything that night. The smoker car opened and they both expected it to be Lindsay, but it was Bailey come in on his canes.

He came up and leaned into their table. You know, Pascoe, I didn't mean anything the other night when I started in about herders.

Walter told him he hadn't thought about it since.

And he doesn't want to think about it again, McPheters said, snickering.

It was just something to say.

Let's leave it at that, Walter said.

McPheters scratched at his leg persistently and would not look up.

Bailey nodded and then left the car without taking a drink or a smoke.

When their drinks came McPheters still hadn't touched his first one. He picked up his second one and began palming it.

You all right, Mac?

Just making sure they're warm, McPheters said, taking up his first whiskey glass and pouring it back. I could go at this all night. You know he's really just a pussy, that Bailey.

Walter drew on his cigarette and settled deeper into his chair.

No sense waiting on yours, Walter. It's on ice.

Walter smiled. I got it, Mac.

This is good here, McPheters said and nodded, taking in the whole car. It is, isn't it.

You figure you'll hold up? McPheters asked, scratching his leg again after a long silence between them.

I'll find something to hold me up.

You will, won't you. You been like that from the start. That shivering you do. The way I see it, you are just starting to itch with whatever it is you got to do. It keeps you in your skin. It's not anything more than that.

Convinced Bailey was gone back to the sleeper for good, they talked about him too. You think Bailey's coming undone? Walter asked.

I think he will, Lindsay said, sauntering up and smugly setting down a glass of bourbon. But he might prove better off than the rest of us.

Coming home without a leg? McPheters said.

People got a reason to feel for him, believe he lost something, you mean? Walter said.

That's right, Lindsay said.

Pretty heavy price to pay to get a taste of sympathy, Walter said.

But it makes sense, don't it? Lindsay said.

I suppose, Walter said. Can't say I'd want to be riding home on one leg, though.

McPheters was going quiet into his drink.

None of us would say so, but I think we all thought about it, at least that it might be easier somehow, Lindsay said.

You mean it might be better than the compensation the rest of us get, our five cents a day for every day we were away.

He gets that too, McPheters said bitterly.

Another round. To compensation, Lindsay said, raising his empty drink and beckoning the bartender for another.

You might be right, Walter said and smiled, but he wasn't picturing Bailey anymore. He was thinking where Trina'd be standing on the platform when he arrived, which way the wind would be blowing across her, what color the light would turn her hair. Somehow he let himself believe she'd be there, when it was his very own doing that would keep her away. He saw her getting word somehow and saying, To hell with it, I've waited this long for him. And then he saw her eyes looking him up and down like they'd done from the beginning and every time since.

What took you so long to wake yourself up, anyway? Walter said.

You were waiting for me?

Nah, Mac said.

I've been with the green dress girl, Lindsay said.

That so? Walter said.

A lot of lips and hands and not a lot of leg and thigh. But she was sweet.

How'd you do it? Walter asked.

The noise is inconceivable in a berth, but there are draperies to deaden the sound.

McPheters shook his head. He's wondering where you found her?

233

Think they compensate the dead? Lindsay said.

Pay 'em, you mean? McPheters mumbled.

That's right.

Wouldn't do a hell of a lot of good, McPheters said shortly.

Their families, I mean.

McPheters poured back another drink while another one warmed before him. His insides were hot and piqued and he seemed tired of Lindsay and slowly without looking at him he told Lindsay he could be pretty damn smarmy. As if to prove his point he shifted his upper body so he faced Walter and then he spoke without looking at Lindsay.

Patrick told me the first week out, he didn't want to come out of there alive, McPheters said, looking Walter straight in the eye. I told him to shut the hell up and fight.

You had to, Walter said.

Did I?

You reckon he was in shock when he said it?

I reckon I was.

Can't think of it that way.

How you supposed to think of it then?

We did what we had to do, Lindsay said.

McPheters looked down, as if Lindsay had silenced him. He drank off his drink and Walter started in.

From the second we put on those uniforms, we signed a contract and we had a job to do, and the second any of us started thinking about how we'd come out of the whole thing was the second we started getting blown to pieces. Reason some of us didn't come out, Walter said. Reason some of us going to come undone yet.

You really think you knew what you were getting into? McPheters said.

They both shook their heads.

What was there to know? Walter said.

So how'd you sign the contract? McPheters asked.

How could I not have?

And you didn't care what they asked you to do?

Not really.

So you're as foolish as the Germans.

Maybe. Depends how you mean it, Walter said.

And we all thought you'd stand us up even if our legs were blown up and tell us to walk. Hell, we thought we'd see you walking one day with your legs blown off and you'd still be waving us forward. Now you're telling me you did it all for some goddamn contract, McPheters said. He set his glass of whiskey down too hard and the ice rattled and then spun around.

Mac, I can't say that I've heard you properly rant, not ever.

McPheters leaned back in his chair, his face softening just slightly, and for a minute Walter thought they might have given in to one another enough to let it go.

I carried Bailey out of Flanders on his one leg, didn't I, Mac? Walter said.

You did, Lindsay said.

Legless bastard, McPheters said.

Just don't tell me what I would and wouldn't have done for you or anybody out there, Walter said, looking at McPheters.

What if I told you I knew he'd die with his boots on.

I'd say you're a lying bastard and that you didn't know, Walter said, pushing his drink away toward McPheters.

You ever thought some men are just born into the world with no sentiment? Or maybe they wake up and say, All that's over now, no more sentiment from here on out, McPheters said, casting his thick arm out to the side of him, directing all the space before them. And that makes one's options pretty damn simple, doesn't it. Maybe he figured it out quicker than the rest of us.

Lindsay gave a confused look and started to stand up to leave, but McPheters started up before he could go.

Here and now I declare that all along, death was the secret of Patrick's life, that he lived for the purpose of dying. He died to demonstrate the impossibility of living. Hear, hear, McPheters said, lifting his glass. He set his drink down and did not drink to his own toast. He ran the back of his hand over his forehead. He stopped looking at Walter though, and through wide-open eyes, blue, diamond like, a motionless gleam cast from them, he stared at the car's ceiling.

Then Walter knew McPheters was afraid, afraid to move.

235

Steel shrapnel ripped him up. That's what they say, McPheters said. Just missed his heart. Lacerated piece of artistry. His heart choking on itself.

Mac, take another drink, Lindsay said.

His forehead to the ceiling, McPheters raised his hand and the attendant came to him and Walter pointed at the empty glass.

I don't get you, Pascoe, McPheters said, and a shiver or tremor ran through him, and he clenched his elbows to his sides.

That's it, Mac. There wasn't anything to get out there, Walter said.

That's not how you made it look, McPheters said.

I couldn't make it look any other way.

And you're really going to go back and herd you some sheep? McPheters said.

Don't act like you don't know what we're both going to try to do, Walter said, looking straight at McPheters.

McPheters sat there for a while, and then he seemed to mistake Walter's drink for his own, for he picked up the whiskey and put his thick finger in it and spun the ice around fast, until a bit of the drink spilled over onto his pant leg. Lindsay handed him a napkin.

Going to try to walk a straight line across open ground in broad daylight. That's what we're going to try to do, Walter said, and when McPheters's bourbon came he drank it off.

Chapter 23

THE NEXT MORNING the train whistled and sounded the coming stations, Rexburg, Blackfoot, Burley, and after not more than two hours' sleep, Walter rose from his berth, washed, and dressed. His head hurt and his joints were cold, but he had put the night behind him, as had Lindsay and McPheters, and no one spoke of it. At half past ten in the morning when the train arrived in Shoshone, McPheters and Lindsay stood behind Walter when he stepped down onto the platform, as if their sole purpose had been to see him delivered home.

In the end, they were simply three friends who traveled across the country, across the world, and a bit farther than that and now they were returned. They'd shared more and seen more of this life than most men would care to admit, but that didn't seem to matter right then. They said good-bye, and they knew they would probably never see one another again, but they didn't say so, for the war was nothing to which you really said good-bye.

For a fleeting instant, as the train slowed under screeching brakes, Walter wondered to ask Lindsay and McPheters if they thought he'd recognize Trina, wondered if she'd ever been. He knew he loved her and still ached for her, but in his heart there resided an enmity for the coldness that had not been able to empty him out, an indignation that he had not been seized or resigned away into a state of dullness through the war, but rather had been made cold and intractable in certain estimations of the world and its inhabitants.

There was the cold of flesh antsy to be warm with another body on a harsh, bitter night, and then there was the stealthy cold of flesh ebbing away to find a kind of death. Not so long ago he'd thought his hands able to tell the one cold from another. He had put his hands to soldiers' chests laid open with gaping wounds and known they would live, and he had put these same hands to another man's bare chest and it was like skin given way to gauze, numb. Either way, you did not ask another man to tell you what you would or wouldn't feel in your own heart.

Walter stepped down onto the platform. He wanted to come back to the land slowly and for it to rise up on him not so quick and sudden, as it might if he were dropped in the middle of it.

He stood on the platform and the train began chugging off and suddenly the shade of the train pulled away from him. The light fell from the sky in chasms of pure transparency, and the sky was blue and immobile, and over it there were the country dogs baying at mystery and the brilliance of the found daylight throbbing on this sound and making the day seem brighter still, so that finally Walter lifted his hand just above his brow to shade his eyes and see what lay before him.

Bolles was nowhere to be seen and the station was empty but for spindly mounds of tumbleweeds rolling end over end across the hard brown dirt. He went to the east side of the station wall and stripped naked. He saw where his arms shivered and a slight tremor ran the length of him, but then in the warming sun he stilled himself and it was as though his bones were metal rods set into a branding fire and his insides grew hot. From his duffel he pulled a new pair of dungarees and boots, an undershirt, a long-sleeve shirt, and a hunting vest, all of which he'd bought in Richmond. He dressed and then he took his Colt .45 service pistol from his bag and buckled his service holster around his waist. Then he felt through all his pockets and removed all identification from his army clothes before putting them back in the duffel.

He waited what seemed like over an hour for Bolles, and then he was there, as if he'd been there the whole time and it was Walter who had somehow missed him. Bolles was standing just west of the platform, opposite where Walter had dressed, and he was leaned up against a rail, twisting his mustache and spitting in the dirt, taking his time watching Walter.

You just get here? Walter yelled.

Pretty near to it, Bolles said as he walked to where Walter stood.

Those cars are nothing different than being on a ship as far as I can tell.

I wouldn't know. I haven't been on either.

Not a bad thing to admit.

Bolles gave him a sheepish look of incomprehension and finally said, Good to have you back, Walter. He extended his hand and the two men shook hands.

I say the same to you. Good to see you around.

Bolles studied Walter and looked too long at his trembling hands.

Did you expect me to be carrying my rifle still? Or is there something wrong?

Nothing's wrong. Bolles turned quickly around behind him and pointed. There she is, he said. I done just like you said. I didn't tell anyone.

Tied to the back of his own horse was a black liver mare with four white socks and a blaze down her face.

I done all right by you? Bolles asked.

Walter went to the mare, gently stroked her face, felt along her crest and down her shoulder where the muscles narrowed and tapered to bone and then he squatted to the ground to be nearer to her still, as he traced his fingers along her cannon bone and around her fetlock. He smoothed his hand down her legs so he might know how she was put together.

He stood and leaned into her and he could feel the mare not so much leaning back into him as staying put. He stroked her neck with the back of his hand and again leaned into her and she was warm and her coat soft and slick. Her hindquarters were dappled and shone gold in the sun. He nodded to Bolles and waited.

I worked her over with some cattle getting her tuned up. She's just four.

She settled?

Broke and ready to ride.

Walter nodded and pretended to look her over some more. Trina didn't want to come?

I thought it might come down to this.

Come down to what?

You asking me if I come and brought her when you told me not to. I thought it peculiar.

You did right.

Why'd you say it?

Just thought I'd ask.

She knows you're coming.

Figured she would.

But she didn't know what day.

Good. Sort of how I wanted it, Walter said and started to mount up, but as he lifted his leg it began to twitch and he set it back down. He ran his hand quickly over the top of his leg to still his muscles but made like he was brushing dust from his pants.

I'm sorry about the baby, Bolles said.

Walter looked at him askance. What are you talking about?

Looks like you're out of practice swinging the old leg up. Then Bolles looked down. I'm sorry. I figured you'd have heard.

Heard what?

She lost your baby back in January. I don't think it's my place to say more.

But Walter told him he would say more and it was not rendered as a decision but a rule of procedure for a decree that would not be reissued. Bolles looked to him and told Walter what he needed to know, and the men stood looking at one another.

I think I might take a smoke now, Walter said, turning around slowly. They sat cross-legged on the ground facing the rails. Bolles held a match to Walter's cigarette and Walter breathed in and the ember was red. Walter went to resting his hand on his knee, and there he twirled his cigarette like a baton between his two fingers. The sage rolled for miles before them, ridge after ridge. Ground squirrels lifted their heads to scout the surface before ducking back into the earth.

Walter asked Bolles how he'd been and they talked about horses and the weather and the sheep being driven south again for winter. Bolles asked Walter some of what he'd seen and Walter told him in as truthful account as he knew how. Once, Walter, not paying attention, brought the wrong end of his cigarette to his lips and jerked his head back and cursed what he'd done. He set the cigarette to the ground and put it out with the heel of his new boots and they went silent together.

I think I might like to be leaving now, Walter said. When Walter tried again to mount his horse, his leg twitched all the way to his hip and he simply couldn't reach the stirrup.

Bolles went and stood beside him and, interlacing his fingers, he made a step for Walter to mount up from.

Seated in the saddle, Walter looked across the hills laden with sage and the bold sloping lines of the benches and foothills beyond. And with the sun behind the clouds for a moment, a distant field of alfalfa looked to be burned and yellow splintered. Already things were coming alive in contrast and there was a sort of entering in and issuing forth taking place within the landscape.

I figure you won't be wanting any company, then, Bolles said, unconvinced it was right to leave Walter alone just yet.

Thanks for showing up here today, Cliff. I realize you didn't have to.

Walter, it's what I do. Besides, I did this for John as much as anybody.

I know that. And I've noted it as kindness all the same. Meant something to me.

You watch yourself moving through the lava rock this time of the year. Fall's late and the rattlers still been seen sunning themselves.

I'll keep my eye out, he said, and then he turned around, nervously casting a glance behind his shoulder.

What are you looking for? Bolles asked, confused.

I guess it was nothing, Walter said. Which way you heading?

West.

Why's that?

The direction of the world, Bolles said and smiled.

We're face to face with the west as it is. You looking for the sea?

Bolles placed the reins over his horse's head and set his foot in the stirrup and swung into the saddle. A field of hay. I got a late cut of hay waiting for my approval in Fairfield, before they move it to my place. If you want to ride, you're welcome, he said. Might do you good.

Walter sat still in the saddle and seemed to consider Bolles's suggestion. I'm heading home, he finally said.

Just offering, Bolles said, and he turned and began walking the horse west in the direction of Fairfield. I've got some business down that way and then I won't be far behind you.

Aren't you going to give me a price? Walter called out to him.

I've taken care of it, Bolles yelled, waving the back of his hand in the air, dismissing the offer. He kept going and did not turn around.

241

Walter started to say he didn't feel right about doing business as such, but then he realized Bolles wasn't doing business with him any more than he'd been doing business with Annette, the first day she drove Walter and John to Ketchum to buy the Rosina horse. He was still settling his debt with John and there wasn't anything Walter could do about it. He watched him go like he were someone he ought to keep track of, and then he turned.

He rode the horse north, testing her stride as he moved her between gaits. She was light in his hand and he hardly had to shift his weight and she'd angle off in another direction. He could tell Bolles had worked the horse over himself and got her just how John liked them, swift and surefooted, cueing off the slightest bit of rein.

He spent the larger part of the afternoon working her at a lope, breaking her into a trot as they entered land cratered with rock. She easily wove in between charcoal gray lava knolls where the volcanic rock had seeped up and when the land finally smoothed he lengthened her stride. Now that he was riding he had no plans of stopping to eat or to sleep. Both seemed like such unnecessary extravagances, urges unknown to him on this ride that was now everything about covering ground.

Nearing Silver Creek in the coming dusk, they walked through a boggy meadow, high with burnt orange grasses. At the creek he dismounted for the first time since they started their journey and he let her drink. He watched the sandhill cranes tower over and beyond themselves scrounging for food in between the heads of cattle grazing. The cows lifted their heads now and then to stare at him before setting them down to the ground, taking no mind of either horse or rider. Just upstream Walter could see where the creek was lined with cattails that rose above his head and he rode in that direction. The ground turned boggy, and the grasses, so high the bladed tips flicked her neck, made her quiver as if the flies were after her. He halted her and untied the duffel from behind his saddle and there he left it.

Downstream a heron, blue-gray and weathered like wood, landed in a tree. He shifted from leg to leg, stretching his barefoot presence. Silence ran through him. He cocked his head at Walter once before his wings spread wide, cooling the branches he barely touched as he headed for the sky, vanishing.

Then Walter was on again and nearing closer to the land he loved. It was land that had born him, raised him up high, leveled him, and sent him off into the world. He registered it and sized it riding up a ridge with towering rock extensions and thought it to be not so very changed. What he could not know was the land would not bear its misfortunes up again simply to make him better understand what had passed in his absence. He ached to be of the place and not entrapped there, to be nowhere and everywhere, almost ghostlike. He tried to recite the passage of days, the construction of events in keeping with the seasons that might reconstitute him and make him of the land. He became tired and still more hungry in doing so.

Just north of Gannett he spotted a herder's wagon on a knoll just east of him. He rode toward the wagon, driven by his mounting hunger and the prospect of receiving his first supper meal at a sheepwagon. There were no sheep in sight, but he figured they might be grazing on the other side of the hill, but as he neared he still did not hear their bleating calls.

Anybody home, he called when he was within a few paces of the wagon. The door was propped ajar and a sunken chested man came forth to stand in the doorway. He stepped down dragging a leg and then it seemed it was just a stiffness for the man limbered up and walked evenly toward Walter. His hair was dark and matted to the side of his head as if he'd just risen from bed and his face was bristled with the start of a beard. He took one hand to his face and scratched his cheek and then dug inside his ear with his finger. His other arm hung at his side covered by a pinned-up shirt sleeve.

Walter held out his hand and the herder waved his hand and shook his head furiously. Yeah, yeah. I'm Baptie and you're?

Walter Pascoe.

Fine. Walter it is. Forget the greeting and I'll get you some grub. It's what you want, isn't it? he muttered. He was a quick little man who did not look annoyed so much as he did agitated with himself.

Walter said it was indeed why he'd come.

He tied the mare to a metal ring clipped to the wagon, pulled the saddle off her, and then Baptie led him to the other side of the wagon where rocks were piled in a fire ring. Walter sat on the ground and leaned back into his saddle to watch as Baptie kneeled on his hands and knees and lit and then began to blow at the base of a small pile of burning kindling. Baptie stayed there for some time and Walter passed him brush and twigs piled near the ring and the fire grew.

Later they heated black beans, and they ate them with dry, leathery tortillas under the stars. During the meal Walter asked Baptie where his sheep were and he said he didn't have any.

Baptie? I heard of a Baptie, Walter said. It seems a long time ago.

Baptie did not seem to hear as he took a pinch of herbs from a tiny jar and sprinkled them into the beans. What remained on his hands he brushed into the fire.

Baptie passed Walter the last tortilla and told him to eat it. Then he explained to Walter that he didn't keep sheep because he moved too much. He told Walter he was back from the great war and that startled Walter and he held the tortilla in his mouth trying to figure what had been said. Slowly he began to chew again.

Baptie held out a flask to him as if he had something caught in the back of his mouth and Walter drank off the burning liquid, a stealthy moonshine.

Then Baptie pushed his long sleeve up his arm to reveal his gnarled stub that seemed itself to flicker in the firelight.

Some kind of dream-hell it is walking amongst the wounded, Baptie said.

Walter watched Baptie and felt his head nod in agreement, to what, he could not say.

Baptie clutched the knotted end of his arm. The cold fights over it now, he said, like dogs over a bone. And when it's not the cold, I can hear the motor convoys rumbling down the road and the tramp of feet marching. I can hear the war going on. The mouth of a cannon got me.

Listen to you talk, Walter said. He'd meant to stop him right there. You're a herder.

Baptie was still holding onto the stub of his arm. He shook his head.

Walter saw that out of nowhere there were tears leveling in the man's eyes. Boy, you is just lucky to have been spared. There were heads and knees and mangled testicles. There were chests with holes as big as your fist and thighs. And eyes sick as cats and mouths that couldn't say what they were. And so many of these things and parts, there were no men. All the while Baptie held the stub of his arm with his empty hand.

Walter spat the remaining tortilla from his mouth into his tin and coughed and set it at his feet and Baptie held out his flask again and Walter shook his head.

I suppose I could make an effort to figure out who you are, but I haven't done that in several years, Baptie said before standing. He left and went into the sheepwagon and rifled around in a canvas knapsack and pulled from it a uniform from the Spanish War. He called to Walter, telling him he had something to show him. A lantern was lit and the door creaked shut behind Walter when he entered. Baptie was holding a uniform to his own face to smell and then to Walter's before letting it drop to the ground.

You've been there too, haven't you? Baptie said. I seen it in your eyes.

Walter stepped back, but he was already against the door. He looked at the man whose finest hours were so far behind him they could not be dredged up. He felt his fists numb with the death they'd held, and though he clenched them tight, he did not feel for the man enough to use them on him.

Baptie's eyes moved wildly.

Walter reached behind him for the handle and began to turn. The room was distilling around him and his hand held to the door.

Despairing and more desperate now, Baptie was close against Walter's back, nearly touching him. There is no God, Baptie said. You must have learned that.

Walter could think only to call him a drunk and force out a laugh, when he wanted to call him a cripple. He pivoted around and faced the man. His eyes were deep-set and scarred and suddenly he felt the closest thing resembling a feeling in some time and he took pity on the man. It was not a noble feeling and he could not say he left Baptie in good faith, but he let him alone.

Disagree? Maybe you'll be thinking you're God himself.

Walter peered dizzily at Baptie, felt then that his own anguish and life were bound in a low-pitched ring sounding through the sheepwagon.

He mounted the mare and rode, and with him he carried a found resentment, bore into him through the war, a sense that the victory of any party over another fueled resentment that inculpated some and retarded others with a sense of incapacity. And there was no birth seed to be found to claim ownership for any of these feelings and maladies. It was the very reason that in this place, this earth, this war, which would be any and every war, could not be given a name. It had swallowed all of them, earth made itself human, made itself malign in its willfulness to exact intention on the world. It occurred to him that perhaps the finest hearts already lay at rest beneath the earth, for they were the stillest with their unsounded power naked in bare soil.

He saw the man he was looking for as he wound around Lookout Mountain and then angled his way east where the contours of the mountain merged with Seaman's Creek and the land furrowed into itself like a sunken vein running a twisty lifeline, and as far east as he could see was the creek gone dry. Dust rising out of the creek bed and gully in clouds that appeared as heavy fog in the dusk that was turning to dark, for how the cattle milled about in the cool of the coming night. He breathes in the wind and lifts his shirt to cover his mouth as if the wind smells of something burning and then suddenly of something so sentient it's not a burden to be walking through enemy land and he lets his shirt fall back around his neck. He looks around, and where he is seems so large, even though it is chiseled out of a larger part of an even larger run of land, and this thought begins to repeat itself. The stars so faint overhead as they are just coming on. They are like burning-out lights.

The man he is looking for is clothed in his horsehide shotgun chaps and bent over with his horse's hoof wedged between his knees and a small pick in his hand to work free a stone. When he stands his sawtooth roweled spurs tinkle as they spin and his legs are barrels for how wide his stance. They see one another and it is undivided quiet spread between them and the fusing of what light is taking away. There are no shadows. Cow paths wander the leveled-out slopes where the hillsides climb and the two men are seen to be in the lowlands of this scene, rising out of this thin basin, marking the makings of some venture terribly impoverished and yet more ennobling than the world that bore it.

The bark of a small stand of aspens is white even in the dusty haze and just beyond it a fox lopes out of nowhere and finds a place of hiding, and his red face and black eyes peer at them deftly. He drew the pistol from his service holster and pointed it and shot the man he'd found in the head, watching him to go down in the final bleed of light where crows were caught in the sky and ravens hung on the wooden fence posts, or perhaps they stood upright eyeing the scene with a crude sense of certainty. They cawed at the night sky and sounded off no great urgency, only great importance. The importance was itself sad and itself terribly small, for it bore up a map of scars and hollow bones and awesome bones not yet stripped of flesh. All the while the bats were whirling out of the uneasy night air.

He no longer wanted rest and so he rode toward the rim before him where the sun was fallen beneath the earth. He kept up at the mare, pushing her without telling her when to stop, not knowing himself when to stop. He was riding home and holding on with as much conviction as one has looking ever so softly up at a strip of fading blue sky. He spurred her sides harder than he might have, but she was well conditioned and showed no signs of wearing.

And he rode her still farther, the white sweat gathering on her neck like a lace garland, where the leather of his reins struck her coat. Her mouth frothed, and he could see the red in the corner of her eyes and she seemed all eyes and nerves, and still he lengthened her stride, giving her head and letting her fill the rein. They moved with a kind of blind ambition now with her forelegs striking the ground, splitting it apart.

They were moving across wide open ground in flat light, with the mountain walls pressing in on them. It was growing even darker and he did not see where they rode and so he shut his eyes and began to count each time her right foreleg struck down, certain he would hear the land moving past them faster and faster and he would know where he was.

He rode on and on like a man fallen in and out of the holy shudders and a light sleep. He was raveling together the pieces of himself he carried, bringing to bear the recognition he was coming to and falling back into the purpose for which he felt intended. He thought how McPheters and Lindsay were probably off the train by now. He imagined McPheters working at an orchard until he could save up enough to buy one. He tried to picture Lindsay moving from city to city and couldn't quite imagine where he'd end up. Just maybe he'd get off the train with the girl in the green dress. They might take a room together. And he thought of a baby buried in the ground.

He saw Trina walking. Her hemline broke just below her knees and her legs were slender and her calves round and white as she walked barefoot toward him. Her face was soft and she smiled and her lips moved to say something he could not hear. He leaned into her as she clutched him and he felt he knew himself again and it was a profound calm. She did not speak but seemed amazed at him for whatever he'd done. There was beauty and rhythm and music to be listened for so they could hear their insides uttering those wants too fierce to be damaged by the haunt of memory. She held his hand, and they were alone together in the yellow light falling across a black field, him holding onto her gently enough so as not to frighten her.

Wind falling down on them all like still falling snow, like ice glittering in the sunlight, like a season unsure of itself, all the while transforming sorrow into something that does not feel pain, only longing of a kind felt far worse than pain. Everywhere there is the quiet flicker of light going backward.

A NOTE ON THE AUTHOR

Heather Parkinson is twenty-seven. She lives in Idaho. This is her first novel.

A NOTE ON THE TYPE

This old style face is named after the Frenchman Robert Granjon, a sixteenth-century letter cutter whose italic types have often been used with the romans of Claude Garamond. The origins of this face, like those of Garamond, lie in the late fifteenth-century types used by Aldus Manutius in Italy. A good face for setting text in books, magazines and periodicals.